TWISTED REUNION

MARK TULLIUS

VINCERE
P R E S S

Published by Vincere Press
65 Pine Ave., Ste. 806
Long Beach, CA 90802

Twisted Reunion

Printed in the United States of America
Second Edition
ISBN: 978-1-938475-23-8
Library of Congress: 2015917301

Cover design by Michael Squid www.mrmichaelsquid.com
Cover of Each Dawn I Die
Cover design by Luis Vega vegaluis24@gmail.com
Graphic Design by Florencio Ares aresjun@gmail.com
Cover of Every One's Lethal
Cover design by Brian Shepard
Graphic Design by Florencio Ares aresjun@gmail.com
Cover of Repackaged Presents
Cover illustration by Martin Kelly
Cover graphic design by Brian Esquivel

"Out There" first published by On the Premises, 2007
"Group Session" first published as "Judge, Juror, and Executioner" by Meat Grinder Press 2006
"Split Decision" first published by Wild Child, 2003
"The Artist" first published by Nossa Morte 2008
"Bad Habits" first published by Black Ink Horror #4, Sideshow Press 2008
"When it Rains" first published by Abominations, Shroud Publishing 2008
"To Feed an Army" first published by Black Ink Horror #0, Sideshow Press 2006
"Instant Terror" first published by Dredtales, 2005
"Midnight Snack" first published by Wicked Karnival, Sideshow Press 2005
"Shooting Flies" first published as "Drawing Flies" by Black Ink Horror #1, Sideshow Press 2007
"Surviving the Holidays" first published by Black Ink Horror #5, Sideshow Press 2008
"Shades of Death" first published by Magus Press 2007
"Book of Revelation" first published by Bound for Evil, Dead Letter Press 2008
"Every Precious Second" first published by Vincere Press 2014
All other stories first published by Vincere Press 2015 in Every One's Lethal and Each Dawn I Die

Criminally Insane
Words and Music by Jeffery John Hanneman and Kerry Ray King
Copyright (c) 1986 by Death's Head Music
All Rights Administered by Universal Music - MGB Songs
International Copyright Secured All Rights Reserved
Reprinted by Permission of Hal Leonard Corporation

For Olivia, Jake, and Bailey
The brilliant sparks of light that keep away the darkness

TWISTED

REUNION

"Night will come and I will follow
For my victims, no tomorrow"

– Slayer

TABLE OF CONTENTS

A NOTE FROM THE AUTHOR

Half of the short stories you are about to read were previously published in small magazines, ezines, and anthologies between 2003 and 2008, the other half hiding on my hard drive because they just weren't good enough. It was difficult rereading these older stories, but tons of fun reimagining them. Villains switched jobs, motivations, and methods of murder. Some settings were rearranged and a couple good guys changed names, but they all faced the same ending. The same ending we will all face. The reason I wrote these stories.

Each Dawn I Die

The girl he called Laura buried her face in the pillow, her crying returned to full-blown sobs. Vic stroked her shoulder and tried to shush her, wished he could remember her real name. She eased up a little with his touch. "There you go. That's better," he said. "It's not that I don't like you, but I gotta sleep by myself."

She jerked away from him.

"It's nothing personal."

She screamed into the pillow. "I know!"

Vic stopped pretending with his nice voice. "You need to get up." He grabbed the stained wipe-up towel and wrapped it around his waist.

She peeled her face from the pillow and looked at him, her face a black mess of smeared mascara. Sounding much younger than the eighteen years she claimed, she asked, "Where are you going now?"

Vic opened his bedroom door and called to George, who was passed out on the couch. "Hey, I need you to help me out."

"No, I don't want anybody in here," the girl pleaded.

George had been Vic's boy for nearly a decade. They'd met in Principal Jenner's office after getting caught buying ecstasy. George rubbed his eyes and ran a hand over his shaved head. "Come on, lady, you gotta go."

"Oh my God," she said to Vic. "You're such a jerk!"

Vic turned to face her. "I'm sorry, but I have to get up early. George will take you home."

"I can't go home! I told my parents I'm staying at Amy's."

Vic rolled his eyes at the ridiculousness. He needed to start doing a better job of checking IDs. As he headed for the bathroom, he told George, "Handle this quietly, please." He could hear her yells with the door closed, even with the shower running. The sound of the radio, though, made her disappear.

1

When he walked out of the bathroom she was still gone. He slipped on his boxers as he fired up his laptop, opened the website. Fifteen thousand views. *Not bad for a half-dead fish in the sack*, he thought. Vic had been running his site, *Maybe Legal,* for two years. The numbers had been on the uptick for the past nine months. All of Vic's girls were real. Real homely, real naïve. Some were real ugly, but most importantly, they were real virgins. Virgins weren't easy to come by these days, but Vic made do by prowling the malls and local water park. Their first forays in porn were then broadcast to fifty-three countries. Vic got fan mail from all over, none stranger than the one from a guy in Bulgaria asking if he could shoot a video with a girl riding a GI Joe action figure.

Three quick knocks at the door, and Vic jumped to his feet. He checked the eyehole. Too many of the girls came running back for their phone, panties, or just to see if he'd call them the next day. Most never wanted to see him again, but he was shocked at how many did.

George entered, hand pressed to his ear, a small trail of blood running down his neck. "Stupid bitch."

Vic asked, "What the hell happened to you?"

"She bit me, man! She fucking bit me!"

"Bit you?"

"Yeah, I was telling her how good she looked, thought maybe I'd get some seconds. And she fucking bit me!"

George went to the bathroom to clean up, and Vic laughed, grabbed an energy drink from the fridge. He cracked it open, and took a long swig. Not really caring, he asked, "She say anything?"

"She said maybe five words the whole ride. 'Right here. Left there.' Didn't seem too happy."

"Can't please 'em all."

George came out of the bathroom a few minutes later, three bandages awkwardly taped to his ear. His fat frame filled the doorway as he flicked on the light. "Holy shit, looks like you killed someone."

Vic chuckled, took a swig, and sat down at the computer, as George snapped photos of the bloody bedspread.

George yanked off the old sheets, pulled a new set of silk linens from the closet, and slid them onto the mattress. He smoothed them down, arranged the pillows. "She any good?"

"Eh, all right." He refreshed his website and said, "Oh, shit; I guess no one cares. She got 34,347 views. Not bad for two hours."

George shoved the old sheets in the trash bag and twirled it closed, tied the end in a knot. "She was superhot though." He nodded at the cabinet with the recording equipment. "She know?"

"I don't know."

George joined Vic in the living room. "Any new prospects?"

"Yeah, this chick's dad's a pastor."

"Crazy."

Every new girl guaranteed a few new members, but subscriptions were skyrocketing. Tonight, "Laura" had already brought in seventy-four at twenty bucks a pop.

George shook his head, helped himself to the fridge. "I don't know how the hell you do it."

Vic wanted to say it was because he made them feel special, but even he didn't believe that anymore.

"Got anything lined up for tomorrow?" George plopped down on the couch, smacked his lips with each bite of yogurt. "Need me to stick around, or can I ..."

He was interrupted by pounding on the front door.

"Did you not lock the gate?" Vic asked.

"I did. I always do."

Vic shook his head, got up from the computer, but reconsidered answering the door. "See who it is." He headed into the bedroom. "I'm not here."

Another bang.

George took another bite of yogurt. "They're not here for me."

Vic was too tired for this. "How much do I pay you? You want to get a real job?"

3

George muttered under his breath and headed to the door. He opened it and said, "He's not ..."

An old woman in a dark brown dress barged across the threshold, backed George to the wall without so much as a touch, her decrepit finger and long, brittle nail inches from his lips. He pointed towards the bedroom.

Vic threw on his robe and barely beat the woman to the doorway, not wanting to get trapped in his room with her. The woman looked middle-eastern, like her leathery brown skin had been blown dry by wind and sand. Her angry eyes were cold and red from tears.

Vic motioned towards the door. "You need to get out of here."

The woman brought her hand to her mouth, spit in it and flung the saliva toward Vic. She shouted something he couldn't understand, but the hatred translated perfectly.

Vic wiped the spit from his face, pushed the woman toward the front door. "Get out of here before I call the cops, you psycho bitch."

Vic looked to George, but George didn't move. The woman did, turning her back on Vic. She stopped next to George and spoke in broken English. "You part of this?"

He shook his head and kicked the trash bag. "I just clean up."

Vic's face still felt wet, but his hand came away dry. "I'm calling the cops," he said, heading for his phone. "So you better get the fuck out of here!"

The door slammed. The woman had already left and George threw the deadbolt.

"Why'd you let her in?" Vic said.

George's face was whiter than the time he'd thought he had testicular cancer. "Who was she?"

Vic hurried to the sink and splashed water over his face. "How the hell would I know?"

"You've never seen her?"

There was a large Lebanese community on the south side of town, but Vic rarely went down there. Something about her seemed familiar, though. "Maybe from a restaurant. I got no idea."

George pointed to the computer. "You probably screwed her granddaughter. That wasn't just some random nut job."

"Chill out."

"I bet you anything," George said. Vic waved him off and George grabbed the trash bag and camera. "I'd be careful, Vic. She could come back."

"Then maybe I'll have to get someone over here that could actually do something about it," Vic said as George left.

Vic had hired George because he was big and didn't ask for much money. Maybe Vic needed to spend some serious cash for legitimate protection. The number of girls on the site had climbed to sixty-three, and at least half of them probably had dads in the picture. Vic threw the deadbolt and walked over to the computer. He wasn't worried, but it'd be good just to make sure.

Another fan had called him the "Virgin Slayer." He liked that, thought about adding it to the masthead, then scrolled through the photos. He was three months deep when Becky's profile and bloody sheet popped up. She'd been his waitress. They'd gone out drinking. He'd brought her home.

Waitress. Shit. The old woman had been at the counter. Becky had introduced her as her grandmother. George had been right. But how had she found him here? Had Becky actually told her grandmother about what had happened? It'd been three months ago.

Vic couldn't sleep. His bedroom was pitch-dark. There was a loud noise outside; it sounded like something scraping his shuttered bedroom window.

It's not the old lady, he told himself, ashamed to even think of something so stupid. He was on the third floor. It was probably a bird on the window ledge. Still, the old bitch had been in his head all night long.

It was almost six o'clock. The sun was about to come up and he needed to rest for a heavy day at the gym. Vic grabbed a pair of earplugs and a sleep mask from the nightstand. He had one earplug in when the scrape came again, deeper and louder.

Stop being a pussy. Vic pulled back the shutters, saw the first rays of light washing away the last of the predawn shadows.

He didn't see it right away, not until the scraping continued, a tendril of black mist slowly swirling in the air on the other side of the window. Three beings took their forms, each floating. The one in the middle looked closest to human, a pale face wearing a black medieval doctor's mask. He wore a dark robe, his bony hand gripping a scalpel. On either side of him were his henchmen, with the heads of jackals and talons for hands.

"I'm fucking dreaming," Vic said aloud to snap himself out of the nightmare. The trio floated forward, seeped through the edges of the glass. Vic slammed the shutters, but the thick black mist poured through the cracks. They began to solidify, once again taking their previous forms.

The henchmen each grabbed an arm and dropped Vic onto the bed, pinning him down, their talons ripping through his flesh. The doctor produced a curved, metal tube from his dusty robe, inserted it between Vic's lips. It clinked against Vic's teeth, tore into the back of his throat.

Vic studied the doctor's pale, rotting face, searching the black sockets that should have held eyes. The beast's chuckle paralyzed Vic as the blood poured down his throat.

The doctor whispered something unintelligible, produced a glass jar filled with spiders and scorpions scrambling over each other. He unscrewed the lid, held it to the tube. Vic's mind screamed as the creatures poured inside him; his body bucked against the henchmen who were holding him down.

Soon the container was empty. The death doctor tossed it aside. Vic never heard it hit the floor. He couldn't breathe, his windpipe clogged, thousands of bristly feet finding their way up and down every path, fire-filled stings blurring his thoughts. Vic had never wanted to die until this moment.

He opened his eyes and found the death doctor's decaying face just inches from his own, his foul breath tinged with rotting meat seeped through the mask. He pulled the tube from Vic's throat then slid a magnifying monocle from his robe, placed it where his right eyeball should've been. A small silver dot in the eye socket grew larger in the glass. The doctor pinched Vic's cheeks and peered down his swelling throat.

Vic couldn't understand the doctor's words, but he recognized the language. It was the same nonsense as the old woman's. And he didn't have to speak the tongue to understand the evil dripping from those words.

A distinctive, metallic click pulled Vic out of the panic. The doctor had just tapped the blade of his scalpel to the bedpost. Vic stayed conscious just long enough to see his belly split open, the fading doctor and his henchmen smiling as the creatures skittered out from his intestines.

Vic shot out of bed, his mind racing, trying to get his bearings. He was in his house, the house his parents had left him when they'd passed. He saw the tripod in the closet. It was all a dream he thought as he placed his feet on the floor. A sharp pain shot through his big toe. A shard of glass was sticking out of it. He plucked it out, looked at the ground. Dozens of spiders and scorpions were racing around a pile of broken glass.

This was no dream. It was late afternoon. He opened his shirt, felt the stitches running down his chest. "What the fuck, man?" *Maybe I'm still sleeping?* But he wasn't. The blood trailing behind him as he pulled himself to the living room told him that. His computer was still up and running. Becky's profile was on the screen. But he'd turned it off, hadn't he?

The old woman's laugh echoed in his head. Had she slipped him something? She'd gotten spit in his mouth. Maybe it'd been laced?

He ran back to the room hoping the spiders and scorpions were gone. They were still crawling over his dirty underwear on the floor.

The old bitch had done something. For the next few hours he tried to figure out exactly what. He called George, but there was no answer and his voicemail was full. Vic paced as Becky's eyes seemed to follow him around the room. Finally, he deleted her profile and videos.

Still, he felt her judging from somewhere.

He threw on his jeans and a shirt, and grabbed the gun under the sweaters in the closet. He got in his Porsche, drove to the alley across the street from where he'd dropped off Becky. It was dark except for the light in the girl's house. He didn't bother locking the car, the .357 tucked in his belt, the baggy shirt hiding it. He stopped in front of the white picket fence and stared at the snarling pit bull on the opposite side.

The old woman's gravelly voice jolted Vic. She stood on the porch staring at him through dark cataract sunglasses. "You came," she said, sounding pleased.

Vic realized he hadn't thought about what to say. He felt silly and exposed out here on the street. "It doesn't look like he likes me."

"Oh, he will. At least the taste of you."

The old woman loved seeing him squirm. But he couldn't show his true emotions. He had to be smart. Diplomatic. If that didn't work, there was always the gun.

"I need to see your granddaughter."

"I have no granddaughter."

"The young girl that works with you. She introduced us. That's why you came over."

"That's not why I came over."

"I want to apologize." It actually felt good to say that, but the look of disgust on the old woman's face made Vic want to shrivel up and disappear.

"You don't even know her real name, but you suddenly feel the need to apologize. Why?"

The girl's name came back to him. "Gabby, her name's Gabby."

8

"Gabrielle."

"I already took her off my website. I destroyed the recording."

"How thoughtful." The old woman spat on the ground.

"I can pay you. She deserves that. Five grand?"

"That's the filthy money you made off of all those poor girls. Using them like they were trash."

"I didn't use them. I gave them …"

"You lied to them."

"I'm sorry if you think I … Can I please talk to her?"

The old woman shook her head. "She didn't come down for breakfast one morning. I went to her room and saw the computer was on. There was a movie playing on the screen. I watched ten seconds of the filth and turned it off. I heard the water running. Gabrielle was in bathroom. The bath water was so red I couldn't see her legs. She died as the sun came through the window."

Vic placed his hand on the fence. He felt sick. The pit bull growled and leapt for his hand, snagging his knuckle. Vic jumped back. "I'm so sorry."

"And you'll remain sorry for the rest of your life."

There was no reasoning with her. The pit bull rammed itself against the fence. The beast was going to break through.

Vic whipped out the gun as a black mist surrounded the woman. It flew at Vic, swirling around the gun until it pointed back at his own face. He felt his finger tensing. There was nothing he could do.

The old lady said, "There will be no end." The gun fired.

Vic lifted his head from the piss-stained pillow in the abandoned house he'd been squatting in. It'd been a solid six hours since his last death, his seventy-sixth in a row. The taste of hydrochloric acid sat on his tongue as Vic slipped out of bed and headed straight for the recording equipment piled on the moving box. Vic played the footage from last night and turned on the small monitor.

On the screen, Vic moved around the dark room then fell asleep on the bed. He fast-forwarded a few minutes and slowed it to when he rose to check the oncoming dawn. When his recorded self turned to the door, no one else could be seen on the video, but his body was miraculously lifted into the air and slammed onto the bed.

There was no need to relive the experience. Vic turned everything off and headed into the bathroom. He grabbed the bottle of Listerine, filled his mouth, and gargled. He made the mistake of glancing at the mirror. He was only twenty-four, but the dark bags under his eyes were getting bigger and blacker every day. His full head of dark brown hair had gone bone white and started falling out. He'd considered dying it and getting Rogaine, but what was the point? A few more dawns like this, and it'd all be gone.

Maybe that was part of the curse. To end up looking like that damned woman. All he needed now were the liver spots.

Vic spat the mouthwash out and grabbed his toothbrush. If the Listerine couldn't kill the taste of the acid, he doubted the toothpaste would help, but he gave it a shot. The sight of his emaciated arm moving back and forth made him break down and weep. He was falling apart.

He'd lost over fifty pounds since the curse. With his withered frame, he would never again seduce a female, but that was the last thing he wanted now. He just wanted this to end. How nice it would be to fall back to sleep like a normal person and wake with the sun pouring through the window. He used to sleep in every morning. Now he was lucky to get a couple hours of fitful rest each night.

Vic threw on his jeans, put on the blue tank top that used to showcase his biceps, but now only exposed his atrophied arms. Death did not exist. Not for him. Whether it was the doctor and his henchmen or by his own hand, the permanence of death couldn't happen. He'd tried everything. Slitting his wrist. Jumping off skyscrapers. Bridges. He'd driven his car off a cliff and eaten more bullets than he could remember. Sleeping pills didn't work either, always wearing off at first light.

Vic had fled west in an attempt to escape the dawn, but the bastards had followed and flooded his throat with a steady flow of viscous oil. They lit it on fire in Illinois. They forced razor blades through his trachea in Albuquerque. Then the doctor took a chainsaw to his chest in Wyoming. There were the Dobermans in Cheyenne. Being ripped apart by dogs had been the worst.

He'd lost everything within the first month: his house, his bank account, every one of his so-called friends after he shut down the website. He traveled the country seeking out the girls he'd betrayed. Some forgave him; most did not.

It didn't matter where he was. Each dawn he died. Usually he was alone, but a few times there were spectators. He avoided crowded places because the doctor never left witnesses. Good Samaritans, thinking he was having a grand mal were torched and gutted. So Vic stayed in the darkness. He ate whatever scraps he found in dumpsters, drank his belly full of cheap wine, hoping to numb the pain, but the doctor would leech his blood until he was sober enough to feel the blade. Vic prayed for natural causes to eventually strip him of his strength, prayed the doctor would one day grow tired and find someone new, but each morning he'd rise and see that wretched sun.

This was his life and it would never end.

Wrong Side Tavern

Paulson logged off the computer and shut down the Amtrak's controls, what Hank would've been doing if it hadn't been for that damn van. The grisly accident outside San Diego had delayed his run by more than two hours. Overtime was always a pleasant addition to his engineer's salary, but the long day had taken its toll on him and he was ready to get home.

Hank waited until all the passengers were gone before he stepped off the train. A few of his porters nodded their good nights and Hank headed for the escalator instead of the employee parking lot. His truck was in the shop, and he lived within walking distance of the station. It would've been easy to grab a cab, but Hank wasn't in a hurry now that he was off the train. Plus, he could use the exercise and, with any luck, the midnight air would clear his mind. The wreck was still heavy in his thoughts. The woman's head poking through the windshield. It'd been the van's fault. It had slammed right into her Camry, and knocked her car through the crossing gates. Hank couldn't have stopped in time.

Hank looked up and down the block, not quite sure which way to go. He'd never used the pedestrian exit or actually walked home. The blinking yellow traffic light, barely visible through the fog, had to be First Street. All he had to do was cross the tracks, go left at the light, and then walk another six or seven blocks. He'd be home in half an hour.

Three teenagers wearing blue bandannas were hanging out at the corner. Hank didn't know if he should nod, make eye contact, greet them, or just keep his eyes down. They kept staring at him, letting him know he had no business being out on their street. Hank opted for studying the sidewalk and the broken glass before turning left at the corner, his hard soles clicking on the concrete. His footfalls weren't the only ones though. The teenagers' footsteps echoed close behind him.

Hank walked a bit faster, fighting the temptation to turn around and ask why they were following him. Did he disrespect them by not looking at them, or was he simply an easy target? Why the hell hadn't he called a cab?

They matched his speed. Hank crossed the deserted street, didn't bother to look both ways. Two sets of footsteps crossed with him. The third thug stayed on the other side, walked directly across from Hank, who could see him out of the corner of his eye. Hank took both hands out of his pockets in case he had to defend himself and accelerated his stride. He flinched when one of the guys behind him cleared his throat.

"I just love this speed-walking shit. Great way to stay in shape, huh, Deuce?"

"Nah, Player, it just gets me all sweaty," the other said in a deep voice. "And when I get sweaty, I get pissed."

The intimidation tactic was working, but Hank wasn't about to give up his wallet just yet. Despite his pounding chest and burning legs, Hank kept up the pace. He searched both sides of the street for any sign of life, tried to remember passing any gas stations or liquor stores whenever he drove through this rundown stretch of town. Whether it was his nerves or Deuce and his partner talking behind him, Hank couldn't recall anything being open this late. The only lights ahead of him were traffic signals.

If Hank tried to run, he'd guarantee a beating, or maybe worse. He only had a hundred or so dollars in his wallet, which he would gladly part with if they would leave him alone, but now that'd he'd led them this far, Hank didn't think they'd just walk away.

A small neon sign flickered up ahead. Wrong Side Tavern. Hank had never noticed it before. Below the sign was a flashing arrow pointing down the alley. Hank figured he could call a taxi or cops from inside the establishment, if he could make it to the entrance.

"Where you headed, white boy?" Deuce called. "You don't want to head down there."

Hank kept walking, prayed he hadn't just made a terrible mistake and trapped himself in a dead end. Another glow was coming from halfway down the dark alley. Not caring what the thugs thought of him, Hank took off running toward the flashing neon.

The sound of his slapping shoes and thundering heart blocked out all other noise as Hank raced past dumpers and inky puddles. His lungs were on fire when he reached the entrance. Hank grabbed hold of the handle and yanked the door open. Much lighter than it looked, it flew open and out of his hand, banged against the wall. Hank caught the door on the rebound and slammed it shut behind him.

Gripping the handle, he braced for a tug-of-war, but no one tried to pull back. There weren't any noises in the alley either. But people in the bar were talking, probably wondering what kind of drug he was tripping on.

Hank let go of the handle and headed for the counter, accidentally bumped a man on crutches. The man, missing a leg, continued toward the back of the dimly lit bar, mumbled something about Hank needing to watch where he was going.

Hank walked toward the bar, unable to remember ever being in a place so grim and depressing. Still, it was better than being mugged or even killed. He studied the empty tables with their dingy white tablecloths. The joint wasn't dirty, but it had a bad feel to it, unlike any other dive bar he'd been inside. The patrons slouching in the booths that lined both walls weren't here to watch a game or pick up chicks. Their dejected faces told him they came to this bar for one reason. To forget.

"Would you mind calling me a cab?" Hank asked the burly bartender with thick glasses. His right arm was missing just below the shoulder. Hank didn't mean to flinch.

"That was quick. What is it?" The bartender sniffed at his armpit. "Do I offend?"

"Oh, no." Hank looked to the grimy window, unable to see anything in the alley. "I just had one hell of a day."

The bartender said he understood and picked up the phone. "One at the Wrong Side." After a pause he thanked them and hung up. "They're on the way. Care for a drink while you're waiting?"

Although he'd promised himself he was done with that, at least on a work night, Hank said, "Why the hell not? Gimmie that stout." He had a lot on his mind: the thugs outside, the paperwork he'd have to face in the following weeks, even though he couldn't have avoided the wreck. If anyone in the bar deserved a drink, it was him.

Hank took a seat on a stool and noticed that a track ran the length of the counter. He pointed at the rails and asked, "So who's on the wrong side, you or me?"

Only having one arm didn't slow the bartender. He set the mug between two rail ties and sent it sliding to Hank. "I'm afraid it's everyone who sets foot in this place."

Hank raised his drink and took a long swig. "That's not very uplifting."

"Yeah, but it is a catchy name, don't you think?"

Hank nodded and took another drink. He tried to sound nonchalant when he asked, "Is there a back door to this place? Maybe somewhere else the cab can pick me up?"

"Nope, there's no back door." He motioned toward the entrance with his stump. "That's the only way in or out. Why you ask?"

"I'd hate for the cabbie not to find this place."

"No worries. They'll come down the alley right up to the door." The man scratched his stubbly black beard and studied Hank, the hint of a smile on his lips. "Let me guess. Someone follow you?"

"Yeah."

"Three black guys?"

"How'd you know?"

"If they keep scaring people into here, I'm gonna have to start tipping them. You're lucky though. I've heard about a couple of people who didn't make it in here. I won't say it was them for sure, but it wasn't pretty, and Deuce is known to be good with his blade."

Hank tried not to look at the stump. "They ever mess with you?"

"No one ever messes with us. That's why we like this place. It's almost like we don't exist."

Hank looked around the sparsely populated bar. "I don't mean to be rude, but isn't part of running a bar wanting people to come in? You know, attract more business?"

"The thing is that ever since my accident, money hasn't meant a thing to me."

"That must be nice." Hank finished his beer and checked his watch. "Did they happen to say how long it would be?"

"They always say twenty minutes."

"Are they ever on time?"

"Might as well make yourself comfortable. Looks like you could use another drink."

Hank set his empty glass between the rails and slid it toward the bartender. It tipped over and shattered against the tie. "Ah, shit, I'm sorry," Hank said. The already quiet bar was now completely silent. He tried to help pick up the large pieces of glass, but the bartender waved him off.

"Don't sweat it." The bartender held up a fresh mug and asked, "Another one?"

Hank nodded and the man filled the mug, set it between the rail ties and slid it across the counter. Hank picked up his drink. "You make it look easy. I didn't think I threw it that hard."

The bartender leaned forward and whispered, "Glass gotta be full."

Hank emptied his second round in three healthy gulps and handed it back. "Maybe one more."

The bartender poured another glass. "Hell of a day, huh?"

"Hell of a year is more like it."

"Work?"

Hank nodded, tried to block the images from earlier in the day.

The bartender slid the mug over. "Whatcha do?"

"I'm an engineer."

"What kind? Mechanical?"

"Actually, I'm a train operator."

"Dude, it was a joke. Take a look around." He pointed out the railroad signs plastered on the walls, the crossing signal next to the bathrooms, the various train paintings hanging from thick iron spikes jammed into the walls. "I know what an engineer is."

"Sorry, my head's somewhere else." Hank took another drink.

The bartender told him not to worry about it and then excused himself to serve the wino in a wool hat at the far end of the bar. Hank looked at the large painting above the shelves of booze. He shuddered and set down his drink, afraid he might drop it.

What kind of sick bastard would think the depiction of a train derailment was appropriate to display anywhere, especially in a place like this. Body parts scattered on the ground, some lying underneath the overturned engine car. Hank closed his eyes to block it out, but the death and destruction from the painting evoked images of today's accident, swirled together in a crimson collage.

It didn't matter if the thugs were outside waiting for him. Hank slid off his stool, threw a twenty on the counter, and turned for the door. A beautiful brunette sat at the nearest table, her bright red blouse and matching beret a sharp contrast to the white tablecloth.

Hank turned back to the bar, scooped up his money, and downed the rest of his beer. When the bartender returned, Hank asked who the woman was.

"She's in here by herself if that's what you're asking."

"No, she just looks familiar."

"None of my business who you know." He polished a glass trapped between the counter and his waist. "Why don't you go talk to her?"

Hank stole a glance at the woman, and then asked for a whiskey. He promised himself he'd stop after this one. Hell, the taxi would probably show up before he even had time to finish. "You wouldn't happen to know what she drinks, would you?"

"Can't say I've ever seen her in here before. That'd be another question for her."

"That's fine. Give me a screwdriver, another whiskey, and a water."

"You're the boss."

Hank balanced all four drinks in his hands and approached the table. She was beautiful, her eyes so blue. Hank stumbled on his pickup line. "One thing I can't handle is seeing a woman in need of anything, and I noticed you were without a drink."

In a melodic voice, she said, "Thank you for noticing, but I don't drink."

"The good news is that I do. These three are for me." Hank set down the alcoholic beverages. "This water is for you though."

Her smile almost made the horrible day bearable. "That's thoughtful of you."

"Mind if I sit?" Hank asked.

"Didn't think you'd want to."

Now it was Hank's turn to smile, though he got the feeling he was missing something. As he sank into the chair, his legs disappeared beneath the long tablecloth. The woman didn't touch her water, but Hank started on his whiskey and asked, "So what in the world are you doing in a place like this?"

She adjusted her beret and said, "I don't know. I was on the Four-fourteen and then something told me to come here."

Hank wondered if he'd heard correctly. "The Four-fourteen?"

"That's the one. Why?"

"I just can't believe I didn't notice you."

"You take it, too?"

"Actually, I operate it."

"No fooling?"

Not wanting to appear conceited, Hank said, "It's really no big deal. The thing practically runs itself."

When he asked, the woman said her name was June. She patted the back of his hand. "Oh, I'm sure you're just being modest. You have so much responsibility."

"I suppose it does take its toll." Hank finished his drink, set it down.

"How do you mean?"

Hank pulled over the screwdriver, but didn't take a drink. No need for her to suspect he was an alcoholic. Cranking up the emotion, like a sad insurance commercial, he said, "Sometimes bad things happen, but you just have to deal with it and go on."

"What happened, Hank?" She gave his hand a light squeeze. "Did something happen today?"

Hank let out a long sigh, nodded, and gulped down half the screwdriver.

"What? An accident? Was it an accident?"

"Yeah. Some van plowed into a woman stopped at the crossing, and caused me to hit her too."

"What was he doing?"

"He was probably high or just stupid, maybe texting. They'll find out in the autopsy."

June took his hand in both of hers. "How can you stand it?"

"The funny thing is that I don't feel that bad. This one wasn't my fault. I braked. Hard. Almost all of them couldn't have been avoided."

"You've hit others?"

"There are over a thousand deaths a year on the rails, and I'm afraid I've got eight of those."

"And you haven't quit?"

Hank finished the screwdriver. "That's what I was saying. The people I've hit don't bother me that much. Most of them are strung out on drugs and want to die. Instead of suicide by cop, it's suicide by train. Decent person will just slit their wrists or pop some pills. Stay indoors. Why mess up everyone else's day?"

"That is pretty selfish."

"Why do you think so many trains are delayed and cancelled?"

"I never thought of it like that."

Hank took a swig of the second whiskey. "I feel worse about the animals. When I honk they usually either freeze in fear or run directly down the tracks. Imagine that. Imagine seeing someone's poodle sprinting for its life, knowing you can't do a thing to stop the tons of metal bearing down on it."

June shook her head. "That's awful."

Hank wiped his hand on his pants and smoothed the wrinkles. "Would you mind if we talked about something else?"

"Of course not. I'm so sorry."

Hank smiled and told her not to be silly. "So what about you? Is there a lucky guy waiting for you somewhere?"

June shook her head so hard her hat nearly came off. "Oh, no. No one wants me."

"Are you serious?"

June cast her eyes down. "I don't have a lot to offer."

"Don't say that. You're beautiful. That's something."

June looked up, tears welling in her eyes. "I know what I am."

"You're talking crazy." Hank got up from the table and said, "I'm going to get you a drink."

At the bar, while Hank was clearing his tab, a loud squeaking came from the rear of the bar. An elderly man pulled a rusty red wagon toward the bathroom. It was hard to see in the dim light, but it looked like he was carrying a pile of dirty clothes.

"Here you go." The bartender handed Hank his change and said, "That's just Jimmy. He's harmless."

Hank carried two drinks back to the table. He took his seat and placed a bright green cocktail in front of June.

"I can't. Really." She pushed it away from her.

Hank took hold of her hands. "Just try it. It's a Midori Sour, almost no alcohol in it."

"I'm such a lightweight, Hank, and this stuff will run right through me."

"You need it. We both need it." He eyed his whiskey and said, "Come on, beautiful, what do you say?"

June sighed and stopped pushing away the drink. "I guess one won't kill me."

"That's more like it." Hank casually slipped his leg under the table, sticking it out to see how she'd react. If she pushed back against his foot, they'd be back in his bedroom within the hour. If she played it cool and moved away, it could take a date, maybe even a dinner or two.

He was still blindly searching for her leg when the squeaking started again. "What's with this place?" Hank sat up, the mood ruined. "They give discounts to cripples and crazies?"

June threw her head back in laughter. It was so loud it was almost terrifying. Not knowing what else to do, Hank asked, "Are we going to do this or not?" He held his glass up for a toast, mildly surprised when she joined him. He finished his whiskey and noticed a steady dripping sound. It was coming from under the table.

June set down her empty glass and asked Hank if he was okay.

"I think I must have spilled something."

"I'm sorry. It was probably me. I can be so clumsy sometimes." She licked her lips. "Would you mind looking for me?"

Hank lifted the tablecloth and stuck his head under the table. A puddle of bright green liquid pooled around the legs of her chair. He was about to warn her to move her feet out of the way so they wouldn't get wet, when he realized she didn't have any. The green liquid dribbled out of June's exposed intestines that dangled a few inches below the ragged edge of her severed torso.

Hank bolted upright, the back of his head slamming into the table. His mind filled with darkness. June's icy hands shocked him back to reality. She held both of his wrists, smiled as if nothing was wrong. "I told you it runs right through me. At least since this afternoon."

"Let go of me!" Hank tried to pull his arms free and get up from the table. *At least since this afternoon.* Wait. He did know her. She was the woman from today.

"Where are you going, Hank?" June squeezed his wrists, his tendons and bones grinding together painfully.

Hank shouted for help, looked around the room, anywhere but at June, that beautiful face he'd seen sticking through the windshield. June

21

wouldn't let go of him, even as he continued to back away. Her torso slid across the table, leaving a bloody trail as she knocked over their empty glasses. June's hat fell to the side, revealed her crushed skull that looked as if someone had hammered away at it with a brick. The skull he'd seen poking through the glass. But he hadn't done that. The van had hit her. It'd run the flashing lights, slammed into her ... Or had it? No, the woman had been stalled out on the tracks. Hank had seen her before the van came barreling at her. The van had been trying to help. Hank hadn't been able to hit the brakes in time.

June crashed to the ground, brought the table down with her. Hank ripped his hands free, backed into the counter, and spun around. He yelled to the bartender, "Call the cops! Call someone!"

The bartender smiled and scratched at his beard. "And why would I do that?"

June dragged herself toward him on her elbows. Hank screamed, "Look at her."

"But you said I was beautiful," she wailed.

The squeaking of the wagon made Hank freeze. The old man pulled the rusty red thing to the front door, dropped the handle.

"To hell with you!" Hank shouted to June, to the bartender, to the patrons oozing out of their booths. He ran to the wagon and kicked the back of it, the pile of rags in the back falling out and somehow tangling around his legs.

The rags were heavy, anchoring Hank to the floor. He tried to kick them off, but both of his legs were pinned. He looked down and saw a mixture of flesh and cloth, the raw meat nearly indistinguishable from the mangled jeans the woman had been wearing earlier today.

Hank pulled on the door, but it would not open. June kept calling him honey, creeping closer. The bartender whistled, tossed a sharpened rail spike in the air as he made his way over. The forms of disfigured patrons advanced upon the entrance that would never be an exit.

Woodshop After Math

The bell rang and Tyler was out the door before Miss Conner finished saying she hadn't excused them. Tyler hated pre-Algebra, another reminder he wasn't living up to his father's expectations, that he had wasted the last three years of his life. But that wasn't why he was in a hurry to leave, at least not today. It was Friday, Sam's birthday, and he had to see her before school let out. Then he had to get to his appointment with Dr. Heckman.

Sam's present in one hand, his math book in the other, Tyler moved through the stream of students pouring out of their classrooms. He snaked past two football players punching each other in the arm, then a group of Goth kids passing a vape pen. Tyler focused straight ahead. He wasn't in the mood to see their stares, to hear them mumble and call him "freak." He'd only started school one month before but that's not why they talked about him.

The hallway branched, right to the administration building and his appointment, left to Sam's locker. Dr. Heckman's warning not to be late echoed in Tyler's head. He turned left, hoped Sam would be there so he'd make it to his appointment in time.

Sam, of course, wasn't there. She was never on time. Tyler set her present on a small desk in the hallway and wiped his sweaty hand on his shirt. What could he say that wasn't lame? *Happy birthday. How's your birthday going? Did you get any cool presents? Here you go. Here's the present I made you in woodshop. I spent the last two weeks making it. Look what a dork I am. Do you know how pretty you are? Do you still like me?*

A few kids ran down the hall and a crowd formed outside the bathrooms. Someone shouted. Tyler picked up Sam's present and found himself at the back of the crowd when he heard a girl plead, "Stop it!"

It was Sam. Tyler pushed his way into the middle of the throng. Bradley, a pompous prick who would have been in tenth grade if he wasn't so stupid, stood over Sam who was on her knees trying to retrieve a pink bakery box from the ground. Every time she went to grab the box, Bradley nudged it out of her reach with his boot. Her fair skin flushed red and Tyler felt the hair on his arms rising when she told Bradley to leave her alone.

Bradley kicked the pink box against the wall.

Tyler surprised himself when he said, "Back off, Bradley."

Sam and Bradley both looked toward Tyler. Then Bradley grabbed her hair, turned her head, and pumped his groin at her face. Sam swatted at his arm and flailed to get away, but Bradley wouldn't let her go.

"Bradley, I'm not kidding," Tyler said, trying to keep his voice from cracking.

Bradley talked so loudly everyone in the hall could hear. "What are you going to do about it, Psycho?"

"Yeah," Hector chimed in from behind Bradley, his raised middle fingers a clear indication of what he thought about Tyler. "What are you going to do, pull a Newtown?"

Kent, their little dork follower, stood next to Hector, grinning his idiot grin then twisting his face into his rendition of a psychopath. "No, man, this guy's all Virginia Tech. He's like the Energizer bunny. He'll just keep going and going."

Three-on-one with a whole bunch of kids to watch him get his ass kicked, but Tyler wasn't walking away from the only girl who'd ever stood up for him.

A locker slammed shut at the far end of the hall and Hector jumped. Tyler dropped Sam's present and his book. It didn't matter if he was smaller than all of them. It didn't matter that he was by himself. Bradley chuckled, kept Sam down with his hand on her shoulder. "Are you serious? Check this loser out."

Tyler said, "Let her be."

Bradley stared down at Sam's chest. "She's a big girl. She can take care of herself."

"I'm not telling you again."

Bradley let go of Sam and took a step toward Tyler. "Or what? What are you going to do, you little psycho?" Bradley stuck out his chest, what they called puffing in juvie. Kids did that when they were scared deep down, and they were usually the ones who got their butt kicked. That's what Tyler tried to tell himself as he looked up at Bradley.

Pretending he was someone else, someone stronger and more confident, Tyler said, "I'm not scared of you, or your little buddies."

Ooh's and *aah's* came from the crowd. Before Bradley could respond, Tyler took a step toward him. "Donnie was a lot bigger than you are," Tyler said, his voice flat and dead.

No one said a word. Bradley looked like he wanted to say something, but kept his mouth shut. A teacher that Tyler hadn't seen before came out of a classroom and yelled for them to break it up before she called the principal. Tyler couldn't help but notice she focused on him the whole time. Even teachers he didn't know had heard about him; they were convinced he was the monster the papers made him out to be.

Tyler turned back to Bradley, but the punk and his friends were walking away, heads held high as if they hadn't just chickened out. If Bradley really wanted to fight, he would have done it in front of the teacher. In juvie, Tyler had witnessed one kid jump another one right in front of an officer, stabbing that kid's neck with the sharpened end of his plastic fork, one, two, three, four times before the officer pulled him off.

The rest of the crowd dispersed while Tyler helped Sam off the ground. She thanked him, but didn't need to. The way she looked at him was enough to make him take on a dozen guys. She was the one person who didn't believe he was a monster, who knew he was innocent, who believed he wouldn't want to hurt anyone for no reason. She knew the Tyler prior to his juvenile hall stint wouldn't ever do something so vicious, but that kid had been forgotten by everyone else. They only saw the Tyler who had spent the last three years locked up. He looked different. Maybe he was different. He'd learned that sometimes people needed to be hurt.

Sam picked up the mangled pink box. It was filled with brightly decorated cupcakes, most of which were squished, their frosting splattered on the dirty tile. "You shouldn't have done that," she said.

Tyler tried not to stare at her low-rise jeans as she stood. "I'm glad to see you, too."

She swiped the hair from her eyes and said, "Sorry. I'm just surprised to see you." She kicked her locker closed. "Don't you have your appointment today?"

Tyler wasn't listening. He scoured the floor for his present, spotted it by a row of lockers. Luckily, it hadn't met the fate of the cupcake box. He picked it up, gripped the wooden cylinder, not sure if he should give it to her.

Sam repeated, "Don't you have your appointment?"

"Yeah, but I was passing by and thought I'd see you."

Sam motioned toward his math book. "You passed Admin on the way from Pre-Algebra."

"What can I say, I'm still new here." Tyler forced an awkward laugh. "Haven't got the place figured out yet."

"You should get going. The bell's going to ring any minute, and you can't be late."

"Then we better hurry." Tyler grabbed her hand. "I'm walking you to class."

Sam hesitated before following. "You can walk me down the hall. I don't want you to ever get in trouble because of me again."

Tyler almost said that he would do anything for her, that she was worth it.

"What's that?" she asked, indicating her present.

He almost offered it to her and wished her a happy birthday, but he saw the clock. Less than two minutes. Sam told him to just go. Tyler began to pull her in the opposite direction. "Woodshop's over here. I said I'd walk you to class."

Sam complained, but not too much, and hurried with Tyler to the lone building outside the double doors, where the loud noises wouldn't disrupt the other classes. At the door, Sam looked down at her mangled box of cupcakes.

"These are ruined. I worked so hard on them," she said.

"You made your own cupcakes for your birthday?"

Her look said she was surprised he remembered.

Tyler said, "I thought you hated Jenkins. Why take the cupcakes to woodshop?"

"I need all the brownie points I can get. Jenkins hates me. Especially when I don't wear a skirt he can look up."

Tyler changed the subject, worried he wouldn't be able to talk if he thought about her smooth thighs peeking out from under a skirt. "You do just as well as any of the boys in there."

"You'll find out that doesn't always matter."

Unable to think of anything clever to say, Tyler simply said, "Well, that sucks."

The bell was going to ring any second, but Tyler didn't care. He tried to remember if Sam had always been so beautiful, if she'd always been so quiet. He wondered if her dad still drank too much. If things had gotten any better at home.

Fifteen feet from the door, the bell sounded, signaling the start of the seventh period. Tyler opened the door and held it for her.

"Will you just go?" Sam begged. "I really don't want to see you get in any trouble."

Tyler nodded started jogging backwards. "I have a present for you. I'll give it to you after school."

She smiled before she turned to head inside. Mr. Jenkins, with his creepy mustache and safety goggles, ushered her in. Someone inside the class whistled. It was Bradley who was sitting at the table closest to the door. The prick patted the empty chair next to him, telling Sam he had another place for her to sit if she didn't want to sit there.

Tyler headed back, didn't care that Mr. Jenkins was in the middle of roll call. He pushed open the door all the way. "Excuse me?" Mr. Jenkins said, clearly pissed.

"Go take your Ritalin or whatever it is they give nut jobs like you," Bradley said.

Hector and Kent laughed. Mr. Jenkins snorted.

Tyler didn't waste any words, just headed straight for Bradley. The look of surprise on Bradley's face was priceless as he pushed back in his chair, struggling to get to his feet. If Tyler had been a hair quicker, and if Sam hadn't yelled at Tyler not to do anything stupid, Tyler would have embarrassed Bradley in front of the entire class.

But Mr. Jenkins was quick. He blocked Tyler's path, a two-by-four in his right hand, his left hand extended like a crossing guard. "Don't you have somewhere to go?"

"Yeah, go see your shrink." Bradley pointed at Tyler. "You and I will talk after school."

Tyler imagined how good it would feel to rip the wood out of Jenkins' hands and bash Bradley's face.

"Ignore him," Sam said. "I can take care of myself."

Without looking at her, Bradley, Hector, Kent, or any of the other assholes laughing at him, Tyler spun around and headed for the administration building. He was late. His heart was pounding. He took deep breaths and practiced Heckman's positive thinking drills, told himself that Bradley wouldn't really try to fight him after school, that the punk would end up chickening out. He tried to forget about Mr. Jenkins threatening him with the lumber, and concentrated on the smile Sam gave him when he told her about the present.

Tyler pulled out the wooden cylinder he'd only finished the night before. He hoped Sam would notice the effort he put into the picture-perfect alignment of the bracelet she'd given him back when he was in the detention facility. *Sam and Tyler: Best Friends Forever,* the bracelet said. He wondered if she knew how happy he had been to get it from his mom when she visited him. He wondered if she knew that bracelet was what got him through so many lonely, scary, miserable nights. Maybe, someday, she could be more than just a friend.

Tyler entered the office, nodded at the secretary, and headed to the last door on the left. He stopped in his tracks when he saw that his mom sat across from stuffy old Heckman.

"What are you doing here?" he asked. This couldn't be good.

"Your mother is here because I asked her to come in." Heckman folded his wrinkled hands. "The real question is, why are you late?"

"I forgot I had to come today. I got all the way to woodshop before Mr. Jenkins reminded me."

Heckman glanced in the folder. "You have woodshop first period."

"I …"

"I'll have to put this into my report to Officer Wright. I warned you that I would."

Tyler shrugged his shoulders, trying to seem like he didn't care, but he did.

"Should I also add insolence?"

"It doesn't matter what I think, so do whatever the fuck you want."

"Tyler!" his mom said. "Watch your language!"

"And have a seat," Heckman said.

Tyler did as he was told, well aware that Heckman would love to bury him in the progress report to Tyler's probation officer. Tyler took a deep breath and said, "I'm sorry I'm late, but I did forget that I had this appointment."

"That's a convenient excuse."

Not about to take the doctor's bait, Tyler sat quietly.

"We've talked about this, Tyler. Making excuses is one of the road blocks to your recovery."

"I thought I was recovered. Why else would they let me out?"

"Your rehabilitation is ongoing. We're to ensure you never do to anyone else what you did to that boy."

Tyler wondered if a high school junior Donnie's size should be considered a boy, but he kept the question to himself.

"Not taking responsibility for your actions, that's been an issue for you, hasn't it?"

Tyler felt his mother's stare and nodded.

"Only by taking responsibility for the wrongs you have committed can you begin to respect yourself, and only then will others be able to respect you."

"I'm trying. If I screw up, I try to admit it." He turned toward his mom. "Right?"

"Well, for stuff around the house you do. Like when you forget to take out the trash or don't clean up after Lucas." She turned to Heckman. "That's our blind Labrador. Tyler's real good with him."

"But that's not what we're talking about, Tyler, and you know it," Heckman said.

"I'm not admitting to something I didn't do. I just forgot."

"Tyler," Heckman began.

"Okay, I was talking to a girl. I'm sorry. Happy?"

"A girl?" his mother asked. "Not that Samantha."

"No," Tyler said way too quickly.

His mom was silent for a moment. She looked at him and said, "What did we do wrong, Tyler? Your dad and I did our best to raise you right. How did you get like this?"

Before she became hysterical and started to cry, Tyler said, "Nothing. You guys did nothing wrong!" Then he looked at Heckman and added, "Neither did I."

Heckman cleared his throat. "Then why were you arrested? Why did the judge sentence you to three years in juvenile detention?"

"Because no one believed me. Is it so hard to believe that I'm telling the truth? That I didn't do anything?"

Heckman shook his head. "The facts are the reason why no one believes you. You were found covered in his blood."

"I was trying to help him."

"After the damage you'd done."

Tyler tried to remain calm, tried not to think about every humiliating experience in juvie. "You can't even consider that maybe Donnie fell down?" He looked at Heckman and then his mom. "He did have epilepsy."

The doctor pointed out that the tests proved Donnie didn't suffer a seizure that day.

"Maybe the test was wrong? Ever think of that?"

"What he did have was a history of beating you up and teasing you."

Tyler shook his head. He wasn't going to convince Heckman or anyone else, even his mom. Only Tyler and Sam knew that he hadn't hurt Donnie. And only Sam knew what had happened before Tyler arrived.

Tyler had been on his way home from elementary school when he heard the scream coming from the alley. The second scream he'd recognized as Sam's. He'd run full speed toward the sound of her cry.

He'd never told anyone that part of the story, and he wasn't about to now. Heckman wouldn't have believed him anyway, and he couldn't bring up Sam in front of his mom, who always said there was something wicked about that girl. His mom was right, but she didn't know the whole story.

The doctor asked Tyler's mom some questions, leaving Tyler to his memories. He remembered racing into the alley, his heart thudding against his chest, seeing Donnie on his back, flopping around like a fish. In Donnie's clinched fist was the cherry donut Tyler had given Sam earlier in the day. It was smashed just like the cupcakes in her pink box.

Hearing his name, Tyler snapped back to the present, realized Heckman was asking him something. His mother started speaking when he interrupted her. Tyler told the doctor he didn't feel well. "I need to go to the bathroom."

Heckman excused him with a wave of his wrinkled hand. "Make it quick."

The memory replayed as Tyler left the building and jogged past the bathrooms. Sam had been standing over Donnie, her shirt ripped, her cheek an angry red, a palm print still visible. Donnie's face was red, too. His blond hair was red. The concrete was red.

Donnie's eyes were wide, staring at Tyler. Donnie was scared, his expression begging for help as he raised his own head off the ground and smashed it into the concrete with a sickening thud, blood spraying everywhere. Without a word, he brought his head up again and smashed it back down, over and over, again and again. Sam just sat off to the side with her eyes closed.

Tyler's jog turned into a sprint, the woodshop building still fifty yards away. He hoped he was overreacting, that Sam wasn't doing it again. He was probably just imagining things. But if he wasn't, this time he would do the smart thing and take Sam away. He wouldn't listen to her cry while he tried to make Donnie stop bashing his brain into the ground.

Running faster, the distance closing, Tyler's heartbeat sounded like the thud, thud, thud of Donnie's skull. He remembered how Sam stood and watched Tyler try to restrain Donnie from hurting himself even more.

"He tried to kiss me," Sam had cried. "He tried to kiss me and touch me. Don't tell my dad, Tyler. Please. He'll say it was my fault."

Now only ten feet away from woodshop, Tyler heard the scream of machinery. That was not unusual, but Tyler still hesitated to open the door. He gathered his courage and entered the building. Most of the students were bunched together in the far corner, staring at their feet or at the back of the person in front of them, their hands clapped over their ears.

Hector was the closest of the three boys who were not lucky enough to be part of the herd. He stood in front of the planer, both of his pinky fingers on the floor looking like bloody sausages covered in sawdust. His face twisted in a horrified grimace, but he just stood there letting the whirling blade tear through his fingers a millimeter at a time.

Kent was on the machine to Hector's left. He kept feeding his fist into the grinder, a slow soggy push.

Tyler spotted Bradley over at the rip saw. He was on his knees in front of the massive blade that was spinning, whirring, inching closer.

Bradley looked at Tyler with his wild eyes as he pumped his groin into the spinning saw, chunks of meat and cloth and blood spraying everywhere.

Jenkins was overseeing it all, shaking in the corner while his favorite pupils mutilated themselves.

Sam was sitting behind Jenkin's desk. Tyler ran over to her, pleaded for her to stop. She told him to leave, her voice cold and calm, nothing like it'd been with Donnie.

"Why, Sam?" Tyler asked. "Why?"

"They were going to hurt you."

It took Tyler a moment to find his voice. "You have to stop."

"I can't let you take the blame again. Plus," she motioned toward the other students, all the eyewitnesses she let live, "it's too late for that. Now go."

Tyler knew she was right, that there'd be no way out of this incident, but he wasn't ready to leave her. While Hector took off his remaining fingers, the grinder polished Kent's forearm, and Bradley completed his evisceration, Tyler took the wooden cylinder from his pocket and placed it on the desk.

"Happy Birthday, Sam."

Sam smiled, stood up from her desk, and kissed Tyler on his cheek. A few of the other students ran from the building. Sam told Tyler, "Go."

Tyler could only think of the kiss, the kind words, not caring of the carnage surrounding them. "I'll stay."

"No, you won't. I need you to leave. The cops are going to show, and I don't know if I'm ready to let them take me. You can't be here for that."

Tyler tried to stay, but Sam forced his feet towards the door. Her control over his body weakened when Tyler stepped outside. He jammed his foot in the doorway and tried to call Sam's name, but nothing came out. All he could do was watch as Sam focused her attention on Mr. Jenkins who'd just started the jigsaw.

Twisted Memory

The key wouldn't turn. The goddamn lock was always sticking. Tom slid out the key to examine it, making sure he had the right one, then he shoved it back in. The deadbolt still wouldn't move. Tom pounded his fist against the door. "Gina! Open up!"

That bitch must've changed the lock while he was out. He banged his fist again.

A man shouted from inside the apartment. "What the hell's going on?"

She had a man in his apartment? "Open the goddamn door!"

Huge, clonking footsteps came toward him, and the door whipped open. A heavyset Hispanic man filled the doorway. With a scowl on his face, he asked, "What the hell's your prob —"

Tom's heart was pounding so hard he didn't even hear his fist striking the man in the mouth. The man stumbled backward into the apartment. Tom followed, slammed the door shut behind him, and ran after the guy, who was trying to hide behind the couch.

Tom grabbed the man's collar and looked into his soulless eyes. Gina and this asshole probably laughed about Tom when they had sex. Before the bastard could ask for forgiveness, Tom threw a devastating elbow at his head. A loud crack filled the apartment. The man's legs gave. Tom dropped him and rammed a knee into his chest, then shoved him into the cheap particle board entertainment center.

An ancient, thirteen-inch, tube television set crashed to the floor next to the broken man. Tom wondered where his forty-two-inch flat-screen and the mahogany piece it sat on had disappeared to. Figuring Gina had let her lover sell Tom's stuff for crack money, Tom yelled for her. "Get out here, Gina!" He stood over the crumpled man, woke him with a kick. "Get out here now, Gina, or you're gonna end up like your boyfriend."

The man spat out a mouthful of blood and held his jaw as he mumbled, "No one's here. Fuck, man, you got the wrong place."

Tom kicked him in his thigh. "She's got ten seconds. You better call her."

"There's no Gina here. Never even heard of her." The man used his shoddy entertainment center to get back to his feet. He motioned to the frames on the wall. "This is my place. Look at the pictures."

Not about to look away and get sucker punched, Tom pushed the man's chest, sending him into the hallway. He planned on knocking the damn liar out when he rebounded off the wall, but the bastard must have seen it coming, somehow stopping himself and taking off down the hallway, racing for the bedroom.

Tom flew after him before the man could get hold of Gina or call the cops, but the guy was already shutting the door behind him. Tom threw his body at it before it closed all the way.

A loud grunt came from the other side of the door as it popped open, spilling Tom inside the strangely decorated bedroom. There were balloons all over the walls, something Gina must have done earlier that morning. The intruder spun his arms and stopped himself before hitting the crib. *Why is there a crib?* Tom thought, as the man picked up the cordless phone in his left hand and a baseball bat in the other.

"Put my shit down. Now!" Tom yelled even though he didn't recognize the bat. It was bright red. Tom realized it was plastic

"I'm calling the cops."

Tom could barely contain a chuckle. "You're gonna call the cops on yourself? I don't think so. Put my shit down and maybe I'll let you leave."

"Back off." The man waved the bat back and forth. "I mean it."

Tom took another step, the length of the crib between them. "So do I. You got any idea how fucked you are?"

The deluded guy looked down at his bat. Tom lunged forward, placed one hand on each end of the bat, and twisted, the robber's wrist snapping in a satisfying crunch.

The robber's surprised cry was silenced when Tom chucked the bat and began pummeling the side of the man's head until his arm grew heavy, the loud smacks splashing blood over Tom's face. The man was begging him to stop through his sliced lip when a baby cried.

Tom let the man drop next to the light-blue dresser and walked over to the crib. A baby, red-faced and squishy, wailed. "What the hell is this?" Tom asked.

"It's my kid, man. Come on, please, I don't know any Gina."

A quick search reassured Tom that Gina wasn't there for some unknown reason. He picked up the brown leather wallet that the amateur had left on the entryway table and stuffed it into his front pocket, figured he should hold onto it, just in case. He didn't even know. His head was spinning as he walked out.

The midmorning sun blinded him when he walked onto the sidewalk. Disoriented, he looked up and down the block, searching for his convertible Boxster. He clearly remembered parking on the north side of the street, but his car was nowhere to be found. *I drove it, didn't I?*

Tom could still hear the baby crying in his head. He dug his keys out of his left pocket, tossing aside a one-way bus ticket from Folsom he must've picked up by accident. He went to press the panic alarm on the remote, only to realize there was no remote. His shiny apartment key and a worn key for Gina's Honda were all that was left. The Porsche key must have fallen off the ring earlier that morning. Some rotten son of a bitch must have come across it and stolen the car.

Instead of making himself sick thinking about it, Tom decided he would file a report with the police after he found Gina. He had to make sure she was okay. If he was so materialistic that he placed his car above her, he didn't deserve to be called her boyfriend.

A cab turned the corner. Tom had his first break of the day, flagging it down with a wave of his finger. It wasn't until he slid into the passenger side of the back seat and the driver asked him where he was headed, that Tom realized he had no idea where he could find Gina.

The bald cabbie looked into his rearview. "You doing okay, brother?"

"My girl. I need to find her, make sure she's alright."

"Not a problem. Where's she live?"

Tom motioned toward the apartment building he'd just come out of. "With me. At least she did until this morning. Her stuff's gone."

"Damn. Tough break." The cabbie turned his attention back to the street. "So where you want to go?"

"I ... don't know. Someone stole my Porsche."

After a brief hesitation, the cabbie asked, "You got any money, because I ain't running a charity carriage."

"Yeah," Tom said, having no idea if he did or didn't. With everything that had happened, he was scared to look in his wallet. Then he remembered the guy and the baby. Sure enough, two hundred bucks and some change.

"So where to?"

Tom looked back at the street, at the apartment building. It did look different than he remembered.

The cabbie said, "Any idea where she might be? I kinda gotta get moving."

Sirens sounded in the distance. "Go ahead and drive up the street a bit."

"You got an address? I need to radio it in."

"Her sister lives in Santa Clarita, pretty close to Six Flags. Gina might be with her."

"That's an hour away."

"I got the money." All that mattered was Gina.

Tom took the cash and waved it in the air for the cabbie to see. Raising his voice so he could be heard above the approaching sirens, Tom said, "This is more than enough. Here's a twenty in case you think I'm gonna stiff you. I just need to stop at a phone booth first to get her sister's address."

The cabbie told him to keep it as he started the meter, pulled away from the curb, and headed north.

When Tom put the bills back into the wallet, he noticed the back of his hand was speckled with bright red drops.

By the time the cabbie found a phone booth with a directory inside it, Tom had wiped the drops off his hands, did the best he could with the spots on the front of his denim jacket. It didn't take him long to find Gina's sister in the book, but there was a surprise. Her address was listed as Pasadena, not Santa Clarita. Gina had never mentioned her sister was considering moving.

Tom ripped the page from the directory and got back into the cab. "Good news. She's not far from here."

"Sure it's the right person? Want to try calling her?"

"It's her. I'd rather just show up."

Ten minutes later, the cab stopped in front of an unfamiliar house. The cabbie motioned toward the red Porsche 911 in the driveway and chuckled. "Is that your car?"

"No. Why?"

"You said yours was stolen. I thought maybe your girl took it."

"My car's in the shop. I hate blue."

"Yeah, all right." The cabbie checked the meter. "That'll be sixty dollars." The cabbie studied Tom to see if he was aware that he was ripping him off.

Tom tossed him a hundred and got out of the cab. "Do me a favor and keep it running. I might need a ride back." He headed for the porch before the cabbie could say no.

The front door opened. Joanne, whose hair was now streaked with gray, was on her cell phone. Her jaw dropped midsentence when she recognized Tom.

"Surprise," Tom said. "I didn't know you guys moved. You shoulda told me."

She sounded like a robot when she said, "I've got to go." She hung up and started dialing someone new, probably the cops.

Tom ripped the cell from her hand, tossed it on the grass. He was about to ask about Gina when he noticed the silver necklace around Joanne's neck. "That's Gina's."

"No, it's mine."

"I gave it to her for our anniversary."

Joanne slowly shook her head. "You shouldn't be here. I can't believe they let you out."

Not knowing who "they" were or from where they had supposedly let him out, Tom focused on the necklace. There was no denying the G-inscribed heart pendant belonged to Gina. Tom took a step into the doorway. "Where is she?"

Joanne shrieked and tried to slam the door on Tom. Not about to let some nutty chick get the best of him, Tom lowered his shoulder and drove forward, knocking Joanne back into her house. He shut the door and pinned Joanne against the wall before she could scream.

"What the hell's your problem? I'm looking for Gina to make sure she was okay. She wasn't at home."

Joanne tried to slap him, but he knocked her hand away.

"Stop it," he said. "I'm trying to protect her. Where is she?"

Joanne tore at his face with her free hand. Tom grabbed each of her wrists and crushed them against the wall. "Tell me where she is!"

"You sick fuck!" Joanne kneed Tom's groin, folded him over. He lost his grip on Joanne and she dashed to the phone in the kitchen, picked it up, and punched three buttons.

Tom ignored the pain, fought the urge to vomit. "Hang up the phone, Joanne."

Joanne backed up to the wall, her eyes looking around her, probably searching for a weapon. She took a deep breath and said she needed help. She said Tom's name.

Tom stepped toward her. "Tell them you called by mistake and that everything's okay."

"He's a convicted murderer. He killed my sister twelve years —"

Tom yelled, "Hang it up. And give me Gina's necklace!" He kept screaming, trying to block out Joanne's words repeating in his head. *Killed my sister* ...

Joanne begged the dispatcher to hurry. Tom didn't ask any more questions. She obviously wasn't ready to tell him where Gina was. He tore the landline off the wall, wrapped his hands around Joanne's throat. It was so soft. Just like Gina's.

Tom closed the front door behind him, then got back into the cab. The driver eyed him and asked if everything was okay.

"No, but she was here." He held up the necklace and said, "She left this by accident. Her sister asked if I could return it to her."

"So ... where to?"

Tom stuffed the necklace into his pocket, noticing he hadn't gotten all that sticky red paint off. "Her mom and dad live nearby."

Mommy's Big Boy

Stacy held her one-year-old on her lap, cooing and trying to get her boy to say the name of her latest man. "Say it for Mommy. Come on, Brendan. Say, 'Harry.'"

Brendan tilted his head to the side and gazed into his mother's eyes. *Babies always look like little drunks*, Stacy thought. Brendan's eyes were glossy and trying to focus.

"Look, he's about to say it," Stacy said.

Harry didn't take his eyes off the baseball game, even when he took a sip of his Bud Light. "Cool."

"Come on, Brendan. You know how to talk," she said. "One time. Say, 'Harry.'"

Brendan's blue eyes sparkled and a grin spread across his face. "Airy."

"He did it! He said it!" Stacy cheered, bouncing Brendan into the air to celebrate.

Harry turned up the television, gulped the rest of his beer.

Stacy saw she'd been annoying again, apologized for being too loud. "I'm going to put him to bed. It's early, but maybe we could have some alone time."

Harry actually glanced over at her. "That don't sound too bad." Harry used the remote control to scratch the side of his neck.

"All right, I won't be long." Stacy stood with Brendan. "Who's Mommy's big boy?" Stacy gently tossed her little guy in her hands. "You ready for bed?"

Brendan shook his head and used sign language to say that he was hungry. Stacy had taught him how to do it after watching a rerun of *Oprah*. Brendan had taken to it quickly. It gave him a voice, and Stacy liked that. Just now wasn't the time.

"You don't need to eat. It's time to go to bed. I'll feed you in the morning."

Brendan squirmed and squealed, trying to wiggle out of her hands. Stacy had to sit back down to catch him. Before she could control him, he turned sideways and positioned himself under her breast.

Stacy laughed as Brendan tried to lift her shirt. "Quit it, Brendan."

Brendan screamed when she held down her top. His scream grew louder.

"What the hell's he crying about?" Harry asked.

"He wants me to feed him."

"Get him a bottle if it will shut him up."

"No, look at him. He wants *me* to feed him."

Harry waited for the commercial before turning around. "That's disgusting. I don't want to see that."

"It's perfectly natural."

"I don't care. I can't handle the thought of some kid sucking on your tits."

"It's not like that. It's no big deal."

"Yeah it is. It's gross. Don't ever do that around me. Don't even talk about it." He turned back to the TV. "And get him to shut up. Little fucker's giving me a goddamn headache."

"I'm sorry," Stacy said to both Brendan and Harry. She got out of the chair and walked Brendan to the bedroom. "I'll put him to bed. Be back in a minute."

Stacy laid Brendan in his crib, but in no time he was up on his feet, rattling the top railing. He continued to scream. She gave his cheek a gentle squeeze and smoothed his fine blonde hair. "I'm so sorry, Brendan. Mommy's sorry. Just do this for me. I wish you could understand. Harry's not a bad guy and I want to keep him around for a bit, but he won't stick if you keep on crying like that. He'll like you. I swear it. Oh, baby, please. Stop crying, will you? I need you to go to bed, sweetheart. Please."

Brendan unleashed an ear-piercing shriek.

"I'm sorry, honey." Stacy forced herself away from the crib. "You need to go to bed. I'll see you in the morning."

Before she changed her mind and picked up her screaming baby from the crib, Stacy walked from the room, leaving the door open an inch so she could peek in later without waking him. When she returned to the living room, she heard Brendan wailing over the baby monitor positioned next to the television.

Harry glared at her and then the monitor. "Come on, Stace. I gotta listen to this? Are you serious?"

Stacy grabbed the monitor and lowered the volume. "I'm sorry. I forgot about it."

Harry turned up the television. "I can still hear him."

"I need to leave it on. This is so I can hear him."

"I don't buy that. What about all the babies before those stupid things came out? They all came out fine. My mom didn't have one of those things."

"It makes me feel better." She sat on the couch, lowered the monitor so she could barely hear Brendan's cries over the baseball game.

"Does that little bastard always scream like that?"

Stacy winced. "The funny thing is he never used to. Even right after his dad died. It wasn't until last week that he started throwing these tantrums." Brendan's dad had passed eight months earlier. He and Stacy had already planned on splitting, but it still tore her up to think about his death.

Harry shrugged his shoulders and returned his attention to the game. "Probably does it because you baby him too much. Treat him like a man, or he'll grow up to be a damn sissy."

"He's only one."

"Put him on a schedule and don't treat him like he's helpless. He'll stop crying, trust me."

"You're probably right."

"I am." He clicked off the game, which ended with the Tigers winning by three. "So now that he's in bed, how about showing *me* some attention?"

"I'd love to." She hurried over and sat on his lap.

Harry looked down and noticed the monitor in her hands. "What about that alone time you were talking about?"

She had left the door cracked and promised herself she'd keep one ear listening for Brendan. "There, it's off." She kissed him on the cheek and set the monitor on the coffee table. "How's that?"

"That's a start." Harry pushed Stacy off his lap so he could dig into his jeans pocket. He held up a plastic baggie. "I brought us a little snack."

A pile of shriveled brown objects sat at the bottom of the bag. "What are those?"

"Mushrooms. Ever tried them?"

"*Mushrooms*? No way."

"Never? You have no idea what you're missing out on."

Stacy's cousin had tried to get her to take them in high school, but one taste had nearly made her puke, and she'd spit it out. She tried pulling Harry to his feet. "We don't need that to have a good time. Come on, I'll show you."

Harry pulled away from her grasp, but kept eye contact. "Just try one. It'll bring us closer. You've got to try it."

"But what about Brendan?"

"He's asleep." Harry slid his arm up Stacy's forearm, gave her goosebumps.

"But what if he wakes and needs me? And what about nursing him? Can it mess up my milk?"

Harry yanked his hand away. "Goddamn it, Stacy! What'd I say about that crap? He's a boy, not a damn glass figurine."

"I don't want to do anything that can hurt him."

Harry opened the bag and placed two of the shrunken mushrooms on his palm. "It's fine." He placed one in his mouth and held the other one out to her. "They've done all kinds of tests on it."

"You mean studies?"

"That's what I said." He surprised her and stuck the other mushroom in her mouth. "Just take it."

Stacy was about to spit it out, but then Harry said, "You were the one who said you wanted to keep me around a bit. That I wasn't so bad."

Stacy was going to deny it, but he pulled her into his chest. He stroked her cheek, forced her mouth closed. "There you go. That's good. Just chew it up and relax. You deserve this. Lie down on the floor. Here, let me put this down." Harry spread a blanket over the worn carpet and flipped on the radio. "We'll just relax and watch some music for a while. That's right, just come down here and get comfortable."

Stacy stopped chewing the nasty stem, lay on her back and stared up at the ceiling. Nothing happened for a while, but then everything began to spin.

Harry just kept stroking her arm, telling her to relax. He crawled on top of her, slid his jeans past his knees. She woke a few minutes later — or was it hours – to the sound of a salesman announcing the best deals at Pete's Pontiac. Still half-asleep, she blocked out the radio ad, rolled onto her side and spooned Harry's sleeping body. She saw movement in her peripheral vision. Through blurry eyes, Stacy saw Brendan standing next to Harry's head. Brendan was struggling to hold a potted plant. He lifted the pot into the air and took a step closer to Harry's head.

Stacy cried out for Brendan to set the pot down. He turned his head so fast that he lost his balance and he fell onto his side, the pot breaking on the floor. Brendan got to his feet and shoved his finger against his tiny lips. "Not a word, bitch," he said and ran toward his room, his little legs struggling to balance his chubby body. Stacy told herself she was hallucinating. She closed her eyes and drifted off again.

Brendan's high-pitched screams and an eyeful of warm sunshine woke Stacy from her deep sleep. The clock told her it was already past seven o'clock. Brendan always ate by five-thirty, six at the latest. No wonder he was screaming bloody murder.

Although her head was pounding and her lower back was killing her, Stacy picked herself off the floor. She hurried to Brendan's room, afraid the baby's cries would wake Harry, who was still sprawled naked on the floor.

Brendan stopped crying and smiled at her. As she went to pick him up, Stacy bumped into the tiny chair someone had placed next to the crib. Using the bottom of her shirt, she wiped the tears from his eyes and the snot from his lip. "Hush, big boy. Mommy's here. I'm sorry, Brendan. You must be starving."

Brendan smiled and gestured in sign language that he wanted to eat. She sat on the rocking chair and pulled up her shirt so he could feed. She was thinking back to her crazy dream of Brendan holding the potted plant, when Brendan bit down on her nipple.

"Ow! What're you doing?" Stacy pulled him away from her and stood him on her lap. "Don't bite. That hurt Mommy."

Brendan shook his oversized head and stared disapprovingly at her and clearly said, "How about you wash your tits after letting that scumbag slobber all over them? If I wanted to taste shitty beer and stale cigarettes, I'd ask you to kiss me."

Stacy held him at arm's length. It took her a few seconds to find any words, but when she did, she screamed for Harry. Brendan smiled as Harry crashed about the living room, yelled for her to calm down. Harry appeared in the doorway, looking worse than Stacy felt.

"What the hell is it?"

Stacy kept Brendan at arm's length. "It's him. He talked."

"You woke me up because of that?"

"No, no," she cried. "You don't understand. He talked like an adult. He had a man's voice and was so mean. This isn't my son."

Harry looked at the smiling baby and back at Stacy. "You're out of your damn mind. It's just the shrooms."

"No. I was feeding him and he bit me. He said …"

"What did I say about that? I told you not to mention that crap."

"I'm sorry, but …" Before Harry could interrupt her, she said, "He bit me and said my boob tasted like beer and cigarettes."

Harry laughed and slapped his thigh. "Jesus, Stacy, you're still tripping. Put the kid in the crib. You need to get your head straight."

"You think it's the mushrooms? I'm still high?"

"What do you think, brainiac? Come on. Put him down and fix me some breakfast. It'll make you feel better." Harry left the room and said, "Wake me when it's ready. I want eggs."

Stacy set Brendan in the crib and stepped back. She studied her giggling boy and felt disgusted with herself. He was adorable, and he couldn't speak. He was one, and she was high. She bent down to nuzzle her son's cheek, whispered his name lovingly.

A sick grin spread across his face. "Why are we whispering?"

Stacy stifled a scream, reminded herself she was still experiencing the drugs. She looked at the chair next to the crib. "Did you get out of your crib last night?"

Brendan nodded. "And you aren't going to say a word, are you, Mommy?" His voice was so deep.

Stacy gasped and pinched herself, hoped the pain would snap her out of this horrific illusion. When it didn't, she said, "What were you trying to do?"

"Let's just say that prick got lucky. If it weren't for these fat baby fingers, his brain would have been mush."

"H-harry!"

"What now?" he asked from the other room.

"He's doing it again."

"Get out of there, Stace," Harry ordered. "You're tripping. Drink some water and fix some goddamned eggs. And don't make 'em all runny."

Brendan waved a mocking goodbye as Stacy backed out of the room. In the living room she noticed the pot, cracked and on its side next to where Harry had been sleeping.

"Oh my God. The pot."

"Relax." Harry covered his face with the blanket to hide from the morning sunshine. "I think I kicked it when I got up. It's your fault though. You scared the crap out of me when you yelled like that."

"You broke it?"

"Who cares? The thing was ugly anyway. Go buy a new one if it bothers you so much."

Stacy wanted to tell Harry about her dream, but it would only upset him even more. Instead, she did as she was told and cooked breakfast. The sunlight was intense, but she felt she was regaining some sobriety. After she slid the plate of fried eggs in front of Harry, Stacy took a bottle of milk into Brendan's room. She was relieved to see he was curled up under his blanket.

Stacy walked to the crib and set the bottle on the nightstand. She was about to pull the blanket down when she heard a noise behind her and whipped around.

Brendan was a few feet away trying to pick up a pair of scissors from the floor.

Before he could cut himself, Stacy snatched the sewing scissors and set them on the cabinet. She turned back to her son who cursed under his breath, looking down at his hands.

"Stupid goddamn fingers," he said.

Keeping one eye on Brendan, Stacy lifted the blanket and saw the pillow underneath it. "What were you trying to do, Brendan?" Her voice shook.

"Let's just say we call you lucky this time."

Stacy picked Brendan up, holding him as far away as possible, and took him into the living room. She set him in front of Harry and said, "Please watch him for a minute. I need to take a bath. I don't feel good at all. My mind's all screwed up. When's this stuff going to wear off?"

"You can't worry about it. If you panic, it'll only make things worse. Hurry up and take a bath. I'll watch him."

"Thanks, Harry. I owe you."

With his back to Harry, Brendan put his fist in front of his O-shaped mouth and rapidly jerked it up and down, showing Stacy he knew how she'd repay her boyfriend. Stacy pretended she didn't see the obscene gesture and ran off to the bathroom. After setting the radio on the ledge and turning on an easy-listening station, she eased into the warm water and tried to relax. She promised God she would never again take drugs. She begged Him to cleanse her mind, take away the evil thoughts. She loved Brendan and hated herself for thinking such terrible things about him.

Stacy had been in the bath for quite some time when there was a low knock on the door.

"I'll be out in a minute, Harry."

The knocking persisted.

"Is everything okay?" she asked. "Brendan's not causing too much trouble, is he?"

The doorknob turned back and forth. Finally, the catch released, the door pushed open, and there was Brendan standing on top of his Rock N' Roll Tigger.

Brendan had opened a door before, doing this very thing, but his sick smile told her the drugs were still coursing through her mind. He got down on his knees and backed off the toy, carefully easing one leg down and then the other so he didn't lose his balance. Before he turned toward her, he picked up his favorite red ball in his right hand, and something else in his left.

"Did you want to play catch?" She looked around the bathroom, actually thinking about what she could use as a weapon before scolding herself. *He's your son. Jesus, get it together, Stacy.* She held her hands in front of her. "Want to throw it to Mommy? Wouldn't Harry play with you?"

Brendan stepped into the bathroom, his left hand behind his back, his right clutching the red ball. "Don't worry about him. That mo-fo got what he deserved."

"What?"

Brendan smiled and moved closer to the tub. "I made a joke. Get it? You're Mommy," Brendan could barely control his giggles. "And he's screwing you. Mo-fo!"

"Brendan, stop this right now. I love you, but you need to listen to me."

Brendan bounced the ball up and down on his palm, his dexterity much improved. "You treat that loser better than your own son. What kind of mom does that?"

"I'm sorry, honey. I … It's just that Mommy's getting older and it's hard to find a decent man."

"You are getting old, and Harry was probably the best you'll ever get. I think I like my chances of getting a foster family. With my angelic face and adorable smile, I'll be picked up quick. And maybe I'll have a proper house, some decent threads." He tugged at the zipper of his ratty sleeper. "These Salvation Army rags aren't flying."

"Brendan, I'm a good mom."

"You named me Brendan for Christ's sakes. You want me to be some sissy boy?"

"Don't say that. Your father named you."

"Oh, what a great guy Daddy was, shaking the crap out of me every night."

"No, he didn't!" Stacy cried.

"Know what else he didn't do? He didn't commit suicide on the bed."

"I'm dreaming." Stacy closed her eyes and shook her head. "This isn't real."

He showed her the fist he had been holding behind his back. "Is this real?"

Stacy stared at Harry's eyeball and screamed. Brendan tossed the bloody orb into the tub. His whole body shook with laughter as his mom slapped it away from her. "Don't worry," Brendan said, "Harry doesn't need it."

Stacy struggled to stand in the tub, waiting for his next move. He threw the ball at her. Stacy moved to her right and then saw the malicious sparkle in Brendan's eyes, realized too late what he'd been aiming for. The radio wobbled on the edge of the counter and fell toward the water before Stacy could leap from the tub. The electricity paralyzed her, and Stacy's eyes fixed on her big boy.

Glory

This was Tony's idea. It always is. He's crouched down beside me behind this juniper, and he won't even look at me. He has his eyes locked on the dimly lit park waiting for us at the bottom of the hill. If the cops drive by, they'll see us running down there. Tony doesn't seem to care.

I whisper to him, "You're going to get us killed."

"What?"

"Nothing."

"I'm going. If you're gonna chicken out, give me the camera and go home."

"I don't think this …" I trail off as Tony turns to me. Even in the dark, I know he's making that face, the one where he's questioning if I have anything between my legs.

"Relax. There's nothing to worry about," Tony says.

It's hard to keep it to a whisper. "What if he's in there somewhere?" I scan the bushes. All I see are shadows, and they're moving. I know it's the ring of flickering red and yellow floodlights, but I can't help but think it's someone lurking.

"There hasn't been a murder since they started locking it up. That psycho split."

"What if he's just waiting?"

Tony ignores me.

I say, "He's probably watching us now."

Tony is focused on our target in the middle of the park. The floodlights encircle the bronze statue of Achilles. It's fifteen feet high, not counting the five-foot stone pedestal. Achilles is holding his spear in one hand, a shield in the other. The top of his helmet looks like a stone Mohawk. His boots rise up to his knees. The rippling muscles of his thighs are almost as impressive as his chiseled arms.

I don't want to sound like a coward, but I say, "He's probably just been waiting for someone to enter the park." I can tell Tony is about to make fun of me when the circle of floodlights flicker in rapid succession. This is part of the display, the new security. The city installed the lights after Christina Peterson ended up with her throat slashed. She was the third teenager who'd been murdered. The killer, they said, could've been a copycat. The first two boys had their eyes gouged out, a different calling card. But all of them died right here.

Tony leans forward. He's looking at something.

"What is it?" I ask.

"Nothing. I thought I saw something."

"Saw what?"

"Nothing."

"Let's just go, man," I say.

"You gotta stop watching those horror movies. The murders stopped when the cops closed up the park. The guy left town."

"You don't know that. No one knows where he is? You want to risk it for some prank?"

"No one knows but the cops. My dad said they didn't release details to anyone. That bullshit going around school is just that; some stupid story to scare little kids." Tony stands and looks down at me. "So are you gonna be a little pussy or are you coming down there with me?"

"I'm not a pussy." I get up and follow him. "But if I hear anything, I'm out."

Tony chuckles. "Not a problem. I'll be the one running right behind you."

We creep down the hill and move from bush to bush. The red and yellow lights playing off of the bronze sculpture of Achilles's massive torso and outstretched arms make it look as if the Greek god is ruling over hell. We get to the six-foot fence surrounding the statue and lights. My head is spinning, and I have to rest my hands on my knees. I listen for noises. All I hear is Tony's breathing, the one thing I can't seem to do right now.

I pull out my inhaler, take two long pulls.

"Dude, keep it down."

"I couldn't breathe."

Tony waits a few seconds. "You ready?"

I've got my face to the fence, checking every shadow for movement, looking for any excuse to bail. "You sure about this?"

Tony grabs my inhaler and chucks it over the fence at Achilles. It clinks off the pedestal.

"What the hell, man?"

"You should get that," Tony says.

"You're a dick."

"I know."

"If we get busted, you're paying my bail." I point to the white and red sign on the fence. "Look, 'No defacing public property – violators will be punished.'"

Tony's looking at the dark bathrooms on the other side of the park. "You read it wrong."

"What?"

"It says prosecuted."

"We're talking about breaking and entering, violating curfew, and vandalism."

"They're not going to do anything. No one's out here."

"But what if they do? I can't go to jail. My parents would kill me."

"You won't go to jail, dumb ass." Tony smiles. "They might take you to juvie, though."

"That's not funny. I know a kid that got raped his first and only night in there, and he was only busted for shoplifting some candy."

"You know a kid who was raped? Who was that?"

I hate it when he calls me on stories. "My cousin Glen told me about it. He used to be a probation officer."

"Yeah, and he told you about a boy being raped?"

"Yes."

"I don't think he did."

"He fucking did."

"Then he was trying to scare you. Guess it worked." Tony gets up, pulls a digital camera from his pocket. He flicks it on and all of the yellow lights encircling the sculpture blink off.

"Why did it do that?" I ask.

"Must be some electrical glitch. No big deal." Tony puts the camera away and motions for me to get up. "Let's go get famous." He points at the sculpture bathing in the eerie red light. "No one's touched that stupid thing since they put it up."

I use the fence to pull myself to the top. "Yeah, for a good reason. No one's dumb enough to come out here."

"We're gonna make a name for ourselves. Now stop talking."

"Fine. Help me over."

Tony laces his fingers. I step up in the makeshift stirrup and look down at him. "You better follow me."

"Just go."

I scramble over the fence, land on the wet grass. Tony lands next to me and the spray cans clank in his backpack. The red lights circling the sculpture flash off.

Tony grabs my arm and I nearly scream. All the lights flash back on and I push him off me.

"I heard something down there," I lie.

Tony shakes his head, eases off the backpack. "No one's in here but us." Tony slips on his mask and holds the camera above his head, like he's going to take a selfie, but instead, he lifts two cans of spray paint in front of the lens and says, "Welcome to Pittsburg." He hands me the green and keeps the black for himself. I adjust my mask and feel the camera on me. There are probably only three or four people watching this and all of them are in our class, but I'm picturing the ten thousand Tony said would be tuning in.

All I want to do is scale the fence and run back home, but I snatch the can and walk down the hill, try not to look scared. Tony following me with the camera doesn't make me feel any better. It's hard to breathe, and my head's on a swivel. We make it to the picnic tables twenty yards from Achilles when every light in the park flickers off. Complete darkness.

I freeze. "What's happening?"

"We're happening, man," Tony says. I don't turn back, but I know he's doing that wide-eyed mug for the camera, the one he's been practicing all week. I hear him hit pause, and I see Tony check his watch. "It just turned midnight. They must be on a timer."

"All of them?"

"That's what it looks like."

The red lights around the sculpture flare back on. Tony hits record.

"So much for the timer," I say.

Tony hits the pause button. "Stop ruining this. Just go. We need some light for the camera anyway."

"You go."

Tony hits record and points the camera right in my face. "Are you ready?" he growls.

I put my hand over the lens. "No way, man. I don't even want to be here. You go first."

"You're going to break it." Tony pulls the camera back, keeps shooting me.

"Who's the pussy now?" I ask.

Tony pushes the camera into my chest, nearly knocks me over. I don't know if he pressed pause or not, but I picture the guys at school laughing their asses off at how stupid we look. Tony tells me to point the camera at him. I do and he pops the top off his can, creeps past the picnic tables, and mumbles that he's not a fucking pussy.

I'm watching him through the screen and trying not to breathe too loud because I know he's gonna rag on it later. So will the guys. *Listen to fat, wheezing Mattie. Surprised he ain't crying.*

Tony steps inside the ring of red lights and the yellow ones spring to life. Tony's almost the color of the statue. He freezes for a second, like he wants to flee, but he surprises me, takes another step toward the sculpture.

The lights begin to alternate, red, then yellow, over and over again. Tony stands at the base of the sculpture and glances back. The lights cycle faster.

I wave him on. "I'm getting it all. Now do it."

Slowly, Tony spins in a circle, his eyes squinting. He says he can't see past the circle of lights. "Someone's fucking with us."

"Do it! Go, man." I zoom in on the statue's profile. Achilles's chiseled features glow in the lights.

I stay on Achilles's upper body, hear Tony take another step. The lights cycle even faster. They begin to strobe. Achilles seems to rock to life as the lights bounce off his bronze skin. The glare is brighter than anything I've seen. "Finish it and get out of there," I tell him. It's hard for me to make anything out. I hope the camera captures something we can use, that we can change the exposure later. It won't do any good for the live feed, but maybe we can fix it in post.

"Are you doing it?" I finally ask.

Tony doesn't answer.

I step toward the circle, the veil of light just as impenetrable as the darkness that surrounds it. "Dude, get the hell out of there."

Again no answer. I take another step and trip on a rock. I throw out my hands to break my fall, the camera and spray can go flying. I pick up the camera, hope it still works. I can't look away from the image on the screen: Achilles's brutal eyes staring directly at the camera; a halo of hellish color swirls around his head.

I don't care who hears me – the cops, the killer, anyone watching this feed. "Come on, Tony! Let's go!"

The lights snap off and the entire park's engulfed in darkness. I don't move, just wait for my eyes to adjust. I see shapes. I hear a hiss. It's Tony, spraying the top of Achilles's head. Tony is on his back, sort of riding the mythic figure. I check the screen. It's too dark right now. I can't see much, so I flip on the night vision. Tony's climbing the statue trying to stand on Achilles's shoulders.

I scream for Tony to go for it, to get up on the statue, although I know I shouldn't be encouraging this. It will sound better for the video though. No one wants to hear the cameraman promoting caution. Suddenly, Tony wobbles; it's like he's surfing, his arms out trying to balance. I slide-step to the left and keep the camera on Tony and Achilles. My feet move slowly, trying to get one of those Michael Bay-type shots when Tony's body jerks back. His foot must have slipped, but it seemed like he was punched or shot by something. He's falling backwards on the other side of the statue.

I hear the sharp crack of him hitting the cement. I keep the camera pointed at the ground as I run over and see Tony on his back. I don't know if he bumped his head, if he's unconscious, but I hope I won't have to call 911. I ask if he's okay. I tell him, "Try to breathe."

There's a noise right behind me. I turn, expecting to see the killer, but it's just Tony's spray can rolling on the concrete.

"Jesus Christ," I say and start to laugh, realizing how ridiculous I feel. There's no one there. Just a stupid can.

The yellow lights flash on. I'm blinded, but I blink a few times until I can see again. Oh God, I wish I couldn't. Something is pooling around Tony's head. It's blood. So much of it spreading on the concrete. The red lights flash on, which makes it all the more vibrant. I want to run away, but it's so beautiful inside the circle. The lights begin their mad cycle, speed to a full strobe within seconds, and it almost seems like Tony is moving. He's not though, and I don't know what to do. I just point the camera at him and keep filming. He's going to be famous.

Mark Tullius

The Infidels' Prayer

Amir signed his name to his latest decree, folded it in thirds, dipped his seal in the calf's blood and turned his wish into law. Pleased with himself, he set the letter at the corner of his desk and turned his attention to the cheap television in the corner of his cramped, windowless room. For two months he'd been trapped here behind the gates. The Americans had gotten too close. He could no longer be seen in public, no longer walk the town square to give coins to the children or to taste the Lady Kabira's dates or cherries.

A loud knock at the door sent Amir to his feet. It was only ten o'clock and he had given orders not to be disturbed until lunch. He didn't hide his irritation when he asked, "Who is it?"

"It is I, Your Excellency, Raheem."

Amir peered through the looking slot. "What is it?"

I'm sorry to disturb you, but we have a problem."

"Americans?"

Raheem shook his head. "It is the prisoners."

Amir opened the door. "Get in here and explain yourself."

Raheem lowered his head and entered the room, his bloody hands working back and forth on a filthy handkerchief. He raised his eyes, looking more like a lamb than the bull of a man he was. "They won't bow."

"What?"

"I'm sorry, Your Excellency, but I cannot bend their will. They say they will not be broken."

"You disappoint me, Raheem. They are but men, barely more than boys. They are not even military. They're infidel."

"Yes, I understand, but they will not budge, and the crowd grows by the minute."

"You can't handle it?"

Raheem straightened to attention, his massive forearms flexing as he clenched his scarred fists. "I can handle it, but my approach may not be as Your Excellency wishes. Especially with nearly the entire town bearing witness."

Amir pointed to the door. "Go and do as you must."

"I have your permission?"

"You have my blessing."

Once Raheem left the room, Amir moved to the three computer monitors lining the back wall. The crowd gathered around the Eastern Court was the largest he'd seen. They'd come to witness the young men who openly opposed Amir. Soon they would discover their fate. That was good. Even the most devoted follower needed a reminder.

Amir admired himself in the full-length mirror. He was the image of excellence, from his perfectly creased beret to his shining black boots. To complete his outfit, Amir removed his sheathed sword from the gilded display case, attached it to his belt, and headed for the door. To hell with the Americans, these people, his people, needed to see his face. Just as he pulled open the door and stepped into the hallway, a loud cheer erupted. He glanced back at the monitors and could see nothing but the maniacal crowd jumping up and down. He hurried to his desk, took out his Browning 9 mm and placed it in its holster.

Amir started down the hallway and saw red footprints marking the carpet. Not only had Raheem proven to be ineffectual, he'd been careless and disrespectful, bringing the blood of infidels into Amir's home.

The crowd roared again as Amir approached the large wooden doors which led to the Eastern Court. Then silence. Slowly, he opened the door.

Raheem rushed to Amir's side, his opened knuckles dripping blood on the sand. "Still nothing." Raheem used the back of his sleeve to wipe the sweat off his creased forehead. "I don't know what's wrong."

Amir looked at the trail of blood Raheem had dragged in from the outer gates. He said, "Take me there."

Raheem nodded and led Amir down the path. As they crossed through the gates, the townspeople looked down on them from both sides. A chain-link fence kept them from getting too close to Amir's greatness. The short path opened onto the Eastern Court, a giant circle of sand surrounded by the quiet crowd.

On the far side of a statue of Amir's father, the man the people had once adored, were three young men. Each was tied to a stake ten feet apart. When they'd been brought in the day before, their facial resemblance made it clear that they were brothers. Now they were unrecognizable, any familial features obliterated under Raheem's heavy hands.

"These men won't bow only because they aren't able to," Amir said. "Untie them and surely they will recognize me."

Raheem shook his head. "They refuse, Your Excellency. Perhaps they will reconsider if you address them."

Amir wondered who should replace Raheem. "Move aside and watch how it is done."

Amir strode forward, stopped a few feet in front of the man on the left, the eldest and hopefully wisest of the brothers. Loud enough for the entire crowd to hear, Amir asked, "What is your name, my son?"

"I am my father's son," the stick-thin man with the mangled face said. His smile revealed a mouthful of shattered teeth. "I am Mikal Marrash."

Amir slapped him across his cheek, the crack echoing across the court. "Do you not know who I am?"

Mikal acted as if he hadn't felt the blow. "I know *what* you are. The same as me and my brothers. Mortal."

Amir unsheathed the sword, placed its point to Mikal's chin before the man could utter another sacrilegious word. "You are as ignorant as you are brave, but neither will serve you in my court." Amir let the tip of the sword drag across Mikal's chest, spilling new blood. "Pray your brothers have more sense."

The next brother, whose teeth and a bloodied piece of his ear glistened in the sand, looked Amir in the eyes, not once glancing at the sword in his hand.

"And what is your name?" Amir asked.

"Zachariah."

"You look brighter than your brother," Amir said, even though he couldn't make out much with the purple swelling. "Would you like for this to end?"

"Very much."

"Good, good." Amir turned to the crowd. "Did you hear that? This young man would like for this to end. He is a man of reason. He will bow down to me."

The crowd cheered, but not nearly as loudly as they had when Raheem had been working on the brothers.

"You misunderstand," Zachariah said. "I bow to no man."

Amir whirled around and drove the sword through the insolent man's thigh. Zachariah's cry was drowned out by the crowd. Amir stuck his face an inch from Zachariah's. "You want to rethink that? I have all day."

Zachariah shook his head, grimaced when Amir pulled the sword out and shoved it through the other thigh. Another cry.

"Pathetic fools." Amir sheathed the sword. The first two brothers groaned and wailed as Amir walked to the third man. "And you," he said to the big-bellied brother. "What is your name?"

"Hassan."

Amir took the 9 mm from his holster and made sure Hassan saw it. "I want you to listen closely. You can save your life and the lives of your brothers. Don't you want to?"

"We're already saved, sir. You can be too if ..."

The blast of the gun cut the sentence short and splintered Hassan's left kneecap. "I can be saved?" Amir fired a round into the other knee, then returned to Raheem, who looked as if he wanted to say something, but wisely remained quiet. Amir ordered him to ready the spears and screamed at him to hurry when Raheem hesitated.

The crowd went wild as soldiers trudged out the six-foot-long spears and inserted them into the metal holders beside each stake. When each of the glistening spears was in place, Amir raised his hand to signal for silence.

Speaking to the crowd, Amir said, "I do not ask much of my people, but I will not tolerate disrespect. Still, as a kind and just ruler, I will give them one last chance." Amir then asked the brothers, "Will you bow?"

Mikal said, "You can hurt us now, torture us every single second for the rest of our days, but it will end, and then we will be welcomed into God's arms and an eternity of bliss. So, no, we will not bear false witness."

Amir signaled his soldiers to proceed. He shouted to the crowd, "I cannot help those who refuse my hand!"

As the soldiers untied Mikal and then his brothers from the stakes, leaving their arms bound, Mikal said, "We are not trying to be disrespectful, but we cannot bow to a golden idol."

"Raise them," Amir shouted. "Raise them high."

Four soldiers surrounded each of the brothers and hefted the men onto their shoulders. Speaking over the cheering crowd, Mikal said, "We believe in one God!" His voice was soon drowned in the cheers as the soldiers pressed them high into the air where they hovered over the spears.

The brothers prayed as one, "The Father Almighty, creator of Heaven and Earth …"

"Impale them," Amir screamed.

The soldiers dropped the young men, the *shlopp* of the spears tearing through fabric and flesh as the brothers cried to their heaven. The crowd crowed their approval as the young men slowly slid down the poles.

Amir was used to men screaming, but not like this, as if they were in the chorus of the damned. All they had to do was bend to him.

Mikal was more than halfway down the pole, only a few feet of blood-slicked steel sticking out below him. Amir stepped next to Mikal's feet, dangling over the ground. The skin over Mikal's upper chest stretched a few inches up the spear, pointing to the sky.

All three of the screaming brothers reached the blood-soaked sand at nearly the same moment. Zachariah's spear had ripped through the side of his neck, a fountain of red flowing on both sides of the steel. Hassan the shortest of the three, hadn't been so lucky, but even he continued to sing despite the spear exiting his right eye socket.

The crowd stopped cheering, the entire court silent except for the brothers' everlasting, "Ahhhh." As if they had planned it, the three men finished their scream, "Ahhhhhh-men!"

Amir turned, found Raheem standing wide-eyed next to the statue of Amir's father. "Lower the spears!" Amir ordered.

Raheem hurried to the switch. Gears grated beneath the ground and the spears tilted toward the statue. Each of the brothers was now positioned to show Amir's father's statue the respect it demanded, but the crowd did not cheer.

As the blood pooled beneath him, Mikal turned his head to the side and looked at Amir. "We are not bending for you, only God."

Raheem ran to Amir's side and whispered, "This shouldn't be, Your Excellency. These men are not natural."

Amir's fury at his first-in-charge blazed in his eyes. The man was no better than a superstitious little girl. "The spears are holding them together. They will bleed out like everyone else."

"No one else has lasted this long," Raheem said. "They should be dead."

Amir backhanded Raheem across his face, stunned the man into silence. "And they will be." To the soldiers, he yelled, "Remove the bodies and stack them here. The rest of you, bring in the wood."

The crowd came alive and cheered the soldiers as they ripped each of the brothers off the spears and sat them back-to-back a few feet from Amir. Wheelbarrows full of wood dumped their contents in a massive circle around the men. The frenzied crowd contributed by tossing branches, rags, and other items over the fence. This would be a fire like no other, an example of the fire that the irreverent infidels would spend eternity in.

Mikal took Amir's attention away from his people. "God forgives you."

Amir didn't acknowledge the blasphemous remark, simply strode to the edge of the court. He pulled Raheem to him and said, "Douse them in gasoline."

Raheem picked up the can by the entrance and walked to the brothers as branches continued to rain down. He said something to the men as he poured the liquid on them, but Amir could not hear the words over the chanting crowd. He didn't need to. Raheem had already proven what kind of man he was this day, but as long as the crowd couldn't hear it, his words didn't matter.

Raheem emptied the can. Amir beckoned a soldier to bring him a lit torch. When no more liquid came out of the container, Amir tossed the torch, and the fire exploded, flames flying fifty feet high. The intense heat drove Amir and the crowd back from the pit. On the outskirts of the blaze, Raheem's body writhed until he was nothing but charred debris for the other soldiers to consider.

A voice from above shouted, "The statue! The statue!"

Amir hoped it was a mirage, a trick the flames were playing on his eyes. The face of his father's statue was melting. It looked like tears. "It's titanium," he said, wondering if the sculptor had lied. "It can't melt."

But the tears continued to drip down his father's cheeks. Amir ordered his men to extinguish the fire. Buckets of water sizzled over the flames when the singing began.

The song was an infidel's prayer. "Stop that!" Amir shouted at the crowd, disgusted that anyone would dare cross his decree. The flames continued to grow and the singing grew louder. Amir turned to his nearest soldier and said, "Take all the men you need and find those who are singing. Toss them into the pit."

The soldier stood staring at the fire and pointed. "From in there. They're in there."

Amir pushed the confused soldier away. He shielded his face from the bright white heat. The statue was gone, a silver puddle spreading across the sand. The song continued, growing louder as three shapes appeared.

Amir yelled to his men, "They're demons! Send them back to hell!"

Most of the soldiers ran. Those that stayed threw down their weapons. Amir fired a round into the closest coward's head. "Kill them!" Amir yelled, aiming his pistol at the brothers in the flames. He fired. The round struck Mikal's forehead. Amir fired again and again, emptying the gun into the flames.

He threw the useless pistol at the figures and pulled his sword, waving it in front of him. "Stay back! Stay back, devils! Go back to the depths of hell. Please." Amir tripped and scooted backwards on the sand. "I am sorry," he said to the fire. "Forgive me. Please. Please …" He pulled himself forward and bowed his head. He recited the infidels' prayer, each word he had banned from his city. He prayed with all of his heart and begged the one God to have mercy on his soul.

When he opened his eyes, he saw Raheem's charred body before him. He saw inside the flames. The brothers weren't alive. They weren't singing. They were dead.

Amir looked at the ring of soldiers, realizing how crazy he probably seemed. He wiped the tears from his face and saw his men training their weapons upon his chest.

Out There

Darrell glanced in the rearview and cocked a thumb over his shoulder. "There she goes. Check it out."

"Man, keep your eyes on the road," Mike said then turned to look out the rain-streaked back window. The small cluster of lights comprising Baker was disappearing. In another fifty yards the lights would completely vanish, leaving them with only their headlights and the occasional burst of lightning to alleviate the darkness of the desert.

They followed the curve up the steep hill, and Darrell snuck another peek in the mirror. "Exactly seventy-nine miles to Vegas."

"Fine, but watch the road. And slow down."

"Stop trippin', man, I got it."

Mike leaned over and checked the speedometer. "Drop it to sixty."

"I'm barely doing seventy."

"I don't care what the speed limit is. I can't see a goddamn thing with all this rain, and the last thing in the world we need is an accident."

Darrell eased up a little on the accelerator, but not without restating his opinion. "We're never gonna get there at this rate."

"Relax. There's no rush."

Darrell and Mike had been sleeping together for almost a year. Their families knew they were gay, but Jimmy didn't. And Jimmy was all that mattered. Darrell turned up the radio. Def Leppard's "Pour Some Sugar on Me" blasted through the speakers.

Mike pulled the phone from his pocket. One bar faded in and out. He figured they'd get better reception once they made it over this next mountain. Mike put the phone away and leaned back in the seat, listening to the pounding rain and Joe Elliot's voice crackling in and out.

Darrell slammed the radio's power button with his palm.

"What the hell? You trying to break it?" Mike asked.

"Might as well with all this static. Look at this car; it doesn't even have a CD player."

"You can deal with it for seventy-nine miles."

"It handles like crap. And it looks like it belongs to my mom."

"Exactly. What'd you want, a bright red convertible?"

"Anything would be better than this thing. And think about all the gas we're using. This thing probably gets fifteen per gallon."

"Oh, now you're an environmentalist?"

Darrell gripped the minivan's steering wheel with both hands, stared straight ahead, and pressed down on the accelerator.

"Slow it down," Mike ordered.

Darrell kept his foot on the gas. Mike punched him in the neck. With a huff, Darrell brought it down to sixty. A moment later they reached the top of the mountain and began their descent.

Darrell couldn't let it go. "We're not going to get there until sunrise, and we're going to be easier to spot."

Mike struggled to remain calm. He couldn't risk drawing Darrell into a shouting match when the hothead was driving. He carefully controlled his voice and said, "Maybe you just don't understand certain things. We're going to be really easy to spot if we get pulled over. And if I'm found in Cali, I'm screwed, which means you're screwed."

"But you got that ID."

"I don't know if it'll fly and I'm not risking ten years to find out."

"We're not getting pulled over and if we do, I'll flash my badge."

Mike tried not to laugh. "You have a badge?"

"Yeah. I'm an officer."

"You're a security guard."

"I'm a security *officer*. I can arrest people just like cops do."

Mike shook his head. "Your badge won't get us out of a ticket, and I don't want anyone searching the car. As far as the gas mileage goes, you're worried about spending an extra twenty bucks."

"Probably more like forty. We're down to a half tank."

"You're making fifteen hundred for an eight-hour trip." Mike turned to the window. "You need to let it go."

The thunderstorm was getting worse. Rain pelted the van with a fury and cloaked the desert. Being stuck in the van with Darrell when he was in one of his foul moods sucked, but at least they were warm and dry.

"When do you think I can go by myself and start making some real money?" Darrell asked.

"Real money?" Mike laughed. "It takes you three weeks playing rent-a-cop to make fifteen hundred."

"You know what I mean."

"Trust me; I want you to start making the trip alone as soon as possible. I really don't wanna get popped for violating. But first a couple things need to happen. Figure on coming out with me at least three more times before Jimmy trusts you. So maybe next month. February at the latest."

"What else?"

"Prove to me that you can chill on these trips. I'd be putting my ass on the line letting you make the run yourself. We're talking major money here."

"I can chill. I'm chillin'. And I like it when you put your ass on the line."

Mike ignored the remark. "No speeding. No reckless driving. No stopping anywhere but for gas. No unnecessary calls."

"Yeah, that's …" Darrell cut himself off and looked out Mike's window. Craning his neck, his eyes followed something they passed on the side of the road.

"What are you looking at?"

"There was a car back there." Darrell checked the rearview mirror. "They're so screwed."

Mike looked out the back, unable to see through the rain. "There's nothing out there."

"It was a car."

Mike sat back in his chair. "Even if it was, it's not on our concern."

"You don't have to be a dick."

"If they don't have a cell, I'm sure the cops will be by and call a tow truck for them."

"They better hurry. That's not the place to break down," Darrell said.

"They're less than ten miles from Baker."

Darrell shook his head. "No, man. You never heard about this area?"

"What are you talking about?"

"You wouldn't believe the number of people that get killed out here."

"Outside of Baker?"

"Yeah. At least fifty deaths in the last year. You have no idea. You're from Vegas. You guys don't care about the crazy stuff that happens out here."

"I'm sure I would have heard about it if fifty people got killed."

"Hell, I'd say at least fifty, and I stopped looking it up."

"You want me to believe fifty people died out here?" Mike asked.

"They found some bones and the rest just vanished."

"Some bones? Vanished? I thought you said fifty died. It sounds more like missing."

"They listed them all as missing, but they're dead. No bullshit." Darrell peered out Mike's window as if he could see something out there. Mike caught himself looking, too, but the impenetrable darkness blocked everything except the two feet of highway to his right.

Mike said, "I bet it was just people leaving and never coming back. If I grew up in Baker, I'd vanish the second I was old enough to drive."

"Yeah, but would you leave your car on the side of the road in the middle of nowhere? Would your bones be found weeks later, picked clean, not a scrap of meat left on them?"

"You're an idiot."

Darrell shook his head. "I'm telling you the truth. There's something out there."

Mike's cell phone vibrated. He told Darrell to shut up before he answered it.

"Where the hell are you?" the gruff voice said.

"What's up, Jimmy? We're ..."

"I've been trying to get hold of you for the last twenty minutes. Where the hell are you?"

"We passed Baker about fifteen, twenty minutes ago. We should ... Hey, Jimmy, Jimmy, you there?" Mike looked at the cell's screen and shook his head. "Frickin' T-Mobile."

"What'd he say?"

"I don't know. Nothing. It's fine." Mike didn't want to think about Jimmy. He asked, "So what were you saying about all the disappearances? You think it's aliens? Chupacabra?"

"It's not funny, man. People die out here."

"I'm sure they do." Another vibration. "Hold on, it's Jimmy again." He answered the call. "What's up, Jimmy?"

"Did you hit state line yet?"

"No, we're still about sixty miles from Vegas, maybe thirty to the border."

"What are you driving?"

"I don't know, looks like a Dodge. Yeah, it's a Dodge."

"A Dodge what?"

"Hey, Darrell, what is this thing?" Mike asked. "What model?"

"Caravan." Just loud enough for Mike to hear, Darrell said, "We could've had a Cadillac."

"Hear that? A Caravan."

"What's the license plate number?"

Mike opened up the glovebox, pulled out the registration, and read off the number.

Jimmy yelled, "You dumb shits! Pull it over!"

"What are you talking about? We're in the middle of nowhere and it's pouring."

"Pull it over!" Jimmy barked.

"You're breaking up. I'll pull over at the rest stop. There's one up ahead a few miles. I saw a sign."

"No, you ass clown! You've been made …"

The signal faded, leaving Mike with a dead line.

"What was that all about?" Darrell asked.

"Jimmy wants us to pull over. I think he said we were made."

"Are you kidding? We can't pull over."

"He said —"

"You said, you *thought* he said we were made. Maybe he was saying something else."

"Like what? He wanted us to pull over."

"Call him back."

Another vibration. "This is him right now. Pull over while I have reception."

"Are you serious?"

"Just pull over. I don't wanna lose him," Mike said. "What's up, Jimmy? You hear me?"

"Pull over, Mike! You've been made."

"You sure? How do you know?"

"Paul got popped about an hour after you left. Vice swarmed the house and they knew what they were looking for. The only thing they found was the money, but Paul must've sold you out. Paul's girl told me about the bust, so I started monitoring police radio. They've got an APB out on the van. Ditch the cargo."

"Tell me you're joking." Mike glanced over his shoulder, ready to see flashing lights coming up behind them.

"You ditch that stuff. Find somewhere safe, go on to Vegas, get another set of wheels and pick it up tomorrow night."

"Where? Where am I going to stash it? I'm in the middle of the goddamned desert."

"Somewhere someone else ain't gonna stumble onto it. And don't leave the van anywhere near it."

"I know." Mike checked the side window, wished he could see more than a few feet through the sea of darkness. "But how are we supposed to get to Vegas."

"Use your fucking feet. Just don't do anything stupid. If you need to, you can crash at my pad."

"Whatever you say, Jimmy. And thanks for the heads up. I'll find a place for this stuff and get back to you."

As Mike hung up, Darrell asked, "So what's happening?"

Mike stuffed the cell into his pocket. "We need to dump the cargo. Cops are looking for the van."

"Dump it?"

"We don't have a choice."

"They won't catch us. And if they did, it's my first offense. They'll let me go."

"We have two hundred pounds. That's trafficking. If we get stopped we're both screwed."

Darrell shifted to park and took his foot off the brake. "So what do we do? Where do we stash it?"

Mike thumbed toward his window. "Somewhere out there."

"No way, man. That ain't happening. How about the rest stop?"

"Too many people. And they've got cameras." Mike peered through the windshield. He spotted a line of cars a mile down the hill. Brake lights. "They've already blocked off the road."

"You don't know that. There could be an accident." Darrell clearly didn't believe that though, because he asked, "You really think they're looking for us?"

"It sure as hell isn't a coincidence. Let's get the stuff out of here before someone rolls by and spots us."

"I can't go out there."

Mike shook his head in disgust.

"I'm not kidding. There're bad things out there."

"Bullshit. Even if there were, I guarantee there are worse things in prison."

Darrell closed his eyes, took a deep breath and let it out. When he opened his eyes, he pulled his Ruger SR40 from his waistband, where he kept it concealed under his bulging belly.

Mike reached over and pulled the keys out of the ignition. "Put on your hood."

Darrell leaped from the van without a word. Mike met him underneath the canopy of the open rear hatch.

"Are we going to bury it?" Darrell asked.

"With what? I didn't pack a shovel."

"So where do we put these?" Darrell asked, looking at the two huge suitcases. At least they were hard-shells and not canvas.

"Those hills." Mike pointed toward a shadowy range running parallel with the road. "There's got to be some rocks where we can hide them."

Darrell stared through the rain. "You have any idea how far that is? No way."

"Hundred yards or so. We'll be there in a minute. Come on."

"No way. That's at least three hundred. We'll be soaked."

"We're gonna have worse problems than that." Mike dragged the first suitcase out of the car, surprised by how heavy it was, and then raised the wheel well cover. Before Darrell noticed, he grabbed the .38 Special he had hidden there and stuffed it into his coat pocket. "Come on, it's letting up." It wasn't, but Mike was already crossing the muddy stretch of road that bordered the highway.

Mike heard the second suitcase hit the pavement and the rear door slam shut. Reluctantly, Darrell followed, but not without finding new combinations of curse words. The complaining didn't last long. Dragging one hundred pounds through the treacherous terrain and torrential downpour wore them out.

Halfway to the hills, Mike set his suitcase down in a clearing. He acted like it was so he could check on his partner, and not because of the burning sensation in his arms and lungs. He heard Darrell's grunts over the rain slapping the hard desert floor, but couldn't see him. A loud hiss sliced through the air. Mike whirled around and backed up looking for the serpent, his hand on the .38's grip, but he couldn't see a thing in the darkness. Still, the hiss sliced through the deluge. When Darrell entered the clearing a few seconds later, the hissing stopped.

Darrell dropped his suitcase onto its side. He was breathing so hard Mike feared his overweight boyfriend would have a heart attack. "Goddamn, this is heavy," Darrell said. "How much farther?" he asked between gasps, looking past Mike toward the hills.

"We got a way to go. I'm tired too, but we need to keep moving. This is still too close."

"We aren't going to make it."

"What?" Mike stepped onto a rock but couldn't see over the small hill that blocked their view of the highway.

"Last I looked they were all over the van. Three cars."

Mike scrambled up the rocky hill, the sight of the flashing lights making him nauseous.

Darrell asked, "Now what? They're gonna be all over this area. What if we make it to the rest stop and jack a car? That's the only thing I can think of."

"They're going to be crawling all over it. They know we're close. The hills are our only shot."

"So then what? What the hell do we do even if we make it?"

"First off, we hide the suitcases. We can't get caught with this. They'll still bust me for violating, but that's better than the alternative." Mike tried to control his shivering. "Let's move before they get a helicopter out here. They'll know we're on this side of the highway."

"Maybe they'll think someone picked us up."

"No way. And watch where you're stepping." Mike grabbed the suitcase and dragged it up and over a large rock. "Snakes are out."

"Nah. They're not out now."

The burning sensation returned to his shoulders. "I know what I heard."

"Well you didn't hear a snake. They hibernate in winter. Must've been something else."

In no mood to argue, Mike pushed forward, leaving Darrell behind. Soaked and exhausted, Mike stopped after a hundred yards. The rain was letting up, but that wasn't a good thing. Mike could see the cops still by the van, which meant they could probably see him. The mountains, which he had thought were hills, were still half a mile away.

Mike crouched down, holding his head in both hands. He'd rest while Darrell caught up and then they'd make one last run for the mountains. They could make it, he told himself. A hiss rustled in the bushes. He looked around. It wasn't rain. There wasn't a drop falling. The hiss grew louder. It sounded as if it were coming from two different directions.

Mike stood and pulled out his piece. He wasn't scared of snakes, and he refused to get bitten and die lying on top of a suitcase of Ecstasy.

The clouds slid over and let the moon shine through. Even with its light, Mike couldn't see much. Sand, brush, rocks, cacti, and more sand. No snakes.

He did see Darrell huffing his way up the slight incline; his face was drenched, only this time from sweat, not rain. Once again the hissing stopped.

"The … choppers … out," Darrell said in between gulping breaths. He dropped the suitcase onto the damp sand and bent over, hands resting on his knees. "We're screwed. That hill won't hide us much longer."

"We need to keep moving," Mike said.

Darrell raised his arms over his head, something he must have seen an athlete do on TV, only Mike doubted the athlete's belly had poured over his belt.

"Come on, Darrell, that's long enough. We have to hit the mountains." Mike left out that they'd already have been there if Darrell had taken care of himself.

"I'm too tired."

"I'll leave you."

"Go ahead." Darrell sat on a rock. "I can't move."

"I'll leave you in the dark with the cops, and the snakes, and whatever little boogie monster you think is out here."

"There ain't no snakes. I told you."

"Well, there's something out here hissing and I'm leaving you with it. Are you coming?"

"Hold on, goddammit. I never should've come."

"I didn't hear you bitching when I asked you before. You weren't complaining about making some cash." Mike picked up the suitcase, hoping it would be easier to carry than it was to drag. "We get through this, and Jimmy will put you on any score you want."

That finally got Darrell on his feet. In the ten minutes it took to make it to the base of the mountain, the helicopter hadn't advanced much. It was too early for Mike to get his hopes up, but it looked as if he might make it out of this thing a free man. Darrell might not, but that was his own fault. If the fat bastard had taken care of himself, he wouldn't be on the verge of passing out as he tried to keep up.

"Now what?" Darrell said.

"We hide the suitcases." Mike pointed to the small cave twenty yards uphill. "In there."

Without a word, Darrell began the ascent. Mike nearly ran into him when Darrell came to an abrupt stop right outside the opening.

"What the hell's the matter? Get in there," Mike ordered.

Darrell whispered, "It's dark."

Mike shouldered past him. "You give gays a bad name."

"I think I heard something."

"What? What could be out here? Mountain lion? Get out your gun and watch your step."

"It sounded like some kind of hissing."

Mike took a few steps past the entrance and turned around. "I thought you said they were hibernating."

"T-they should be," Darrell stammered.

Mike heard the low hiss, but pretended he hadn't. He turned back to Darrell. "You want to make money, you want more responsibility, and you want to do the runs yourself. Why should Jimmy let you? You're afraid of the dark. Afraid of snakes. What else are you afraid of, Darrell?"

"Screw you."

"No thank you. I don't do vaginas."

Darrell finally grabbed his suitcase. Mike told him to take his too, and put them as far back in the cave as he could. "If you want your cut."

"Why don't we each take one?"

"Because one of us should stay out here and keep an eye on that helicopter."

"Well, it looks pretty dark in there. If we both go in …"

"We could get lost. At least you can follow my voice. I'll be right here. Come on, we don't have all night."

Darrell groaned, but did as Mike ordered and picked up his suitcase. "I can't carry both of them," he said.

"Make two trips."

Darrell disappeared in the cave's darkness. Mike sat on his suitcase and watched as the police helicopter circled the desert a few hundred yards away. After several minutes passed, he began to wonder if Darrell had decided to take a break.

Mike took one step into the cave. "Darrell, hurry up. The helicopter's getting closer."

There was no response, so he cupped his hands around his mouth and shouted, "Darrell, can you hear me?"

Again no answer. Mike picked up his suitcase and headed down the dark tunnel, using his free hand to feel the wall alongside him. After a few seconds, he sensed the tunnel widening into a cavern. He called Darrell's name once more. A prolonged hiss echoed through the cave. Slowly, Mike set the suitcase down and pulled the gun out of his coat. When he turned in a circle to pinpoint the noise, he looked out the tunnel and noticed the helicopter's searchlight was closer.

No longer caring where Darrell was, Mike picked up his suitcase and headed for the closest wall. He tripped over something solid and slammed face first onto the cave's hard floor. The hissing grew louder and seemed to be coming from multiple directions. Ignoring his bleeding chin and scraped hand, Mike leaped off the floor before the snakes could strike. He reached for his pistol, but it wasn't there. He got to his knees and felt the floor. When his hand struck plastic, he realized he'd tripped over Darrell's suitcase.

"What the hell's wrong with you? I could've knocked myself out."

Darrell didn't answer, but even if he had, Mike wasn't sure if he would have heard him over the now deafening hisses. He prayed it was the cave's echoes, but it sounded as if he were surrounded.

Mike reached for Darrell's suitcase and felt Darrell's arm draped over it. He squeezed Darrell's hand. "Get up, man." He shook the arm harder and almost retched when it pulled away from the suitcase and fell onto his lap. The arm had been severed at the elbow. Mike reached out but couldn't feel Darrell's body anywhere.

Mike threw the arm into the darkness and heard a grunt when it bounced off something. He scrambled on all fours toward the entrance. The searchlight illuminated the cave's mouth. A sinewy hand wrapped around his neck, cutting off his scream. Mike clawed at the scaly fingers. Deafened by the hissing, unable to move, he stared straight ahead. The entrance was gone. He couldn't see outside, but he knew that the cops were out there. Getting caught meant ten years locked in a nine-by-nine cell. But that decade was gone.

Group Session

"You sure you don't want me to stay, Dr. Hammond? I really don't mind. My mom can watch the kids til eight."

Larry stopped rummaging through the file cabinet just long enough to make eye contact with his overly sensitive blonde receptionist. "I appreciate that, Lisa, but Wagner refuses to come in if anyone else is in the building. You know how some people feel about us."

"So they'd rather live an unhealthy life instead of risking embarrassment?"

He was tempted to say something mean and condescending, but ruled against it. Barton and Richter, the doctors he shared the practice with and who were both already on their way home, wouldn't like him abusing their precious little beauty. Larry had been pulling for a brunette, who actually had real experience, but Barton said that wasn't necessary in this line of work. Barton had the nerve to suggest that maybe after Larry had a few more years under his belt he'd understand.

So instead of saying something Lisa would take the wrong way, Larry resumed his search through the cabinet and said, "At least this guy's coming. For every one of him there must be a hundred others that couldn't be dragged in here by wild horses."

"I hadn't thought about it like that. It just seems like such an inconvenience for you. Wouldn't you rather go home on time and have dinner with your wife?"

Larry pulled out a folder and set it on top of the other two resting on the cabinet. Not knowing why he was telling her of all people, he said, "Actually, that's the last thing I want. We're separating."

There was that predictable look of surprise, accompanied by the gasping of air and her trademark, "Oh, I'm so sorry. I didn't know."

Before she could utter another word, Larry looked at the clock in the deserted waiting room. "It's five-fifty and they'll be here any minute. You really should get going before they show up."

She gathered her belongings. "I thought it was just Wagner."

"I talked him and two others into doing a group session. Should be interesting."

"Do I know the other two?"

"Maybe, but you really need to hurry."

Lisa looked hurt, but Larry didn't care. He'd be able to make a name for himself if tonight's session was a success. There would be papers, talk shows, maybe even a book. If some pretty girl's feelings got hurt along the way, then so be it.

Larry's first client entered the office just moments after Lisa slipped out the back door. "How are you doing, Mr. Petrowski?" Larry held the inner office door open for the little man. "Come on back."

Frank Petrowski, a forty-eight-year-old who looked closer to sixty thanks to his face, which resembled a piece of rawhide that'd seen too many seasons, made his way past Larry and headed for the room. Although this was his fifth session with Frank, it was difficult holding back a smile. Standing four-eleven, it was hard to take the man seriously.

Larry told Frank to make himself comfortable, wasn't surprised to see him sit in the corner chair, avoiding the couch that would make him appear even smaller. When he heard the front door close, Larry excused himself to greet the so-called Honorable Alexander Steele. Always business, Steele brushed by him and said, "I hope they're here. I've got things to do."

"I'm sure you do." Larry followed the bald, pot-bellied judge into the room, anxious to see how he would react to someone in his chair. Obviously perturbed, Steele grunted at Frank and huffed his way over to the couch. "Just one more, gentlemen. He should be here shortly," Larry said before heading back to the receptionist's counter to gather their folders.

The next few minutes were torturously slow. It wasn't quite six yet, but Wagner usually showed up early, as long as he was convinced the building was empty. Hopefully the thought of talking to others hadn't scared him off. Without him, the session would be a bust. Three people composed a small group; only two created an awkwardly confrontational setting. Especially the two in the room now.

And it wasn't just the number of people present that necessitated Wagner's presence. There was something about the man that set him apart from other patients. He was dealing with the same issues as Steele and Petrowski, but he was more willing to accept responsibility for his actions. Without him there would be no group, no published paper, no TV show.

Just as Larry was about to lose hope, the front door swung open. "Evening, Mr. Wagner. I was afraid you wouldn't come."

The muscular thirty-year-old looked about the empty waiting room and peeked into the receptionist's area. "Everyone's gone?"

"Yep. Just me and the other two men I told you about." Wagner seemed unusually tense, so Larry asked, "You okay?"

Wagner said he was fine, but Larry didn't buy it. He locked the front door hoping to take away some of the man's anxiety.

"You mind if we take care of the payment up front?" Wagner pulled a wad of bills from his pocket. "I got some stuff to handle after this."

Larry waved away Wagner's money. "This one's on the house. I expect the session to be very productive, but until we've tried it out once or twice, I wouldn't feel comfortable charging for it. The only thing I ask is that I be permitted to use any material in future papers and books. Of course, I would change all names to protect identities."

Wagner shrugged his shoulders and slipped the thick roll back into his tan pants. "Whatever."

It seemed like some type of thanks was in order, considering he had just saved the man a hundred dollars, but Larry let it slide. As he led the way down the hallway, he asked, "Have you had a chance to look into any insurance yet? I wouldn't want the cost of treatment to prevent you from coming."

"Money's not an issue."

"Good," Larry said as they entered the office, reminding himself to jot down a question for next week's private session with Wagner: *How is money not an issue for an unemployed ex-cop, three years off the force?*

Wagner took a seat on the couch next to Steele while Larry rolled his chair out from behind his desk, positioning it so Wagner was in front of him, Frank off to his left. He noticed Steele checking his watch and apologized to the group for the delay, even though it was only four minutes past six.

"I've brought the three of you together because you're dealing with similar issues and there are no support groups out there for you. I'm trained, just as most psychologists and therapists are, to help give you insight into some of your problems, but this is a subject the medical community has not studied sufficiently. That's why it might be helpful to talk with peers who are going through the same thing." Larry hoped the others hadn't noticed the judge rolling his eyes behind his glasses at the mention of peers. "This is going to be a very informal discussion where each of you will get a chance to tell the group about yourself and ask questions of each other. I'll facilitate as needed, but this will be your time. Why don't we start with our names?"

With everyone acting as if they were at a seventh-grade dance, Larry pointed at Frank and said, "How about we start over here?"

Frank shot him an unpleasant glance but predictably obeyed orders. "I'm Officer Petrowski."

Larry followed Wagner's eyes to Petrowski's waist, where they were probably searching for a badge or gun that verified the diminutive man's claim. Frank seemed to sense the doubt and clarified, "CO, over at Sussex 1 State Prison in Waverly."

"I think this might be smoother if we are a little less formal," Larry told him.

"I guess you guys can call me Frank. I'm used to using last names. I don't think I could name three coworkers by their first names."

"I know the feeling," Wagner chipped in, his earlier tension visibly reduced. "I was a cop in Richmond for four years. The name's Charles Wagner. Charlie's fine."

"Thanks, Charlie." Larry turned to the oldest of the group. "And last but not least …"

"Judge Steele." Before Larry could ask for his first name, the judge grudgingly said, "Alexander. Not Alex, but Alexander."

"So we've got Frank, Charlie, and Alexander. Please call me Larry. What do you say we get started?"

Larry took the group's silence as a green light. "Everyone here has been having a difficult time dealing with their role in death. That said, let's get into specifics. Tell us why you're here, why you've sought treatment. Alexander, will you please start?"

"I came here because my wife said I should."

Larry realized the man wasn't going to say anything more if not prompted. "And why did she suggest you come in?"

Alexander glared at Larry. "We've been over this."

"But not with them. You don't have to go into detail, just an overview."

Alexander thought about it for a second. "I'm a judge. I've condemned people to die. Sometimes it … bothers me," he mumbled.

It was a start. Larry nodded his head and motioned for Charlie to go next.

"I've been forced to take lives. More than one. But the guilt I feel about one in particular has been a little too much, I suppose."

"Good. We'll go into that death later." Larry jotted a note in Charlie's folder. "Frank, your turn."

"Like I said before, I'm a CO over at Sussex 1. I'm on the execution squad. Sometimes it's too much, like Charlie said."

Speaking to no one in particular, Larry said, "Just so you all know, each of you has confided in me the amount of stress these deaths have caused you. I ask that no one diminishes their experiences now that the others are present. Be assured, you are all men and have dealt with your positions and responsibilities remarkably well. You have some of society's most demanding jobs, and you are forced to deal with psychological and moral issues. Feeling guilty or ashamed of things you have done is natural. Not being affected would lead me to believe there was something wrong. Tonight, you need to give these feelings voice. No one will laugh or think less of you. This is a healing process and with that comes pain. Welcome it; don't avoid it." Larry gave his speech a moment to set in before asking, "Frank, can you tell us some more about your problem?"

"Like what?"

Larry checked his watch. At this rate, they'd be here until daybreak. "Why don't you start by telling us about your job? What exactly do you do on this team?"

"I'm on strap-down. The duties are a little different depending on whether we're burning or sticking."

"What's that?" Larry asked.

"Strap-down?"

"No, the burning or sticking."

"Electric chair or lethal injection. They get a choice."

"How nice," Charlie said. "That's one hell of a decision to make."

"At least they only got to make it once," Frank said. "But anyway, like I was saying, I'm on strap-down, so I walk the guy in and strap him down to the table or chair and watch. Kinda like in *The Green Mile* or that one with that colored girl and that retarded guy from *Slingblade*."

Hoping to avoid any racial discussions, Larry said, "*Monster's Ball*."

"That doesn't sound like it. Something else. This one had that girl, the one that's not so bad looking for, you know, being dark and all."

"Halle Berry. Yes, *Monster's Ball*, trust me."

Even though the discussion had gotten sidetracked, Charlie seemed intrigued. "You stay til the guy's dead?"

Frank nodded. "Even after. We get the pleasure of unstrapping 'em and rolling 'em out."

The judge surprised them all by speaking. "How long have you been doing this?"

"I've been a CO for twenty-nine years, on the execution squad twenty-eight of them."

Alexander asked, "Did you volunteer for this position?"

"The warden handpicks the team. Of course, you can withdraw or decline any time."

Larry saw where this was headed, but the judge had already started his question. "So why do it? If you ask me, you only have yourself to blame. If putting murderers to death bothers you so much, then maybe you need a new line of work."

Frank was defending himself before Larry could come to his aid. "I can handle it, and I do handle it, but it is hard. I've helped kill fifty-one people in the last six years, and I've got another thirty-five waiting for their turn after getting condemned in court."

"So now it's *my* fault?"

"Someone's sending these guys to me. I don't go out and find them on the street."

Alexander shook his head. "Judges don't sentence people to death."

"I understand that," Frank said, "but I also understand that a judge has a great deal of influence over the jury. We're second in the nation, only behind Texas, and they'll kill you over there for jaywalking." Frank cracked his knuckles. "So if you're such a fair and just judge, then why are you here? You said you've condemned people to die."

"Only in a manner of speaking."

Larry held up his hand to halt the discussion. "We're not here to pass judgment on each other. We're not here to attack. We're here to listen. Alexander, tell them what you told me before. It's okay."

Alexander pulled a monogrammed handkerchief from his pocket and wiped the sweat off his forehead. He sighed. "I do encourage the death penalty when I believe it's warranted, and I guess I can influence juries."

Frank nodded. "But believing a man should die doesn't make putting him to death any easier to accept, right?"

"I can't sleep some nights. I wonder if I made the right decision, if I should be playing God. I wonder if we've failed as a society when a decision like that rests in the hands of so few."

After a small lull, Larry stepped in. "So, Charlie, why don't you tell them about some of the things you're going through? You don't have to give specifics. Focus on your feelings. How it's affected you."

Charlie cleared his throat. "Sometimes I have difficulty sleeping, too. Almost every night since my revelation." Charlie rubbed his thighs and began to rock. "It's not because of the lives I've taken, though. This was just a one-time thing, but once was more than enough. I helped kill a man that didn't deserve to die."

"When was this?" Frank asked.

"Over ten years ago. I was only nineteen."

Frank said, "You have to be twenty-one to be a cop."

"I wasn't a cop yet."

Larry reminded Charlie that doctor-patient privileges only went so far, but this guy had been a cop and knew that.

Alexander asked the question: "You murdered a man?"

Charlie's rocking became more pronounced. "I might as well have."

"It's okay, Charlie. Try to relax," Larry said.

"I was called for jury duty. First time I'd even heard of a jury. Anyway, I got selected for the trial of Gregory Watkins. Murder 1."

"I remember him," Frank said. "Colored guy. He got stuck a few years ago. For a while it seemed like he'd never leave the row."

Alexander said, "Gregory Watkins. If I remember correctly, that psycho killed over twenty people, all women and children. He wrote on them, too. Carved messages on their backs. Judge Hall ruled on that one."

"Hall? He's a friend of yours?" Charlie asked.

"More like an acquaintance, but we get along."

"If you ever see him again, you can thank him for screwing up my life."

"What are you talking about, son?"

"First off, I'm not your son, or anyone else's." Charlie's hands became fists.

"It's just a manner of speech," Alexander said, his hard edge softened by Charlie's aggressive attitude.

"What Frank was saying about a judge's influence is — Let's just say that Hall practically forced us to give him the death penalty."

"I doubt that."

"You weren't there."

Larry jumped in and asked, "You don't think he deserved the death penalty?"

"Absolutely not," Charlie said.

"Then how was the vote unanimous?" Frank wondered.

"At the time, we all thought he was guilty. Back then I was still a kid. I believed everything they showed us in court. Now I know better."

Frank's furrowed brow showed he didn't understand. "He killed those people. I talked to him about it. Said he had to. Wouldn't even say he was sorry when the needle went in. He was one unremorseful son of a bitch."

Alexander said he had read the same thing in the paper. "The guy was guilty. You feel worse about condemning an admitted murderer than you do about shooting a criminal in the street?"

Charlie looked confused. "I never once fired my weapon."

Frank said, "What about all the lives you said you had to take? Are you trying to tell us you actually beat people to death? Did you use your baton?"

"You were kicked off the force for brutality?" Alexander guessed.

"I quit. I never brutalized anyone on the job! Never once," he said, outraged at the suggestion.

"So you were lying?" Frank hoped.

Charlie jumped to his feet. "I don't lie!" he yelled. "You all lie! Society lies! My parents lied! I don't lie!"

Larry inched up from his chair. No one had ever reacted like this in therapy before. He was almost too scared to wish he had thought of videotaping the session. "Easy, Charlie. Take it easy and have a seat."

"You sit down, Larry. Now!"

Larry flinched and slid back down into his chair. "This is my office."

"Not anymore, Larry."

"Stop saying my name like that."

Charlie didn't sit down but seemed to calm down a notch. "It's about time you start being a professional. Why go by your first name? Are you supposed to be our goddamn friend?"

Frank stood, and in his best I'm-in-charge voice, he said, "That's enough. Now sit down and relax or …"

Charlie glanced at him. "Or what?"

"Or you can leave. There're three of us."

"You're threatening me?"

"No one is threatening anyone," Larry said.

"A Napoleonic racist, a condescending prick judge …"

Alexander didn't get off the couch. "Watch it, son."

Charlie wheeled on the old man and slapped him so hard his glasses went flying off. "I'm no one's son!"

Frank took a step toward Charlie, but stopped the moment Charlie turned toward him. Frank said, "You can't do that. That's assault."

The judge fumbled for his glasses, now somewhere on the floor. Larry tried to calm the melee. "That's enough. Everyone … Let's just calm down."

Charlie wasn't having it. With one step, his chest was pressed against Frank's nose. "I said sit down. Now."

Frank stood his ground, but couldn't control his trembling.

Charlie took a small step back, lulled Larry into thinking his rage had subsided. Then he threw a devastating elbow down and across Frank's nose. The CO crumbled to the floor, curling up with both hands to his bloody face. Larry scrambled to his desk, but Charlie yelled at him before he could pick up the phone.

Charlie said, "Don't do it, Larry. You don't want to do that."

Larry turned, saw Charlie kneeling over Frank. Charlie had a switchblade.

"Charlie, you need to listen to me. Look what you're doing."

Frank tried to rise up, but Charlie applied pressure to his neck. More blood leaked into the expanding pool. "I didn't say you could get up."

Larry said, "He needs a doctor."

"You're a doctor, and you're not helping."

"And you're not a murderer; you're just upset. Let me call for help."

"No one's calling anyone, Larry. None of us deserves to be saved."

"He's bleeding, Charlie. Look at him."

"Yeah, the carpet will need to be replaced." Charlie saw Larry's hand. "If you pick up that phone, there will be a price."

"What do you want, Charlie? What do you hope ..."

Alexander yelled at him, "Don't try to reason with this sick bastard."

A huge smile spread across Charlie's cheeks. "He's right you know. I'm not reasonable."

The judge slid his butt toward the edge of the couch. "We can fight him."

Charlie laughed maniacally. He raised the blade, and Larry charged, lowered his shoulder and tackled him off of Frank. The two rolled into the wall. Charlie's breath was warm against Larry's neck. Larry pulled himself off of Charlie and saw his eyes, wild and filled with pain. Larry looked down, saw the knife shoved into his patient's chest.

"Oh God," Larry said, realizing what he'd done. Charlie's lungs were filling with blood. He leaned into the knife.

"Hey, doc," Charlie gasped, "now you're one of us."

Reunion

Derrick sensed the moment was right, leaned in for a kiss, hating himself as he did it. Beth wasn't ugly. She didn't stink, if you disregarded the cheap wine. But he had no desire to kiss her. He just needed her to stay. For that, he needed her to feel wanted. It was already after eleven and way too late to find a replacement.

Beth welcomed his advance. Derrick matched her intensity and pressed himself against her, as passionately as he could feign, tried to ignore her fat tongue jabbing in his mouth.

Finally, Derrick backed off from the kiss and grinned. "Wow. I wanted to do that all night. Sorry if it was too much."

She ran her fingers through her bleached blonde hair, her cheeks flushed. "Are you kidding? That was perfect." She tugged down her shirt to hide the little roll of her tummy. "Just like old times."

Derrick looked around his mother's outdated living room. He said, "Ten years. Feels like nothing's changed."

They were sitting on the same couch where he and Beth had had their first heavy petting session when they were juniors in high school. None of the old furniture had been upgraded, and none of the pieces had moved since he was a kid. The pictures on the mantle and walls were untouched. A lot of things had changed in ten years, but not this house. His mother seemed stuck in the past, refusing to change anything, especially Ronnie's room. His brother's room was precisely as it had been the day he disappeared. Nothing had been moved, not even the poster of a half-naked Cindy Crawford above the bed, the one their mother had said made the place look like some nasty frat house.

The most significant thing that had changed in this room was Beth, the girl Derrick needed to convince to stay the night. She was a little heavier, but so was he. She was still bone-white, and her years of partying were peeking out from behind the layers of makeup. But she'd lost some of her shitty attitude, the insecurity. She had matured.

Beth cleared her throat, interrupting his thoughts. "This isn't your first time back, is it?"

Derrick shook his head. "I come back once a year to house-sit when Mom visits her sister in Philly. I'd rather not do it, but she refuses to let a stranger stay here. She won't go otherwise."

"What about your dad?"

"He split a year after Ronnie."

"You see him at all?"

Derrick shook his head. "The coward didn't even leave a note."

Beth rubbed his arm and said, "I'm so sorry."

"It's fine," he said. "It's just not something we talk about. Mom wanted me to keep it quiet."

"Wait a minute." Beth pulled away a little. "You've been back every year and now, out of the blue, you decide to call me?"

If Derrick hadn't been expecting the question, he might have answered honestly. He might have told her that she wasn't his first choice, but all of his other old girlfriends were gone. He'd run through each one on nights just like this.

"It's hard to explain." He pretended to be embarrassed, took a quick swig of the wine he'd picked up at 7-11. "It's just that with you, I was always afraid to call. I thought about you all the time, but I was so sure you would laugh at me and tell me to get a life. I know it sounds corny, but even though I never called you, I always had the dream of you sitting right here." He ran his fingers over her thigh.

"Ohhh," she said in her whiny little voice that still irritated the hell out of him. Another thing that hadn't changed. "That's so sweet. You shouldn't have worried, though. I'm thrilled you called." She slid up against him for a smothering hug. "I couldn't wait to come over."

He was grateful. It wasn't like he could tell any of his old friends the real reason he wanted their company. If he told anyone why he needed them to stay, he knew they'd laugh. He was twenty-seven years old — way too old to be afraid of a house. Of a room. Of Ronnie's room.

The thought sent shivers up his spine. Beth mistook the spasm for one of pleasure. "You like that, huh?" She ran her fingertips across the nape of his neck. "Thought I didn't remember?"

Derrick had never liked it; in fact, he hated it, but he couldn't tell her that. Even though she was dressed sort of sleazy, in a good way, this was by no means a sealed deal. Now was not the time to speak his mind. Instead, he snuggled closer.

"Just a sec," Beth said as she turned to the oversize purse that had yet to leave her sight. She took out her phone and swiped it on.

"You expecting a call? I'm afraid the service in this house is terrible."

"I've got one bar, but I was just checking the time. It's almost eleven-thirty. Getting kind of late."

Derrick's heart almost stopped. His mind raced as he tried to think of a way to convince her to stay. He'd shed tears if he had to, but he hoped it wouldn't come to that. Maybe he had misjudged her. Maybe she had developed some morals over the last decade. Maybe she was still sore over the way he'd dumped her the week before prom.

Before Derrick could come up with anything to say, Beth said, "You wouldn't mind if I took a quick shower, would you? I had a long day and came over right after work."

"Of course not. Do you have somewhere to go?"

Beth slipped the phone into her purse and played with her hair. "I was hoping your bedroom, but if you don't want me to I can go home."

"No, no," he said. "I just didn't think you would ..."

"We're both adults, right? And I figured that's why you called. It is, isn't it?"

He hesitated briefly. "Yeah, I mean, sort of, but I guess I didn't think you would really want to."

"Are you kidding? That was the best thing about us. I mean, you were always kind of — don't take this the wrong way — a little weird. But you were amazing in bed."

"Oh ... really?"

"Yeah. And I also know, even though you would never admit it to anyone, it must be real hard for you to be here. All those memories. Look, I don't want to ruin the mood, but you never did find out what happened to your brother, did you?"

Derrick shook his head, wished the conversation hadn't taken this turn. He finished his wine and set the empty glass on the coffee table. "Ronnie didn't run away like people think. He just disappeared. There was no forced entry, but I know he never would have let anybody in the house."

"You were home, huh?"

"We all were. We didn't hear a thing. It was something … with that room." As he said it, he wondered just how much he should be admitting to.

"You don't believe that?"

"I do."

Beth laughed, which made him feel small and angry. "He was a kid," she said. "I remember he used to say there was something under his bed, but you never believed him. Please tell me you don't know."

Derrick forced a smile. "Of course not. It was a joke." He pulled her in by the waist, his thumbs lightly pressing on her tummy, knowing it made her self-conscious. "We have to sleep in his room, and I guess I wanted to freak you out a little so you'd get that much closer."

"Very funny."

"No, seriously. It's either in there or on this couch. Mom locks her room whenever she's gone and mine was turned into a study nine years ago." He told the lie easily, knowing his mother hadn't changed anything in his room either. She never stepped foot in it.

"Really? I don't know …"

Derrick leaned in and whispered, "I'll protect you."

Beth laughed, because his breath was tickling her. "Well, if you don't have a problem being in there, then I definitely don't." She ran her finger down his chest. "We'll need more room than this couch."

"That settles it." Derrick got up and filled Beth's wine glass, told her to relax. "Just give me a minute to clean up. I'll get the water nice and warm for you."

Beth said, "You're so sweet," but it sounded fake, sort of like she was making fun of him.

Derrick didn't care. He hurried to the hallway, was hit with the smell of the red roses that sat on the console table beside the door of his old room. There was a second vase on the bathroom counter, but there was another smell underneath the aroma of roses. Derrick turned on the shower and covered the room with orange-scented air freshener.

The bathtub was clean enough, but there was a filthy rag and toothbrush inside the wastebasket. Derrick tore off several streams of toilet paper and tossed them on top of it. The mirror was starting to steam up. He went back and told Beth the shower was ready, that he'd wait for her in the bedroom.

Beth grabbed her purse and disappeared down the hallway. Derrick refilled Beth's wine glass, wondered how much she could drink. This was going to run a lot smoother than he had hoped.

Derrick turned off the lights. The bathroom door was closed, slivers of light outlining the frame. As a matter of habit, Derrick moved to his left and made sure his bedroom door was locked. He rearranged the roses and walked to the opposite end of the hall, snuck a quick glance into his mother's room, just to make sure it was empty, locked it so he didn't look like a liar. Derrick paused outside of Ronnie's door, his hand frozen on the knob.

Derrick told himself to hurry up and get inside the room. What would Beth say if she came out of the bathroom and saw him standing here like a scared little boy? There was nothing in that room that would harm him. Sure, the memories hurt, but he'd slept in this room one night a year for ten years and he'd awakened just fine. Tonight would be no different.

He turned the knob and pushed open the door. The room was pitch-black. Derrick felt along the wall and flicked the switch. The overhead light didn't come on. His mother had asked him to change the bulbs, not knowing all she needed to do was screw them in more tightly.

The dim light from the hallway barely penetrated the inky blackness. Derrick waited for his eyes to adjust. He saw the outline of Ronnie's bed, the one his brother swore had a monster under it. No one ever believed Ronnie. His mother didn't. Derrick didn't. Then Ronnie was gone.

Derrick set Beth's drink on the nightstand, mixed in a little powder from the plastic baggy to help her relax. He turned the table lamp to its lowest setting and looked around the room. Although his mother hadn't changed a single object since the night Ronnie disappeared, she'd cleaned it every week. Ten years of vacuuming and dusting had left this room feeling like a movie set.

The lamp light reflected off the trophy-filled bookcase. Less than a year before he had vanished, Ronnie had led his baseball team to the state finals. Every player got a championship ring, which was the only thing missing from the room. The ring couldn't have cost more than ten dollars to make, but it was priceless to Ronnie. Derrick smiled, remembering how Ronnie polished the fake ruby every morning. He refused to take it off, even in the bath.

Derrick felt tears forming, slapped himself to make them stop. He had to man up before Beth came back. He had to check under the bed for the monster.

Keeping an eye on the dust ruffle that skimmed the wooden floor, Derrick untied his shoes and slipped them off. The shower stopped and he walked over to the doorway, his feet sliding along the hardwood, barely making a sound.

Derrick called Beth's name and she asked what he wanted.

"Your wine's next to the bed. Make yourself comfortable. I've got to grab something from outside real quick."

"Sure thing. I'll be out in a minute."

Before he chickened out, Derrick knelt down beside the bed and raised the dust ruffle. There was nothing underneath. Derrick rubbed his face against the inside of the ruffle and inhaled deeply, the mustiness taking him back all those years.

The bathroom door opened and Derrick slid under the bed, made sure his entire body was hidden. It was too dark to see anything, but he could feel he was directly lined up with the middle of the mattress.

Beth's feet slapped off the wooden hallway. He was going to scare the hell out of her, make her sorry for ever teasing him.

Derrick ran his thumb across the beam directly above his head. He felt the nine razor-thin nicks carved in it. The beam above his chest had dozens more.

The footsteps stopped at the doorway. Beth said, "Derrick? You back?"

Derrick felt further along the beam until he touched the leather mask folded on top of it. He rubbed the mask on his cheek, slipped it over his head. He carefully gripped the razor blade that had been beside it.

She called Derrick's name once more, but he didn't answer. He took the razor and ran it across the wood next to last year's cut: Jasmine. When Beth walked over to the bed, Derrick quietly eased the blade back where it belonged.

Beth sat down, her stubby ankles not far from his shoes. Derrick rolled onto his side, his shoulder pressed into the beam. He could grab both her legs and send her screaming, but that'd be pointless. He needed her. She had to tell him he wasn't a monster. Ronnie was wrong.

Derrick rolled onto his back when Beth brought both feet up and moved toward the middle of the bed, bringing the beams a little bit lower. He ran his thumb across the ten little lines, and his mind returned to the night before they'd existed.

Ronnie had been acting a little weird all that day, had called Derrick back to his room, said he'd wanted to show him something. It was ten o'clock, Dad was blacked out on the couch, Mom dazed in front of the blaring television. Derrick stopped in the doorway, asked Ronnie what was happening.

Ronnie stood at the dresser, kept his back to Derrick and the bed. "I got something to show you." Ronnie sounded strange, almost like slow motion. "Want to see it?"

Derrick was suddenly afraid to say yes. "What is it?"

Ronnie turned around nearly as slowly as he'd talked, kept a hand on the dresser to hold himself up. He opened his left hand, revealed the orange pill bottle.

"What are you doing with those? Are those Mom's?"

It took Ronnie a few seconds to swallow. He nodded yes.

"Ronnie. Did you take any?"

The bed creaked and Beth shouted Derrick's name, yanked him out of the memory. "Where are you?"

She was getting too antsy too soon. Maybe she knew Ronnie had been right. Derrick brought his hand to the beam with the scratches, all the nights he'd spent under the bed. He ran his finger across the top of the beam until he touched the bottle of nasal spray that was wedged there.

"Come on, man," Beth said under her breath. The bed shifted to the right, the wine glass clicking on the table. "I tell him I want to fuck and he goes and does chores," she said to herself.

Derrick brought the Fentanyl spray under his nose, the scent intoxicating. With his other hand, he undid his belt buckle.

"Eww," Beth said. The glass clinked on the table and the bed shifted, Beth's weight directly above him, the wooden beams low enough to lick.

There was no way to know how much of the wine she'd had. Maybe he'd added too much of the powder. Derrick prepared to slip out from the left side of the bed in case Beth ran. She didn't move so Derrick waited, his mind flying back ten years ago.

Ronnie was swaying at the dresser, the orange bottle in his hand.

Derrick had hoped Ronnie was acting, just trying to get attention. "Did you ..." he trailed off. "How many?"

Ronnie tossed the bottle and it bounced under the bed. "She hadn't opened it."

Derrick dove under the mattress, shook the empty bottle, read the label: 30 pills.

Ronnie collapsed, his face smooshed into the floor a foot from Derrick. Talking through half his mouth, he said, "I know it was you. You're the monster."

The bed creaked to the right, ripped Derrick back to reality. The lamp clicked to the high setting, lighting the other side of the ruffle. "Last chance, Derrick! I'm not waiting all night!"

She sounded a little scared, but not at all sleepy. If Beth had drunk the whole glass, she'd be passed out.

The house sat on fifteen acres and was surrounded by trees. Derrick wasn't worried about Beth's screams. He rubbed the tip of the inhaler along the bottom of his nose. He stroked himself and let out the softest, "Mmmmhhhhh."

"Derrick! Is that you?!"

It sounded like she clicked open her purse. Derrick had to assume she pulled out her phone. Playtime was over. It was time to ask Beth the same thing he'd asked his father, all the girls that'd spent the night. But first —

Derrick pulled the lamp's plug, cast the room into darkness. Beth screamed, and Derrick slipped out from beneath the bed. She was backed against the headboard, hands out in front of her. Derrick reached for her face and readied the spray. He asked, "Am I a monster?"

Beth roared as a stream of liquid hit Derrick's chest, neck, the bottom of his mask. He raised his hand to block his eyes, but the stream kept coming, splashing off his forearm, getting in his mouth.

Everything burned at once. His lips, his mouth, his eyes all stinging, snot pouring from his nose. Derrick ripped off the mask, screamed when the pepper spray nailed him in both eyes.

Derrick blindly grabbed where Beth had last been. He couldn't breathe. From out of nowhere Beth slammed into his chest, sent him reeling into the bookcase. Trophies toppled onto his head and shoulders. Derrick dropped to his knees.

Beth was still in the room, but he couldn't tell where, so he just lunged forward and threw out his arm, his hand slapping off her leg. She screamed and kicked, her foot crunching his fingers, knocking the Fentanyl across the room.

Derrick forced his eyes halfway open, saw Beth scramble to her feet, make it to the door. He couldn't let her escape.

Beth was coughing in the hallway, and it sounded like she'd bumped into the wall. Derrick got to his feet, forced one eye open, blew strings of snot down his lips and chin. A doorknob rattled.

Derrick saw Beth, her right hand feeling for the living room doorway. Derrick said, "You can't leave."

Beth screamed, ran full speed, past the living room, towards Derrick's old room, the vase of roses smashing on the floor.

Derrick ran after her. "No! The monster! The monster's in there."

The cheap lock did nothing. Beth stumbled into the room, the door bouncing closed behind her. There was a huge clatter then a crash, Beth grunting like she'd been punched in the gut.

Derrick pushed open the door, flicked on the light. Jasmine's still damp bones were scattered all over the floor, no longer laid out where Derrick could easily assemble her. He'd spent all day digging her out of the backyard and scrubbing her clean, but that wasn't why Derrick stood frozen. He was afraid to make a move for Beth who had crashed on the bed, her shoulder buried in his father's ribs, her face pressed into the moldy mess on the sheets. Derrick shrieked, "Get off him!"

Beth pushed up with her free hand, screamed when she saw what she was inside. Her arm ripped out of the bones, cracking a few. The sternum splintered and landed next to Ronnie's skeleton on the recliner, his ruby red ring pointing right at her.

"Stop! Stop!" Derrick pled, not sure if the tears were real or from the pepper spray. Through half-opened eyes, he sidestepped between Elise and Paula, who sat cross-legged, their skeletons taped to stakes driven through the floorboard.

Beth batted at her blouse and side of her face. She looked for an escape; Ronnie and the circle of seven, all forever facing the bed, keeping the monster on top of it. "Help!!!"

"He has to be on the bed!"

Beth stopped at the panic in his voice. She closed her eyes and pushed his father's skull, popped it off the bed.

Derrick wailed, a sound he'd heard but never made. "You can't."

Beth's voice trembled with fear. She begged him to let her go.

He saw what she was going to do, dove to stop her, but was too slow. Beth kicked down on his father's hips, knocked his lower half off the bed. It crashed in front of Derrick, the brittle bones crumbling on the hardwood. The monster was no more.

Beth backed off the other side of the bed and ripped off Ronnie's arm, sent the rest of him to the floor. She held his arm like a club, swore she'd fucking kill Derrick if he took another step.

It was time to start acting like the man of the house. Derrick laughed at Beth and pointed at the pile of dust and bits of bone by his feet. "You can't hurt me."

Beth took a step toward the doorway, the bone held high, aimed at Derrick's head. "I'll kill you."

Derrick lunged and Beth swung. The rounded end of Ronnie's arm clipped the side of Derrick's skull, shattering both. Derrick lost all feeling and smashed onto the floor. A pool of red spread out before him, the edge flowing farther and farther from his face.

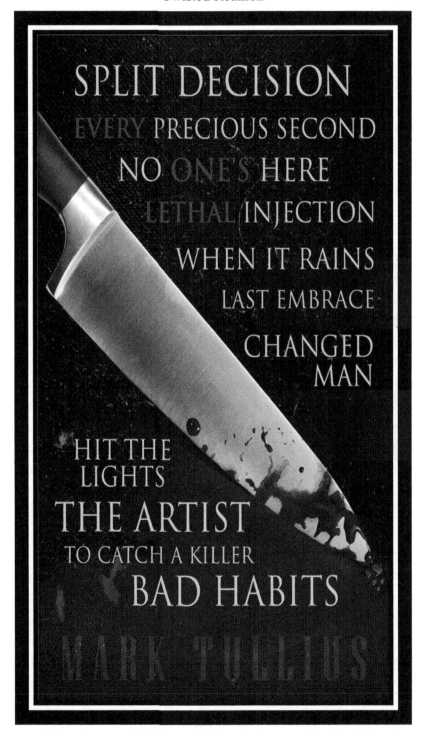

The Artist

The artist climbed the final flight of stairs, opened the door, and then locked it behind her. Today would be a busy day, just like every other one, and she couldn't be bothered while she was at work.

She climbed onto the swivel stool in the middle of the tiny room and turned toward the north-facing window with the easel directly beneath it. After placing a blank canvas on the easel, she looked out the window, admiring the beautiful nothingness before her.

With remarkable speed, she painted the T-intersection where Main Street ran into West Oak Avenue. A few moments later, a row of beautiful trees lined the east side of the road. Their shade spread across the blacktop. The artist sat up and looked out the window, pleased. The deserted streets miles below her were exactly as she had rendered them on the canvas.

Afraid she'd lose her inspiration, the artist brushed a peaceful morning sky, then an elderly couple on Main Street walking hand in hand, appreciating the beautiful sun, each of them aware they only had a limited amount of time left, enjoying every passing moment. On the other side of the street, nearing the intersection, a young mother pushed a bright red stroller and smiled down at her infant daughter staring in wonder at the balloon frozen in the sky.

Knowing the people were outside the window just as she had drawn them, the artist continued. With a few strokes of her brush, she painted an eighteen-year-old boy on his father's Harley out for a leisurely ride. One day, God willing, he would have a bike of his own and a loving son he could lend it to. A few strokes later, she'd painted a yellow bus full of the elementary school honor roll students. The PTA had rewarded them with a day of fun at the beach. Laughter floated through the bus as the kids celebrated a Sunday free from homework, chores, church, and other obligations. They worked so hard every day, and now they finally had a chance to just be kids.

Twisted Reunion

The artist set the painting against the wall and looked out the window. Her creation slowly came to life – the elderly couple sat on the bench, the school bus headed towards the stoplight. Time inched by so she could enjoy every expression, appreciate every emotion of the children pressing their faces to the windows.

The driver tapped the brakes. The biker held up his hand and waved at the elderly couple who were friends of his grandmother. The mother, now stopped at the corner waiting patiently for the walk signal, bent down and smoothed her daughter's fine blonde hair.

Panic didn't set in on the bus driver's face until the third time he tried the brakes. He had no way of knowing the cable had snapped after years of use and poor maintenance, but he did know he was just a few feet from the intersection and the motorcycle that had just entered it.

Even from way up in her tower, the artist heard the blaring horn. The biker brought his hand back to the handlebars and tried to swerve out of the way. It wasn't due to the lack of skill or slow reaction, but the bus struck the tail end of his bike. He flipped over the front wheel.

The bus driver jerked the wheel to the right, losing control of the vehicle. Young screams pierced the crisp morning air as the bus rushed toward the row of trees. At the exact moment the biker sailed into the stroller, the bus wrapped its front end around the trunk of a tall oak. The engine slammed back into the main compartment, severing the driver's legs and pinning him in his seat as tiny bodies flew past him, smashing into and through the windshield.

The artist studied the smoldering wreckage. She cringed at the pained, confused expression of the biker who broke his back against the light post, completely unaware of the mother screaming at him to get off her baby. She counted the little bodies hanging from the bus windows and smashed against the tall tree. She breathed in the familiar scent of gasoline and watched as sparks ignited the back of the bus, trapping the survivors in an inferno. The elderly woman stood in horror, torn between helping the children or her husband of fifty-two years lying on the sidewalk suffering a massive heart attack.

Discouraged with her first attempt, the artist turned to the eastern window and contemplated the nothingness, wondering what she should fill it with. After a few moments, she sat back on her stool and designed an elaborate amusement park. What would take others years, she painted in seconds, each calculation precise, every angle exact. The brilliance behind its design was evident as she looked out the window and admired its grandness.

An amusement park without visitors to enjoy it was the equivalent of the perfect snowflake melting before anyone could see it. Quickly, she moved the brush across the canvas, leaving thousands of bodies in its wake. Eighth-graders raised their hands and screamed as they rushed down the steep descents of a roller coaster, while their older brothers and sisters became better acquainted on the Ferris wheel. Parents in line for the log flume gave their children their first taste of cotton candy. The lines weren't too long and the weather was just right. She had just created the perfect day.

The artist stood at the window and watched parents pull their babies off the carousel and then down beer after beer. She heard the loud crack come from the roller coaster snaking and looping through the entire park.

The first car, occupied by a five-year-old redhead and his father, had just reached the crest of the ten-story climb, about to race down the decline in order to build enough speed to complete the two corkscrews. The father also heard the crack as the car began its descent, pulling the rest of the train with it. When the final car passed the crest, the train zoomed toward the corkscrews. Every passenger raised their arms and screamed as they plummeted.

The broken coupling connecting the first car to the second held halfway through the first twist. When it gave, the first car shot off the tracks and headed for the lake fifty yards away. The little boy hadn't even realized they had left the track until his father's arms were severed by an electric wire.

Both father and son died on impact, so they didn't see the wire fall onto the brown building that housed the fireworks. The father and son didn't see the building explode into a blazing fire that spread in the wind. They didn't see the thousands of people caught in the flames, the crowd panicking and trampling those who had fallen. But the artist did.

She rested her arm on the window ledge and watched the story unfold. She listened to each wail and unanswered prayer and every damning curse. She smelled their fear and the sharp stench of burning flesh. She felt their sadness, their loss. When she couldn't handle any more, she turned to the southern window.

The emptiness begged her to fill it, but she was hesitant to try once again to create a perfect picture. Finally, she decided that sometimes the simplest thing was best. She began depicting the core of the human race: one man and one woman who had taken each other in marriage, vowing to love one another till death did they part.

The artist glanced out the window and watched the disheveled thirty-three-year-old enter their living room and head to the dining room table. Saturday night's business dinner had turned very unprofessional, and all he wanted to do was close the blinds and crawl into bed. His wife was waiting for him at the table, holding a small, unmarked box behind her back, smiling from ear to ear.

The artist returned to her canvas and filled in the details. On the table, a mound of unopened mail that the man hadn't had the courage to open. The white box held a pregnancy test that had finally read positive after so many failed attempts.

The artist remained seated and listened as the wife asked her husband how the dinner went and if he made the sale. He grunted something about the same old bullshit and opened the mail. His wife's next question was drowned out by his curses and the tearing of a letter in two. This was repeated three more times before the artist painted the couple's deceased son's Louisville Slugger. They kept it mounted on the wall, just within the husband's reach.

After setting the finished piece against the wall, the artist listened as the wife broke the good news that they would once again have a family. The husband, overwhelmed by an unsuccessful career, a demanding mistress, and insurmountable bills, didn't tell his wife the baby couldn't be his. He couldn't admit to her that he had had a vasectomy after their son died. He couldn't admit that he'd been lying to her every month of the past five years when she cried because she wasn't pregnant. He also couldn't contain his rage as he wondered whose baby she was carrying.

The artist winced at the first thump. She didn't want to watch what he did with his dead son's baseball bat. Knowing the doctor had botched the vasectomy didn't make it any easier for the artist to watch the wife cower on all fours to protect the baby, screaming for God to stop him. God didn't and the man continued the onslaught until the house was silent except for his heavy breathing, the sound of her blood dripping onto the hardwood floor.

Sickened by the display, the artist took a blank canvas and set it on the easel below the western window. In a matter of moments she had created a glorious church. She looked out the window and studied the pained expression of Jesus hanging on the colossal crucifix. She counted the abundant gold items, wondering how much money the church had spent on them instead of on the hungry and meek it claimed to serve.

A crowd of parishioners filed through the church doors, every type of villager filling the pews. The farmer and his family were in the front row, trying to get closest to God so He would answer their prayers for rain and an abundant crop. Across the aisle, an elderly woman said a prayer for her dead husband and asked when she might be reunited with him, not understanding that she never would. Believers and skeptics held hands as they wished for salvation and survival, peace and prosperity, fame and freedom.

Conflicting prayers bounced off the tower's four walls. The farmer's prayers for rain were just as heartfelt as the travel agent's plea for clear skies. The teenage boy in the back held his girlfriend's hand and prayed she would abandon her beliefs and have sex with him, while she prayed God would give her the strength to hold out until they were married. Some prayers were silly, many were selfish, most unrealistic, but all were heard, and all were unanswered.

The artist studied the canvas. She reached toward it and stroked the hair of a beautiful eight-year-old girl who promised over and over that she'd be good if God let her younger brother walk again. The boy had stepped on a land mine and lost both legs, but the girl truly believed God could change that.

A few strokes later, the artist's brush paused, then peppered the street with her final touches. She listened to the rumble outside and set the canvas against the wall, stood at the window and took in the entire scene. As the villagers set aside their differences and joined hands to say the Lord's Prayer, rebel insurgents crouched outside the building, holding their submachine guns, their fingers anxiously tapping the triggers. The rebels stormed the church, mowed down the farmer and his family, the preacher, the Mayor, nearly everyone in attendance.

The artist shook her head and left the tower. She'd try again tomorrow.

Split Decision

Waking every morning with regret and resentment was taking its toll on Brian. Turning and seeing that lumpy, out-of-shape body, and hearing the incessant snoring, was just that much worse due to lack of sleep. Brian was tired and unhappy with this lifelong commitment. If this was one of his novels, he'd simply erase Joseph and create someone more appealing, or, better yet, allow himself the pleasure of being alone for a while. He'd never been alone, and the thought made him angry.

But it was too early to be angry, definitely not the way to start the weekend. They were supposed to be installing new shelves in the living room. Brian had been putting it off for months, maybe longer. He couldn't remember. Everything had become such a blur of procrastination. He didn't even open his yellow notebook of things he'd promised to do.

He and Joseph had gone to one of those self-help seminars last Christmas. A gift from Joseph, but really a gift *for* Joseph, just like every other gift he gave.

Brian felt Joseph stirring and decided it was time to get up. Brian cleared his throat.

"Huh?"

"I gotta get up," Brian said.

"Hold on."

"Just get up."

"Fine."

Brian shook his head as he slid off the bed. Even when he didn't want to fight, they started off this way. The bathroom mirror verified that Brian looked as miserable as he felt. He wasn't surprised to see his bloodshot eyes and the dark, puffy bags under them, while Joseph's face seemed so fresh and young.

"Goddamn it, Joseph. Some privacy would be a nice change."

"I'm sure it would, but what do you want me to do about it?"

"I gotta take a piss. And don't stand there and watch. That creeps me out."

"Like I haven't seen it before."

"Please, just move. I've got a bad headache and I don't want to argue."

Joseph's face softened. "I'm sorry. I didn't mean to upset you. You're my everything. You're my heart," he said. "I couldn't live without you, you big fucking pussy."

Brian rolled his eyes. He and Joseph rearranged themselves in the cramped bathroom. As he emptied his bladder, Brian made up his mind. Their relationship was over.

Half an hour later, Brian was sitting on a bar stool at the kitchen counter, eating cereal and reading the sports section. Joseph was sitting on the stool to his left, smacking up his oatmeal and trying to read over Brian's shoulder even though he had no interest whatsoever in the football scores. Brian took another swig from his coffee mug.

Joseph said, "I really wish you would cut back on that. All that caffeine is bad for the body."

"It helps me get through the day."

Joseph sounded very hurt when he said, "Now what's that supposed to mean?"

Brian set the mug down and tried to look at Joseph objectively. It was no wonder everyone stared at them as if they were freaks. They were.

"Don't look at me like that. What did I do now? Go ahead then, drink your coffee. You're being such a prick today."

Brian ignored the comment and finished his drink.

"You aren't going to be able to sit down long enough to write anything decent," Joseph warned. "You'll be getting up every five minutes."

"Maybe I don't feel like writing today."

"You should. It helps you relax. And I don't want you to be a dick all night. Plus, I would like to paint later."

"Your stupid flowers…"

"I sold three this year." Joseph's eyes turned cold. "What is your problem?"

Brian took a deep breath to brace himself for what he was about to say. "You know what we talked about? About separating? I think it would be a good idea."

Joseph's too-small mouth hung open. "You're just saying that. You're just angry. Let's get you some eggs."

"I don't want eggs. I think it's time."

"But the doctor said…"

Brian nodded. "I know. And I don't care."

"I love you. You're everything to me."

"I love you too, but I think it will be the best thing for both of us."

"The doctor said I could die."

"He said it was a risk. But so could I."

"So that makes it better?" Joseph said, "I won't do it. Even if I could survive, which I couldn't, have you thought about where we would live? Who would keep the house?"

"We'd have to talk about that," Brian said.

"No, no. I won't do it. I won't go along with it. I won't consent."

Brian turned back to his paper. "Just forget it. Sorry, I brought it up."

Joseph asked, "So are we done talking about this?"

Brian turned the page even though he hadn't read a single word of print. "Yeah…"

Later, while he and Joseph were watching television, Brian used the remote to turn down the volume. He turned to Joseph, who was snuggled up beside him, and asked, "Do you want to give me a hand with something?"

"Sure. What do you have in mind?"

"Let's get those shelves up."

Joseph perked up. "Yeah?"

"Yeah."

The men got up from the couch, walked through the kitchen, and made their way into the garage. After a quick search, Brian located the Skilsaw.

He told Joseph, "You can grab the hammer and extension cord."

"What do we need all this for?"

Brian looked down at the plastic drop cloth rolled up in his right hand. "I need to trim the shelves, and I don't want all the shavings getting into the rug."

They stopped at the cupboard in the kitchen and set down the equipment. Brian pulled out a bottle of Early Times whiskey. He gulped down a longer-than-usual drink from the half-empty jug and then offered it to Joseph.

"Are you crazy? It's barely eleven o'clock."

Brian shrugged and put the bottle away. "Come on, we're being men."

"Well, I wish you would take me into consideration next time you get the urge to drink. Which will probably be in what, two hours?"

"Probably." Brian mimicked Joseph's whiny tone. "Come on, let's get to work."

Once they were in the living room, Brian glanced through the window and noted the neighbor's high brick wall. It was the only time their crappy apartment view didn't bother him. He closed the blinds, and then connected the Skilsaw to the extension cord. "Go ahead and plug your end in down there. And help me lay this down."

The conjoined men bent over at the waist and began unrolling the drop cloth the length of the room. Brian noticed that Joseph was pushing the roll while still holding onto the hammer.

Brian held out his hand. "Here, I can take that from you."

Joseph looked around the room and then at Brian. He kept the hammer and asked, "Where's the wood?"

"What?"

"For the shelf."

"Oh, I forgot it in the garage."

"I didn't see it in there."

"It was next to the workbench." Brian held out his hand again. "Here, give it to me."

Joseph remained still. "Forgot the nails, too, huh?"

"Yeah. We'll go back and get them and the wood. Why don't you just put the hammer down?"

"I think I'll hold on to it for a little while."

"What's the matter with you?"

"Nothing."

"Then stop acting crazy."

"Me?"

The whiskey kicked in and gave Brian the extra push he needed. "Give me the goddamned hammer!"

Joseph took a step back, made Brian stumble. "No."

Brian tried to remain calm. "Hand it over."

Joseph shook his head. Brian felt his smaller self tremble with fear. "I won't hurt you."

"Liar." Joseph backed up again, but Brian was right there with him. Joseph lifted the hammer in his left hand, but Brian's much stronger right pinned it to the wall.

"You're crazy!"

"No. I'm tired." Brian wrenched the hammer from his twin's grip and watched it fall to the floor. "I'm tired of you."

Brian and Joseph simultaneously bent over for the hammer. Brian reached it first and swung as hard as he could, aimed for Joseph's jaw.

Joseph brought his arm up just in time, deflected the blow. Both men staggered backward. Joseph shook his arm and shouted, "You'll kill us both!"

"That's a chance I'm willing to take." Brian swung the hammer again, but Joseph ducked, the hammer sticking into the wall.

Joseph latched onto Brian's arm and fell to his back, pulling Brian down with him. "Fucking stop. Just fucking stop!"

Brian saw the terror in his brother's eyes and finally let go.

Joseph said, "Get off me."

Brian awkwardly rolled his head off of Joseph's neck; the two of them sprawled on their backs, both gasping for air. Brian gazed up at the hammer stuck in the wall, the Skilsaw over on the floor. *Tomorrow*, he thought. *I'll do it tomorrow.*

Lethal Injection

Jack held the phone with his shoulder so he could use both hands to clean his chrome-plated 9 millimeter.

"I'll be there," Brian said. "I was just asking if you were sure about this. I don't even know this guy."

"He's cool."

"I got a bad feeling."

"Don't care." Jack set down the wire brush and checked the gun's barrel. "You should've told me that last week so I could've found someone else."

"You really trust this guy?"

"I already told you he's cool. You need to chill. Can't lose your shit just 'cuz your slip said STRANGER."

"I said I'd be there."

"Good. My rent's due Monday. If this guy's right, we should be able to clear at least ten thousand. How many of your teenage buddies make that in one night?"

"Fine," Brian said. "I'll pick you up at eight."

Jack set the phone down, loaded nine hollow points in the magazine plus one in the chamber. It'd be better if Brian wasn't his sister's stepson, but at least he was trustworthy. Unlike nearly everyone else in Jack's life

The phone rang a minute later. Jack picked it up and said, "You better not tell me you changed your mind."

After a brief silence, a woman asked, "Is Jack there?"

"Who wants to know?"

The voice softened. "Jackie?"

Ashlynn was older now and her voice sounded different, but Jack would never forget the woman who'd stabbed him in the back.

"Jackie, that you? Please say something. It is, ain't it?"

Jack had to sit down. "How'd you get my number?"

"I know you gotta hate me, Jackie, but…"

"Stop calling me Jackie. That's not my fucking name."

Ashlynn stuttered an apology. "How you been?"

"Are you serious?"

"I wanted to make sure you're okay."

"What makes you think I've got anything to say to you?"

"Did you finish up school? I like thinking about you as a lawyer."

"Yeah, finished top of my class."

"Oh, wow, I always knew you'd do good for yourself."

"Glad to see you're just as sharp as ever. I dropped out three years ago." Jack stopped for a second, surprised to feel a twinge of guilt at being mean. He focused on her betrayal and could barely keep his voice from shaking as he said, "Who gave you my number?"

He listened to her pained, amphetamine-laced breaths and eyed the 9 millimeter, wondered what he might've done with it if she had appeared at his door instead of calling. They'd gotten married at sixteen. He'd known it was doomed from the start, but he couldn't let her go, stuck through every stint she spent in rehab. Until she blew everything to shit on his 20th birthday. "I'm hanging up," he said.

"Don't, don't," Ashlynn begged. "I got your number from your Selection Service letter. They mailed it here by mistake."

Jack stayed on the line, unsure of what to say.

"Your slip came with it."

Jack's stomach twisted. Part of him wanted to know what was on the slip, but the other part wanted to slam the phone down, rip it from the wall, smash it into a million pieces.

"You there, Jackie?"

"I'm here." Jack's hand began to cramp around the phone, his knuckles white. He forced himself to relax his grip. "What'd it say?"

"You're not getting drafted."

Jack's hand loosened a little.

"That's good, right?" she said.

"What'd it say?"

"You remember Todd?"

"What do you think?"

She sighed. "Jack…"

"What about him?"

"His slip said GUNFIRE. They didn't even stick him in basic training, just sent him right over there with a gun in his hand, figuring he should take out as many as possible before his time's up."

Jack didn't want to think of the scrawny geek who'd banged her in their bed. "You want me to feel sorry for him?"

"His brother, Charlie, can't get a job. His slip said ELECTROCUTION. He could die anywhere. No employer will touch him."

"Why are you telling me this? What did mine say?"

"Come home, honey. Come back home."

Jack looked around his filthy, one-bedroom apartment, grateful for what he had. "I don't think so."

"Come on, baby. I know I made mistakes, but I love you."

"That means absolutely nothing to me."

"I know you're mad. You got every—"

"You're right. Now, I'm hanging up."

"Jackie!"

Jack was furious at the tears building in his eyes. He shouted, "You just can't call up and expect me to — what do you want?"

"I'm so sorry. I didn't know what to do. I screwed up…"

"You're high right now," he said. "Aren't you?"

"No, no. I'm clean. I swear it. I'm better now, Jackie."

Jack didn't know what to say or how he felt. He set down the gun and wiped his hand on his jeans. "What the hell does my slip say?"

It was Ashlynn's turn to remain quiet.

"If you ever want to see me again, you'd better tell me. Now."

After a moment, she said, "The death penalty. You're going to die from the death penalty."

Jack blew out a breath. "The death penalty?"

Ashlynn sounded too cheerful when she said, "It might not be that bad. Maybe it will be when you're an old man ready to die anyhow."

That's not how it worked, and she knew it. "Holy shit." Jack was now talking more to himself than to her. "This is why I didn't want to know."

"You get used to it." She filled the phone with a coughing fit then cleared her throat. "Sort of."

Jack pictured himself strapped to a gurney, some heavyset nurse plunging a foot-long needle into his arm, feeding the fatal fluid into his veins.

"Will you come home? Please come home."

"I want that letter. I need to see it."

"It's right here. Did you eat yet?" Such painful hope in her voice. "I could make lunch for us."

"I won't stay long enough for that."

"So you'll come by?"

"Same house?"

"Yeah. Same one."

"Fine." Jack hung up the phone, considered calling Brian, telling him they'd have to postpone the plan. But that'd be premature. Maybe Ashlynn was lying; it wouldn't be the first time. She was probably trying to sucker him back now that she was alone. There wasn't a letter. It was only one o'clock. She'd said she'd gotten it today. The mail didn't come that early. She had said today, right? Maybe he should go. He could make it to her house and back with plenty of time to figure out what to do about the job.

The death penalty was the worst way to go. They cut the anesthetics years ago, and shortages had forced them to dilute the potassium chloride. Jack got up from the table and considered leaving the 9 millimeter even though he never walked outside without protection. If Ashlynn was telling the truth, Jack didn't need to worry about being gunned down by anyone. He didn't have to fear for his life. That was already decided. The Selection Service didn't make mistakes.

Jack liked to think of himself as being levelheaded. He'd cooled down a lot over the past year, and he wasn't making any rash decisions until that slip was in his hand. He tucked the 9 millimeter in his waistband and headed for the door. A few minutes later, Jack was on the highway, sticking to the speed limit. He needed to keep away from the law at all costs, and he was in no hurry to return to that house. But at least the bastard she'd cheated with was as good as dead. No more worries about Todd's late night visits to Jack's bedroom while he was out hustling.

As he neared his exit, Jack wondered who he'd kill to earn his death sentence. There was no denying that Jack had done some bad things in order to survive, but he'd never crossed that line. If things ever got heated during a robbery and he was left with no choice, he'd do it, but that was the only way.

He hoped the slip was wrong, even thought about tossing the gun out the window. You can't shoot with something you don't have. He could take certain precautions and try to avoid it as long as possible. At least the death penalty verdict was clear. Sometimes the verdicts were vague, like the one Jack's mother had been dealt.

Jack exited the highway and headed west. He questioned if it was better to know exactly how he'd die. When Jack was a baby, his mother got her slip with one word: COLD. They all assumed it would occur when she was an old woman, but that didn't stop her from consuming every imaginable vitamin and keeping away from anyone with the slightest sickness. They'd even moved to California, and she refused to go near the mountains or anywhere with a walk-in freezer. Then after 22 years of paranoia and pills, one night she rolled off her bed, choked on her own phlegm, and died on the floor. Just a common cold. The same sentence his wife Ashlynn received. Ex. Wife.

Jack pulled the car into the driveway and shut off the engine before he could chicken out and drive away. He hadn't seen Ashlynn in almost two years. The living room curtain was pulled back, revealing the same tragically gorgeous woman he'd fallen in love with. But now her eyes were so ringed in black, he wondered if she'd been punched.

There was no denying she'd lived a rough life. It almost made Jack feel sorry for her. Almost. He got out of the car and slammed the door shut. Just the sight of her sickened him.

She waited on the porch, held open the door. Jack knew she wanted to hug him, but he walked right past her, hands stuffed in his pockets.

"Oh, Jackie." She closed the door and followed Jack into the living room. She smelled like an ashtray and three-day-old sweat. "You're still so handsome."

Jack sat down on the sofa, the same worn-down piece of crap they had since they first moved in together. They swore it would only be temporary. He wanted to tell her she looked like shit, but he couldn't even look at her.

"I made some sandwiches, Jackie. I know you said you weren't hungry, but maybe you want one?"

"I said I wasn't staying long. You have my papers?"

She sat down next to him and put her hand on top of his. He jerked away.

"Won't you at least look at me? I'm sorry," she cried. "I'm so sorry for what I did."

Jack stared straight ahead at the fireplace. "I just want my slip."

Sounding both hurt and angry, she said, "You don't even believe me? You think I don't regret everything?"

"I need to see it."

"I shouldn't have told you. It's better not to know."

"Well, you did, so go get it."

Ashlynn started coughing, her whole body shaking. He scooted away from her as she gagged, almost threw up. She wiped the spit from her mouth and said, "I'm sorry."

Jack made the mistake of looking at her, guilt etched into her thin face. He stood. "Where's the letter? I'll get it myself."

"The counter by the fridge."

Jack moved into the kitchen and read the Selection Service notice. It said he was not drafted, but still qualified to volunteer. Jack folded the letter in half and stuffed it into his back pocket. The other paper, the one he needed to see, was nowhere to be found.

He shouted, "Where's the slip?"

"It should be there."

"It's not."

"Just leave it alone. I'll find it later. Come sit down."

Jack stormed into the doorway. "Get it for me now or I'm leaving."

"I threw it away. You don't need to see it, Jackie."

Jack turned to the white trashcan next to the fridge and took off the top.

Ashlynn yelled, "Don't go digging in there." She tried to come after him and started coughing.

He pushed aside the slimy eggshells and morning newspaper. His heart rate quickened as he rifled through a stack of greasy envelopes and junk mail, but the slip wasn't there. He dug deeper, reached his hand to the bottom of the bag. His finger caught something sharp and he yanked it back.

Jack sucked the drop of blood on the tip of his finger and looked into the trashcan. "What the fuck? I thought you were clean!"

"I haven't used in years."

Jack held up the small syringe. "Then what the hell is this?"

"It's my medicine."

Jack continued his search. Too low for her to hear, he said, "Is that what you call it now?" His hands were disgusting and there was food all over his arms. He kept searching, cursing himself the whole time. He was an idiot for coming over and having to deal with her. "What color is it? It better be in here. If this is some scheme to get me back in your goddamn life…"

"It's white. It should be near the top. I threw it out this morning."

Jack took a deep breath and blew it out. He picked up the folded newspaper and shook it. A small scrap of paper fluttered to the faded linoleum. Jack picked it up. She hadn't lied. His fate was spelled out for him in large, block letters: LETHAL INJECTION.

The kitchen walls were closing in. He stumbled out of the room and leaned against the wall. He shut his eyes, struggled not to be sick. His chest felt constricted as if he were strapped down. His arm ached where that needle would one day plunge. He was going to die and it wasn't going to be pleasant.

Her warm hand rubbed the back of his neck. "I'm sorry, honey. I'm sorry you had to see that. But you gotta think positive." She offered a weak smile. "Oh, you're still bleeding."

Jack looked down and saw the red bead on the carpet. She handed him a tissue. "Here you go." The back of her hand was covered with reddish-purple blotches. Jack looked at her, really looked at her for the first time. Her face was so haggard, her eyes sunken. She was just a shell of the woman he once knew.

He felt nauseous. "What's your medicine for?"

She looked away and shook her head. Tears rolled down her cheeks.

"How bad is it?" he asked.

It took her a moment to speak. "It wasn't my fault."

Jack felt the skin crawling up his back. "What are you talking about?"

"The doctor was just giving me a shot. He had cuts on his finger." She looked at the floor. "They called it a super virus."

Jack threw her hands off his shoulder. He ran for the kitchen and stumbled to the sink. He turned on the hot water and held his pricked finger underneath it, squeezed as hard as he could. Ashlynn was crying, saying she was sorry. So fucking sorry.

No One's Here

I'm no one. Been no one since I was old enough to remember. The name on my birth certificate might read Andrew, but I'm never called that. I'm no one. Mother always said so. It kept me safe, and it kept her from lying. No one's here, baby.

She had two hiding places for me when she entertained men like Desmond. Sometimes she put me under the bed. Usually she put me in the closet. That's how I learned to do it to her like a grownup.

That closet was small and it smelled funny. Not like this one. I've been in here for eight hours and could stay eight more if I had to. But I don't think I will. They go to bed early, and they just turned off the TV.

I won't make any noise. When I was a kid, sometimes I accidentally rustled dresses or bumped into the door. If Desmond asked what it was, Mother would tell him not to worry, that she needed to feel him inside her. If he tried to get up, she'd swear no one was there. No one was watching. Just keep going. Don't stop. Don't ever stop.

I'm never remembered. Nobody will miss me when I'm gone. I blend into the crowd, another nameless face. But I like it. I'm no better; no worse. I'm simply here watching. Like the angels.

Even though people may not know my face, they feel me. When they found Mother, the police knew no one could have crept into Mother's room while she combed her hair. No one could have done such brutal things to her.

And if you asked my neighbors who tortures all the strays, I know they'd say no one does that. And, surely, no one in this city is responsible for the horror happening in the school yard.

The lights are turned off. Now it's just as dark out there as it is in here. I'll give them a few minutes to get settled into bed; no need to rush things now. Everything is set. I already searched their bedroom. I found everything I needed.

No one needs to watch this. They're getting undressed. I hear zippers and buttons and pants falling to the floor. I don't hear anymore talking, just the bed squeak briefly, the covers shuffling. They're probably curled up in bed, whispering I love you. No one should have that kind of relationship. No one deserves that kind of special bond.

This damn door didn't creak like that earlier. I should have oiled it. I don't think they heard it, though. There's no noise. He's probably touching her. Stroking her hair. Her thick brunette hair. Just like the only woman no one ever cried for.

I wonder what her throat will feel like. How soft her skin is. Skin is so thin. God didn't think that one through very well. No one could have done a better job.

This is my favorite part. They can't hear my footsteps on the carpet, but I know they can feel my presence. They always can. They know someone's here. I see it in their eyes. Even in the dark, where no one can see.

She's whispering that she's heard something. I'm in the doorway. She's whispering because she knows someone is with them. The husband's telling her it's nothing, no one's here. He's just as scared, but he doesn't want to show it. But he knows someone is coming.

To Catch a Killer

Tina hitched up her skirt and smiled at the slowing Cadillac. The driver pulled to the trash-strewn curb and lowered the tinted passenger window. With her long legs, generous breasts, and red hair falling to her tiny waist, Tina looked more like a model than a prostitute. But just so there were no questions, her thigh-high boots, black miniskirt, and clearly visible pink panties told the driver he'd come to the right place.

Still not used to prancing around in stilettos, Tina took her time and strolled to the Cadillac, aware the driver was watching every twitch of her hips. She pushed up her breasts and stuck her head through the window, hoped this was the guy she'd been searching for, but doubted she'd be so lucky.

She didn't need to look at the well-dressed fat man to know this wasn't her guy. Even with his overpowering cologne, Tina could smell the stench of sickness. It couldn't be masked by the Caddy's rich leather. This guy was alone and diseased, but he was no killer.

"Hi there, pretty lady." Sweat dripped off his chin and spotted his white button-down. "Care to join me?"

"Maybe you should try the girls over on 17th."

"None of them look like you," he said. "Come on. We'll have fun." He spit something in his palm.

Tina stepped back as cars drove by. Any one of them could be the guy she was waiting for. "I'm sure we would, but I gotta run."

He rolled up his sleeve and revealed the gold Cartier sunk into his fleshy wrist. "I can pay a lot. You don't want to regret this."

"Look, asshole," Tina said. "I'm a cop. So if you don't want to end up behind bars, you better haul ass home."

The Cadillac sped off. Tina walked back to her corner and sat on the bus bench. Her feet were killing her and she dreaded where this was heading. Every night he didn't show was another night she had to walk the damp and dreary streets. Another night she had to pretend she was

124

one of the downtrodden, willing to sell herself for a few measly bucks. Another night she was here. Three months she'd been on this detail. She'd begged for the case, but not a day went by she didn't regret it. She'd looked too long into one of the girl's eyes at the morgue. She got attached. Her sergeant had told her it was a dead end, but she'd convinced herself she could crack it.

Chloe, Promise, Shelly, and a handful of other girls walked the opposite side of the street, knowing they didn't stand a chance of getting picked up next to her. These girls were the real reason Tina wanted to catch the killer. That's what she told herself, that it wasn't all a fucking waste. She used to think of these girls as trash, but as she spent more time with them, she began to realize they were no worse than she was, everyone just looking for some fix to feel less shitty.

Fate had dealt each of these girls a hand they never had a chance of winning. They were destined to be whores, no matter how hard they tried to prevent it. The girls had been raped and molested by parents, uncles, coaches, and teachers. They'd been beaten and abused, made to believe they were completely worthless. The strong ones moved out at an early age to get away from that ugliness, only to quickly learn that the real world was even worse. Strip to make money, do drugs to deal with reality, whore to buy the drugs. Or pay your dues on the force to prove you deserved to be a detective so you can hunt down the type of men who slip pills in your drink, rip your panties, and leave you outside your dorm in the bushes. A vicious cycle that never seemed to end.

This was Tina's forty-fifth night on this ten-block strip of hell and she still had not caught a glimpse of the guy. Even though the police were monitoring every strip club, whorehouse, and corner, the maniac continued to strike. Every morning a different girl, or at least parts of her, showed up.

The killer was confident, and with good reason: over fifty mutilated girls and the department wasn't even remotely close to busting him. It was almost as if someone on the inside was telling him exactly where Tina was going to be.

The police had a sketch given by two pros who'd seen the fifth victim, Dominque, get inside a station wagon. Another girl saw victim number 12 climb into a limo. But that was all the police had to go on.

Tina had no idea what kind of vehicle to look for because the killer always used a different car. He was blatantly daring the department, handing them his DNA in the semen-stained underwear he left behind, always wrapped around the girl's throat. He thought the police couldn't catch him, but Tina would prove him wrong, at least that's what she still told the sergeant.

A small, blue Toyota pickup stopped on the other side of Colton Street. Tina's heart rate quickened when she saw Shelly slip into the passenger side. Before the couple closed the deal, Tina crossed the street, prayed the john didn't pull something out of his pants that Shelly couldn't handle. She was relieved to see the driver was a pimply teenager, his frustrated virginity stamped on his forehead.

Tina continued across the street and asked Chloe if she was interested in grabbing them some food. She had just handed Chloe a twenty when a black van rolled through the intersection and pulled to the curb a little way down 21st. The van was a good thirty feet away from Tina when the driver lowered his window for a young black girl. Tina couldn't remember her name. A strong breeze blew past and told Tina to hurry.

Under her breath, speaking into the mike hidden between her breasts, Tina said, "I think this is our guy. Charlie, you seeing this?"

There was no answer in her earpiece. Tina quickened her pace and called out, "Hey there, honey, you've got the wrong car."

The girl pulled her head out of the window and glared at Tina. "Get your own date. This one's mine."

Tina didn't slow. Although the girl was taller and much thicker, Tina wasn't about to let the girl get in that vehicle. "Let him decide."

"Screw you. Get back on your side of the street."

"I go where I want." Tina bumped the girl out of the way, tried not to choke on her rotten peach perfume. She peered into the van and saw a disheveled guy with a cheap comb-over. Nothing like the sketch, but Tina could tell from the smell this was her guy. Forcing what she hoped was a winning smile, she said, "How about it, sugar? Who's the lucky lady gonna be? Me or Midnight?"

"Fuck you, bitch," the black girl said.

"I'm just trying to let the man decide. Who's it going to be?"

He looked right at Tina and said, "Who do you think?"

Tina whipped open the door and slid inside before the girl knew what had happened. She ignored the ripe scent of death and put her hand on the guy's grimy jeans, rubbed his thigh. "I've got a spot around the corner."

He pulled away from the curb. His breath reeked of alcohol when he said, "No, I need to keep driving."

The thought of the 9 millimeter inside her purse kept her calm. "It's your dollar." She turned around in her seat and looked into the back of the van. Black trash bags were taped over the windows and a black tarp covered a lumpy form on the van's floor. This had to be him, but nothing about the case said he was a drinker. The killer was too methodical to allow alcohol to blur his judgment.

"What the hell you think you're doing?" he shouted as Tina crawled into the back.

"Looking for a place where I can make you happy. Want to pull over here? Or there's a spot right after Orange."

"You deaf? I said we're gonna keep driving."

"I heard," Tina said, "I'm just not sure if I'm cool with that. I need to see the money first."

"I got money and you've got a mouth."

Afraid her tail might lose her, she told the guy, "Don't turn right on Pine. Why don't we just keep driving straight down 21st?"

Without slowing, he looked at her. "What'd you say?"

Tina fingered the clasp on her purse. "Just thought it'd be nicer if we headed toward the hills."

"This ain't a date. Earn your money." He reached back, grabbed the back of her head, and slammed her face onto his lap, her nose just inches from his crotch.

Tina tried to pull up, but he was strong. The smell was overpowering. She couldn't do what he asked, but her gun was out of reach, tucked in her purse in the back.

"What's wrong?" He brought his free hand down to his zipper. "Need me to help?"

Before he could pull it down, Tina grabbed his wrist with her left hand and used her right hand to slam down the brake pedal. The van jerked right, scraped off another car, then stopped. The driver's chest slammed into the top of the steering wheel as Tina's head bounced off the bottom of it.

He ripped her up by her neck. "Crazy bitch, what's your problem?"

Tina reached behind her and blindly groped for her purse, but he pulled her forward before she found it. With his face just inches from hers, he yelled, "Answer me, bitch!"

Trying to sound as if she were in control, Tina said, "I'm a cop. Let go of my neck and place both hands on the steering wheel."

The driver smashed his forehead onto the bridge of her nose. Bright lights exploded in front of Tina, and a river of blood rushed down her throat. Tina fell back, slouched against the passenger door, barely aware that the driver was out of the van and running around to her side of the vehicle. She tried to turn around and lock the door, but she was too slow.

"I should've known it was too good to be true," the driver said. He wrenched open the door and Tina nearly fell out of the van, but she managed to grab hold of the glove box. The driver sank his fingers into her shoulder and yanked on her collarbone, sent her crashing onto the concrete. As her head hit the ground, her vision went blank and the wig flew off. Unable to see, she waited for the fatal blow, but instead she heard the squeal of brakes.

A car door opened and slammed shut. Feet slapped the concrete. The driver of the van said something in protest a split-second before Tina heard the bone-jarring impact and felt the men fly past her and crash down on the sidewalk a few feet away.

Tina flopped onto her stomach to stop the blood from rushing down her throat. Still dizzy, she pushed up to her knees and opened her eyes. She didn't recognize the clean-cut man who was mounted on the killer's chest, pummeling his face. The guy wasn't a cop, at least not from Southside.

Wanting to help, but not yet trusting her balance, Tina slumped against the side of the van. Her hero had everything under control, picking apart her attacker, rifling punches between the man's upraised hands. The cop in her wanted to tell the guy to stop, but then she reminded herself what the creep had done to all those girls and probably would have done to her if this guy had kept on driving.

Her rescuer sat back on the guy's chest to catch his breath. Sweat dripped from his forehead, blood from his knuckles. Rage shined in his gray eyes as he stared into the driver's destroyed face.

Speaking through a mouthful of blood, the driver asked, "What are you doing? Please…"

The Samaritan raised his elbow and brought it down with blinding speed, smashing the killer's cheek, shattering the bone. He brought his elbow up again and slammed the tip into the man's forehead, once, twice, three times.

Tina finally found her voice. "Stop."

Almost as if a switch had been flicked, her hero transformed. He looked at Tina with gentle eyes and said, "Thank God you're alright. I thought he was going to kill you." The man got up and wiped his bloody hands onto his jeans. He walked over and asked, "Can I get you anything? Call someone for you?"

Blood trickled into her mouth. "I'm okay."

The man squatted down and pulled a handkerchief from his back pocket. He smiled and offered it to her. "I'm not calling you a liar, but you don't look okay."

Her inability to accept help from others was something Tina had wanted to change for a long time. She took the handkerchief and pressed it to the corner of her mouth.

The man glanced over his shoulder at the unconscious driver and then back at Tina. "Sorry you had to see that. I'm usually not like that."

"Well, I'm glad you were tonight."

He was clearly embarrassed when he asked her if she knew the man. Tina blushed and told him no.

"I'm not judging." He offered his hand. "Here. Let's see if you can get up."

Still a little dizzy, Tina took his hand and stood. She leaned against him while she regained her balance. With one hand pinching her nose closed and the other holding his waist for support, Tina looked up at him. "I'm really not a hooker."

"I can see that. Come on. You can have a seat in my car. I'll call the cops and make sure this guy doesn't leave until they get here."

"They're already on the way." Tina walked with him toward the idling silver Civic. She smiled at the "Powered by Jesus" decal taking up the entire back windshield.

He opened the door and helped her inside. "You sure? Maybe no one called them."

Tina leaned back in the seat and told him that she was an undercover cop. "My back up should have already been here." She looked down and shouted at the mike between her breasts. "Hear that, you jerkoffs? The suspect is at the corner of Pine and 21st. He's the bloody lump lying on the concrete."

"So you really aren't a hooker? That's too bad."

She saw he was playing with her. "Very funny."

He said his name was Gabe and shook her hand. "If you want, I can take you to the hospital."

"How about a bar? I could use a beer," she joked.

"I'm not much of a drinker, but I'd love to." He pointed toward the van. "You have anything in there? Or do you just want to go?"

She started to get out of the car. "No, I'm kidding. I need to wait."

He put his hand on her shoulder. "You should sit."

Tina closed her eyes and relaxed, noticed that for the first time in years she wasn't able to smell anything. She took the bloody handkerchief from her nose and discovered the pressure had stopped the flow. Her nose was sore to the touch and clogged with blood. She tucked the handkerchief inside her shirt in case it started bleeding again. The loss of her sense of smell scared her, but before she panicked she assured herself that it was just temporary.

She opened her eyes and looked out the windshield at the van. The smell from its interior had tipped her off, but she had been suspicious about the vehicle anyway, and one look at the driver had told her all she needed to know.

"How long do you think it'll take your partners to get here?" He pointed at the guy on the ground. "Maybe you should cuff him."

Tina looked in the side mirror and saw a white truck coming up behind them. They were blocking the road. Gabe pulled his car forward, but the truck still couldn't get around. He took a left, then a right. When she looked out the window, Tina realized she had no idea where they were. Her job had never taken her into this part of the city.

Gabe pointed down the dimly lit road. "We're pretty close to my place. There is a bar just a few blocks away."

"Yeah, okay," she laughed. Her head felt light. He started to say something else, but stopped himself and threw on his blinker. The car coasted to a stop on the side of the deserted street.

"What are you doing?" she asked.

"I think it's the transmission. Always something with this heap. I've been meaning to trade it in." He turned off the car and got out. As he popped the hood, Tina turned, tried to figure out where they'd come from. "I'll just be a minute," Gabe called out.

When Gabe came back, he said, "I'm afraid I had to call Triple A. This is so embarrassing."

"It's fine. I need to get back though."

Gabe asked her if she was okay. "The way you're holding your neck doesn't look good."

The entire right side of her neck burned, but Tina said, "Just tight. I'm sure I'll feel wonderful tomorrow." Her vision was blurring.

"Why don't you turn toward the door and lean back a bit. Let me work on it."

"Oh, no, I'm fine."

"It's going to be at least twenty minutes." His fingers were cool, applied just the right pressure. "And I swear I won't strangle you."

Tina barely felt his hands on her shoulders. "I really need to go. There's a report I need…" Tina trailed off as her tongue ran over the roof of her mouth. It felt numb.

"That was the first time I saved a cop. I think you should be giving me a massage." Gabe began working her upper back. "You've got a ton of knots."

"My job's…a little stressful." Tina started to reach for the door handle, but her fingers missed the latch and fumbled down the door.

Gabe asked about her job, his fingers gliding down her spine, settling on her low back. She knew she needed to get out, but it felt so good; Gabe finding every sore spot, smoothing them away. He said, "I have a bit of a confession to make."

Tina opened her eyes, realized she'd nearly fallen asleep.

"I recognized you back there," he said. "I wasn't sure it was you until you said you were a cop."

"Why didn't you say so?"

He smiled. "I didn't want you thinking I was some kind of sick, celebrity stalker. I read that article on you. *The Nose That Knows*. Pretty catchy. So is it true? Can you really smell a crook a mile away?"

"No," she yawned. Some of the guys on the force had fed the reporter that line. She did have an extraordinary sense of smell, but it hardly helped in cases.

"How about out here? No one's around for miles. Can you still smell that guy?"

Tina inhaled. "Nothing. Can't smell a thing."

"That's good. I was hoping you wouldn't smell the dead guy I stuffed in the trunk."

Tina laughed. "I assumed that was you. Sort of a mixture between Old Spice and Brut." She felt drunk.

"Nope, only unscented roll-ons for me. And don't get me started on colognes. Even the lightest fragrance makes me nauseous."

Tina shook her head to try to clear it. "Ok, we need to go back."

"My car's broken. Don't you remember?"

Tina sort of remembered something about AAA, but that seemed like a week ago. She asked if he was teasing her about his ability. He studied her with probing eyes. "Your smell is pure and sweet. It's funny how a person's scent can reveal so much about them." His thumbs rolled down her low back, his fingers down the outside of her hips. "I can smell that you're aroused by me."

Tina didn't know how to respond. She wasn't sure if she should be angered by his crudeness or impressed by his accuracy.

His hands traveled up to her neck. "I gave that guy the van and five hundred bucks to spend on the red-haired hooker on 21st and Colton."

Tina jerked out of his grasp, but he pinned her against the window, his hand around her throat. Tina tried to fight, but he was too strong. Sparks fired off in her mind. She reached for her purse only to realize she'd left her purse in the van.

"I'll pull away, Tina. But as soon as I do, I would recommend you get out of this car and run for your life. Just to prove to you how good my sense of smell is, I'll give you a minute head start."

Unnerved by his calmness, her voice shook when she said, "I'll kill you."

"Go ahead. You really think you can get back to your gun?"

Tina wondered how he knew she wasn't carrying her 9 millimeter, but her thoughts were fleeting and jagged, everything foggy and removed. Gabe made her decision easier by reaching into his pocket and pulling out a six-inch switchblade.

"You've got one minute, bitch. Let's make this fun."

Tina hated turning her back on the knife, but she threw open the door and staggered out, shook her head, and ran like hell. She wanted to turn and fight him, but images of the mutilated women propelled her feet. Tina was near the end of the alley when she heard a bloodthirsty howl. He had her scent.

Tina tried to flick on her mike, but the wires were gone. He must have slipped it out of her shirt during the massage. How could she have been so dumb? His howl grew louder. She zigzagged through the dark and deserted sidewalks hoping to throw him off. Tina turned left at the next abandoned building. Halfway down the alley, she realized it was a dead end.

Tina kept running, hoped she'd be able to scale the eight-foot fence at the end, but when she reached the wooden boards, they appeared wavy and a mile high. Whatever he'd soaked the handkerchief with was now causing hallucinations. She glanced behind her and tripped. Gabe hadn't reached her yet. She picked up the large brick she had tripped on, hid behind the trash bin. The weight of the brick seemed to be increasing. She could barely keep it in her grip.

Gabe howled again. "I smell you, Tina. Why'd you stop running?" He sounded close, just around the corner. "I love it when you run."

Tina leapt back behind the dumpster just as Gabe's silhouette appeared at the end of the alley. She reached up and slipped the blood-soaked handkerchief in the trash. She leaned back against the stucco wall, blinked a few times, listened to his footsteps. Her other hand tightened around the brick.

"Where are you, sweetheart?" Gabe slowed, his breaths labored. "I have something to show you."

Tina remained curled up behind the trash bin. She listened to Gabe shuffling the soles of his shoes along the concrete. He was taking his time, enjoying this.

Gabe stopped next to the bin and sighed. "Oh, Tina, I thought you'd be a challenge. You really didn't think hiding near trash would mask the smell of your blood, now did you?"

Gabe threw open the bin's lid. Metal scraped the inside of the container as Gabe blindly lashed out. "You bitch!" he screamed. "I'm gonna tear your head off!"

Tina leapt up and saw the surprise in Gabe's eyes. He brought his hands up, the knife in one hand, the bloodied handkerchief in the other. He was too slow to block Tina's swing, and the brick connected with a sickening thud against his skull.

Gabe slumped next to the bin. Tina brought the brick down one more time, stopping the rise and fall of the chest of one of the most ruthless killers Southside had ever seen. But Tina knew she would still smell everything, every homicidal maniac still lurking, every girl falling under the weight of a knife, every child left abandoned in the living room next to her lifeless mother. She smelled it all, and it would never end.

Hit the Lights

A low squeak woke Teddy. He thought the noise had come from the mouse in his dream, a furry little rodent cornered by a cat. Another squeak. It was coming from somewhere in his room.

Teddy wasn't about to take the covers off his head. He concentrated on the new noise; a high-pitched screech that penetrated the bound-up nerves in Teddy's little back. The sound his parents' closet door made whenever he inched it open to peek at his gifts.

Just as he would if it were one of his mom's sacks from Sears, Teddy had to look. If something was coming for him, he needed to know. Thanks to his broken leg, he couldn't run away, but if he saw something, he could scream for help.

Ever so slowly, Teddy pulled the comforter off his head. The second his eyes were exposed, the squeaking stopped. He sat up in the bed, kept the comforter pulled tight against his neck, ready to snap it over his head if anything leapt out from the darkness.

Teddy looked toward the closet door, half expecting to see a set of razor sharp teeth, but his eyes hadn't adjusted to the pitch black of his room and he couldn't see past the foot of his bed. The light of the moon would have illuminated everything if he hadn't closed the shutters and pulled down the blinds. He was too much of a chicken to leave his window open; the thought of only one pane of glass between him and the demons lurking outside was enough to keep Teddy up for hours. He knew if he left the shutters open and the blinds up, he'd wake with a creature's face pressed against the glass. That thought alone was the reason Teddy's mom had to wash his sheets twice a week.

Like every other kid from the neighborhood, Teddy hated the dark. That's when all the bad stuff happened in their tiny town. No one went outside at night, not even the adults. You didn't leave your doors unlocked. And above all, you didn't let evil watch you sleep. Tina Jonas and Danny Kincaid found that out. So did Ricky Oliver.

Teddy looked toward the window, saw the shutters still shut. Another squeak from the closet. He jerked his head toward the sound, ready to scream for his mom. He didn't want to wake her again, but that was a hell of a lot better than ending up in one of the bags they'd found by the Harlen River.

Now that his eyes had adjusted to the darkness, Teddy could see the Obi-Wan Kenobi poster above his dresser. The closet next to it was open. A six-inch strip of blackness stood out against the pale white wall. He never left it open and checked it at least twice every night before he crawled into bed.

He waited for the closet door to move again, and noticed his wheelchair leaning against the bedroom door. When he'd gone to sleep, it'd been just to the left of his bed. It must have rolled on the hardwood floor. That was what the squeaking was. It used to belong to his Uncle Matt, its wheels now old and rusty.

Teddy's dad had left him with one lesson before he abandoned them. He'd always told him there was a rational explanation for everything. The mind was a powerful tool, able to paralyze a person with fear or free them through logic. It was all in how you used it.

Teddy studied the open closet. His big, puffy red coat hanging inside wasn't a demon. The two tiny stubs wrapped around the door near the floorboards weren't fingertips. They were probably scratches he hadn't noticed before or, more likely, his batting glove had slipped halfway out the door.

Teddy concentrated on what looked like half a head peeking out from the top shelf. It wasn't moving. It was a stocking cap. It'd been his imagination. That wasn't a demon crouched on the ground near his stinky tennis shoes. It was probably just his football.

He glanced at his wheelchair, and wished he could Jedi it back over to his side. With his wheelchair all the way by the door, he couldn't get out of bed if he wanted to, at least not without crawling around like a little baby. He would have to call out, wake his mom, and have her get it for him. While she was in here, she could also turn on the lights and make sure the closet was safe.

His mom would be pissed though. She'd told him to just let her get some sleep. That's all she seemed to do since the murders began. Teddy pulled the comforter over his head and settled back into bed. A faint slithering sound came from below, a light tug at the end of the bed sheet. Teddy lowered the comforter to his neck and waited. The room was silent. He squeezed his eyes and told himself to stop being such a baby.

A loud *whoosh* near the window. Before Teddy could blink, the closet door creaked and something moved under his bed. The bed sheet grew tighter across his chest and broken leg. Then it started to slide right off of him.

Teddy yanked the comforter over his head and screamed. "Mom! Mom! Hurry!"

A door creaked open at the end of the hallway. He breathed a sigh of relief, and then gagged as he inhaled the rancid air. The putrid smell hadn't come from him. Even if he ate three bowls of chili with broccoli on the side, he couldn't dream of ripping a fart so foul.

Heavy footsteps pounded down the hallway. Not wanting to look like a sissy, Teddy pulled back the comforter and sat up. The sour stench made him want to puke. He looked to the window, still closed and shuttered. Right below the sill, however, was a dark brown pile. He supposed it was possible he'd crumpled up his corduroy jacket and tossed it on the floor, but he didn't remember doing that.

The door opened. It pushed the wheelchair out of the way. Irritated and half asleep, his mother asked, "What's that doing here?"

"Something moved it." Teddy tried to keep the panic out of his voice. "Turn on the light."

She stood in the dark doorway, her silhouette just visible. "Wow, smells like you shit yourself."

Teddy couldn't believe his ears. His mom had never cursed. "It wasn't me."

"What are you talking about?"

"The smell. It wasn't me. It's from over by the window."

"I can't smell anything," she said. "I said that it sounds like you scared yourself."

Teddy wondered how he could have misheard her. "No, I just had to pee and my chair rolled away. Can you bring it over and turn on the light?"

"Teddy, you screamed."

"I just need my chair. I gotta go real bad."

"That's what you get from watching all those horror movies. That's why you're scared of the dark."

"I'm not scared of the dark." He'd been planning to keep with the wheelchair story, but he knew she wasn't buying it. "I heard something."

"Do you need to start using your Mickey Mouse light again, Teddy Bear? What would your friends say if they saw that?"

"I don't need it."

"This is the fifth time this week you've woken me. I need my sleep, honey."

"I'm sorry, Mom." He looked about the dark room and couldn't see or hear anything strange. It had only been his nerves. "Can you just bring my chair over? Please."

"No problem." She staggered away from the doorway and wheeled the chair over to his bed.

Another *whoosh* by the window. The room filled with the rotten stench of a septic tank. Teddy yelled, "Turn on the light!"

"What's the matter with you, Teddy?" his mother said. "You're going to give me a heart attack screaming like that."

"By the window. You didn't hear it? You can't smell it?"

"There's nothing here. You need to understand there's nothing to be afraid of. Your dad was a pussy, too."

Even though his dad had left them one night without so much as a word, his mom had never talked badly about him. And regardless of how scared he was, Teddy wasn't about to let her start now. "No, he wasn't."

"Yes, he was. He didn't like the dark. Said he used to see things."

"That doesn't make him a pussy."

"Don't you ever use that language in this house! And don't ever say anything bad about your father. Your dad was a great man."

"But you…"

"I said he was afraid of the dark. That doesn't make him less of a man."

"You called him a pussy."

"You're worrying me, honey. Maybe I should take you to the doctor."

Something bumped the bottom of the bed. Teddy screamed, "Turn it on!"

Holding one hand to her forehead, his mom reached up and pulled the chain that switched the light onto its lowest setting. She kept her hand up to block the glare and said, "Happy?"

Teddy looked down. What he had hoped was his jacket was a grotesque jellylike mass quivering in the corner. The foot-high, shit-brown lump opened its one eye and stared at him. It oozed forward, leaving a corrosive trail that ate through the boards. Teddy pointed at the blob just as it opened its mouth and emitted that same whooshing sound. He was barely able to keep down his dinner as the noxious aroma passed over him.

His mom followed his finger and looked toward the corner. "What is it, Teddy?"

"There! Right there!"

She stepped toward the corner and looked directly at the disgusting creature, keeping her hand on her forehead the entire time. "What is it? A spider? I don't see it."

With his mom out of the way, Teddy had a clear view of the closet door. Four clawed fingers were wrapped around the white door, sliding it open. Above the hand, a misshapen head peeked out. The impish creature smiled at Teddy, its row upon row of tall, needle-thin teeth glistening in the light.

Teddy scrunched back against the headboard, and yanked the comforter to his throat. "Behind you! Watch out!"

She slowly stood, one hand holding her forehead, the other closing the top of her blue terrycloth nightgown. "You're scaring me, Teddy."

The spindly-limbed imp crept out of the closet. The crud creature oozed closer. Teddy couldn't scream.

His mom took a step toward the bed. The monsters moved with her. Blood drooled out from the corner of her dark red lips and dripped off her chin. The moment a drop hit the floor, a midnight-black, oil-slicked snake shot out from beneath the bed. The four-foot-long serpent lapped at the scarlet puddle, its barbed tail thumping against the floor in celebration.

Teddy screamed for her to run.

She just looked at him. "Honestly, I don't know who was worse. You or your father."

The serpent wound between his mother's legs. She didn't seem to notice as it coiled around the bottom of her calf, leaving a thick black trail across the terrycloth. Without warning, it shot under the full-length gown. His mother began to moan in rhythm with the serpent's barbed tail as it swished back and forth on the hardwood floor.

Before Teddy could pull the covers over his face, the imp rushed forward, his bony, clawlike fingers spread high above his head, ready to dig them into his mother's back. He ripped the nightgown off Teddy's mother, revealing a skeleton-thin creature, with thick, black quills covering its chest, arms, and legs. Now that it was exposed, the creature removed its hand from his mom's forehead. The thin piece of flesh and scalped hair fell to the ground with a wet thud. The crud creature rushed over and sat on top of his mom's face as the snake thing buried itself further between the imposter's legs, its tail whipping around in a frenzied circle inches above the ground.

Continuing the façade, the monster used his mother's voice as it lumbered toward him. "I told you everything was okay. Now go to sleep, Teddy Bear. But first give Mommy a nice kiss."

Last Embrace

It's good to see your whole family made it. Amazing that they still love and support you despite the things you've done. I wonder if they know how much their presence here means.

They came to offer prayers. They came to offer you strength. But all they really do is make your despair darker, your suffering sweeter. To die in your loved one's arms is one thing. To die helplessly in front of them, is quite another. I suppose it's probably a blessing though, to finally see all this coming to an end.

Look at their faces. Look what you've done. Look what you've reduced them to.

This has to be the worst moment of your mother's life and you're responsible. The lines of fear and revulsion etched into her face will never go away. Your father's not doing much better. Look at the pitiful sight, his crushed macho façade crumbling. But their pain is nothing compared to what your baby sister is going through. She's staring at me, too young to know what she's about to see. She'll never forget this day. And neither will I.

I'm not a mercy killer. I am simply the one lucky enough to watch them pull the switch. I can't wait for tonight. I can't wait to feel your sweat on my skin. You must realize how intoxicating it is, to have a dead man's scent seeping through you.

You have some fight. I like how you pretended to struggle with the guards so your family couldn't see you trembling like a little girl. How cute that you're still trying to be a big boy. You were so tough with a gun in your hand. But that's gone. So take my arm. Squeeze as hard as you like. You can't hurt me.

No? Fine. I wasn't much for holding hands. You don't have a lot of time, so take one last look at your family. Remember their faces. Think about what you've put them through. What you're about to put them through. They won't smell you cooking from out there. They're not supposed to, but this is an old building, and they'll start to believe they can taste the fried bits of you.

The way you're sitting on me says you're going to be a fun one. The way you're arching your back, trying not to touch my chest. The way your legs are trembling as you attempt to keep your ass off my lap. Good attempts, but pointless. I'm all you have now. It's you and me.

I know what you're thinking, listening to the tick of the clock. The governor could still call with that reprieve. That could happen, but it never does. Don't misunderstand me. I am glad they tell you that. That last chance of survival toys with your emotions; it fills you with a panicky hope that won't completely disappear until the first jolt hits.

And I've got a special surprise for you and your family. For some reason, the first surge will only be at one thousand volts. The meter will show it at two, so the guards will let it run for the full sixty seconds. Enough voltage to get you foaming at the mouth, bleeding from your eyes, shaking like an epileptic, but not enough to kill you.

When they stop to determine the problem, you'll renew your faith, hope, and determination to live. They'll think they found the problem right away. I'm old and falling apart. A few quick turns of a screw and you'll be back on deck. And what they won't realize is that I've completely drained the brine out of your sponge.

When they throw the switch again, I'll be at three-quarter power. I'll slowly bake your brain and cook your insides before I take you. When you die, the guards are going to discover I'm back at full capacity and can't be shut down. They'll yell at each other and complain that I have a mind of my own, but it won't matter to you anymore. You won't feel your flesh sizzle, but rest assured that I won't stop until every inch of your skin crackles.

Mmmm. Now you're sweating. Haven't even turned on the fire and you're already dripping. This is going to be fun.

When it Rains

Del followed his boss and two co-workers onto the covered balcony of the second floor and took the chair next to Taylor. It was the seat closest to the kitchen. If they wanted to get wet, that was fine with Del, but he was staying by the door. This wasn't just a mild September shower, a little thunderstorm. On a night like this, there was no telling how much rain the town was going to get.

Lightning flashed, illuminated the entire property. "Holy crap," Martin said with his heavy Swiss accent. He pointed toward the rushing river some twenty yards down the grassy slope. "You see that water? Look at that. Amazing, no?"

Del stretched his neck, looked at the overflowing river, but kept his comments to himself. The torrential rains had transformed the usually quiet creek, upsetting the balance of things. Martin clearly wanted someone to agree with him, tell him it was a beautiful sight, but Del figured he'd leave that to the other ass-kissers who'd say that grass was orange and pumpkins were green if their boss said it was so.

Martin must have noticed Del's indifference because he was quick to ask, "Does this all the time happen? The crazy weather like this?"

Taylor took a swig of his fruity drink. He looked like a clown with his flashy jewelry and trendy clothes. Maybe he fit in Hollywood, but if he ever ordered that in one of the local bars, he'd be laughed out of town. Taylor wiped his mouth and asked Del, "Yeah, what the hell's up with this place? It was nice as shit earlier today, all warm and sunny like L.A."

Del was tempted to mention the gray clouds that had been on the horizon all afternoon, but thought better of it. Instead, he took a chug of his Bud Light and said, "The only difference was the lack of smog, huh? Remember, just last week you couldn't stop raving about how great the clean air was?"

Taylor didn't look away from the storm. "Yeah, too bad the freaking pollen count's sky high. I've never sneezed so much in my life."

"Seriously, Del," Martin asked in his slightly mixed-up English, "the weather gets horrible all time, no? Yes?"

"Over in Ashford and sometimes in Heaven, they get downpours like this, but not so much down here. Every once in a while it'll come down real hard like this, but it's usually just quick showers."

Billy, who'd been unusually quiet most of the night, chuckled and polished off the rest of his Jack and Coke. "Heaven. I can't believe you guys got a town called Heaven." He hawked a wad of phlegm into his empty plastic cup and tossed it onto the floor just a few inches from Taylor's feet. "There's a goddamn church on every corner and one in between them."

"And what the hell's up with not being able to get booze on Sundays?" Taylor asked.

"Yeah, I thought that whole wine-being-blood bullshit made alcohol okay," Billy said, disgust dripping like the raindrops falling off the railing.

Another lightning bolt lit up the sky. Del inched his chair toward the kitchen just in case the next one found its way into the balcony. "People out here like to pray. Most of them got good reasons."

Instead of letting it go, Billy continued, "The whole God thing's bullshit if you ask me."

Martin said, "Maybe you shouldn't be so quick to say such things. Who do you think makes the rain?"

Billy pushed out of his seat and headed toward Del, who scooted his chair out of his way as the muscle-bound bully stomped into the kitchen, mumbling under his breath.

Taylor took a sip of his drink. "What the fuck's that guy's problem?"

"Was he never an altar boy?" Martin asked, seemingly surprised when everyone burst into laughter.

Billy stumbled back onto the balcony, a fresh drink in his hand. "What the hell's so funny?"

"It was nothing," Taylor said. "Just chill."

"This shit's miserable. You know how dirty the Escalade's gonna be tomorrow? We live on a goddamn dirt road."

Another burst of lightning exploded above them. Taylor pointed to the driveway below. "You might want to move it, Billy. If the water keeps rising, you're gonna need to get it detailed. Your rims are gonna be a mess."

Billy pulled keys from his pocket and turned to Del. "Go throw it in the garage for me."

"I'm not going out there."

"You afraid of a little rain?"

"No, I'm just not going out there."

"Come on." Billy took another drink. "Earn your keep, man. You don't pay rent."

"Yeah, and neither do you. Plus, I'm only here during the week."

"What if I turn on the outside lights for you? Maybe Taylor can hold your hand."

Del wanted to tell Billy where he could go; instead, he shook his head and sat back, stared out into the darkness.

Billy stuffed the keys back into his pocket. "Fine. No big deal," he told the group, although his tone said it was. "I can afford to get it washed."

The storm picked up. The rain came slapping against the side of the house. Martin got out of his chair and asked everyone to scoot over. For someone who claimed to be an outdoorsman, he sure didn't like to get wet.

"It ain't gonna melt you none," Taylor said before quickly changing the subject. "So guys," he said, "are we gonna head out or what? I need to get laid."

"You want to go out now?" Del asked.

Taylor said, "Hell yeah. Tonight's college night down at Frank's. The chicks can't hold their booze."

"There's nothing going down anywhere," Del said. "Not in this weather."

"Stop being such a pussy," Billy said.

"Go ahead and go out there. I ain't going," Del said.

Billy finished his drink and dropped his empty cup next to his first one. "The storm will be over in ten minutes."

"I bet my house it won't."

"Shit, it ain't a house, Del, if you can drive it over here and drop it off in my driveway."

Taylor snickered then quickly told Billy, "That's not funny, dude."

"You laughed."

"I was thinking about something else. Don't pay attention to him, Del."

Del cracked his thumb, pictured the gun in his nightstand drawer. "I never do."

Billy leaned forward in his chair and turned toward Del. "What's your problem with me, country boy? You jealous or what?"

Del was afraid of what he might say if he opened his mouth. Martin attempted to break the tension and suggested, "Now, now, fellas, let's be quiet and enjoy this."

"I'm going to head on in," Del said as he rose from his chair. "Gotta get up early." He reached for the kitchen door and was turning the knob when lightning flashed. Taylor yelled and nearly fell out of his chair.

"What's your problem, Taylor?" Billy asked.

"Did you guys see that?" Taylor stammered, pointing toward the river. "Holy shit, did you see it?"

"See what?" Billy asked, sounding bored.

"Look, look!" Taylor screamed. "Down there in the shadows."

Del peered into the darkness. He couldn't see anything, but he was afraid he knew what Taylor had seen. Straining to keep the fear from his voice, he asked, "What'd it look like?"

"Leave the little girl alone," Billy said. "He got spooked by a deer or some shit."

Taylor got to his feet and backed into the wall. "That was no deer. Keep looking down there. I'm not fucking around. Something's out there."

Martin was starting to say that he couldn't see anything, when the lightning struck again. No one said a word, but they all saw it.

Billy got closer to the edge of the balcony and stared into the black of the backyard. Martin turned to Del and asked him what in the hell that thing was.

"A lurker," Del said.

Suddenly Del became the center of attention. Bombarded with questions, Del tried to explain without sounding scared. "I've never seen one before, but that's what it's gotta be."

"You knew about these things?" Billy shouted.

"I told you there were things here, but y'all didn't listen to me. Never do."

Martin nearly shrieked. "What do we do? Who do we call?"

"It's alright," Del said, trying to calm down everyone, including himself. "Just leave it alone and it'll leave us alone. Let's go inside. I don't think it likes to be watched."

Billy returned to his chair. "Screw that. I'm gonna sit right here and watch where it goes. I'm not letting it sneak around until it finds a way into the house. Hell no, I'm not."

Martin ran into the kitchen to get the phone. Del told the other two, "I said you guys were crazy for living so close to the river. No one with any sense has a house near the water."

Electricity ripped through the darkness. The yellowish creature, looking like a man-sized lump of Play-Doh covered in mud and algae, slowly climbed the embankment, the rising river at its feet.

"It's getting closer," Taylor shouted. "You didn't say shit about those things."

"I said there were probably lurkers in the river. That's why I said not to go down there."

"I thought it meant a fucking raccoon or skunk or some shit."

"Yeah," Billy agreed, "or some crazy fish-thing."

Martin ran back onto the balcony, cell phone in his hand. "No signal." Everyone else checked their own. Not a single bar. They went inside and found the landline was dead, too.

"Storm must've knocked it out. Happens all the time," Del said, even though he'd never had it go out.

"Goddammit." Taylor stuffed his phone back into his pocket. "I always gotta go at least ten feet from the house to make a call."

"So go do it," Billy ordered.

"Fuck you. You go do it."

Del said, "It won't do no good no how. Police won't do nothing."

"Why the hell not?" Taylor shouted. "There's a monster down there!"

"Relax," Del said. "They won't bother you as long as you don't bother them. Just stay inside." Del had no idea if this was true or not, but he'd heard it at the grocery store last week from two good ol' boys picking up a carton of chum.

"Absolutely," Martin said. "We stay inside."

"And lock every door and window," Billy said.

Del smiled inside, enjoying that the oh-so-smart city boys were finally paying heed to what he said. "Just to be safe," Del said and walked through the kitchen.

"Where are you going?" Martin asked as a thunderclap shook the house.

"To my room." He could tell they were impressed with his couldn't-care-less attitude and he wasn't about to blow it by telling them he was going for his Glock. If the stories were true, the lurker wouldn't go down easily. The good ol' boys said they'd seen one take three rounds in the chest and still get away.

Del paused to flip on the light before descending the staircase. He hurried down and headed for his room, disappointed at himself for being frightened. Nothing was in the house. The lurker would rummage around the river until it found a dog or cat or some unfortunate creature, and then it would return to its home near the Caniton caves.

After entering his room and pulling his .357 out from under the mattress, Del stretched out on his bed and waited, listened to the raging storm. Twice he thought the loud bang outside his bedroom window might have been something other than thunder, but he reassured himself it was nothing but his nerves. Lurkers wouldn't try to get in a house, especially a locked one with four men inside.

Del studied the window, wondering if he should pull down the shade. He decided not to, figured he'd want to know if a monster was on the other side of the glass. He wouldn't shoot it unless it attacked, but, if it did, he was gonna put a hole in that son of a bitch's head.

Someone upstairs shouted; it sounded like Billy. A moment later, everyone yelled. Del jumped off his bed and ran for the staircase. Bounding up the stairs two at a time, he reached the top and rushed through the kitchen, chambering a round, afraid of what he would find on the balcony. Before he lost his nerve, he kicked open the door and took aim.

He lowered the gun when he realized the three idiots were cheering. Billy held a bow, a quiver of arrows rested at his feet.

"He got him!" Taylor shouted. "He got that motherfucker."

"Right in the goddamned eye," Billy said with his voice full of giddy pride.

Martin smiled and clapped Billy on the back. "One heck of one shot, this guy."

Another flash of lightning. Del looked beyond the balcony and spotted the lurker lying flat on its back, the blue bolt of an arrow pointing toward the sky. He turned to the three men. "Why? Why'd you do that? I told you to leave them be."

"He was coming for the house," Taylor said defensively.

Del didn't want to admit it, but the lurker was only fifteen yards from the house, its body illuminated by the light from the window in the back door. "You still shouldn't have done that."

Thunder rocked the house and the skies opened, doubling the deluge. A muddy stream lapped at the dead lurker's webbed foot. If the storm didn't let up, there'd be flooding in the house within minutes.

"Another one!" Taylor shouted, pointing just beyond the slain creature.

Del followed the direction of Taylor's trembling hand, straining to see through the sheet of pounding rain. A shapeless yellow figure was emerging from the roaring river, extending an arm toward its dead brethren.

Billy nocked an arrow and told Taylor to get out of his way. Taylor did and Billy and took aim. Before Billy could shoot, Del grabbed hold of the arrow. "Don't do it!"

"Look at it!" Billy yelled. His arms trembled as he tried to keep the bow taut. "Let me shoot!"

With his hand on the arrow, half expecting it to fly and rip the skin off his palm, Del glanced over the railing. The creature knelt in the muck next to its dead friend. It looked from the arrow to the balcony; its expressionless eyes studied each of them. Then it lifted its head to the sky and a horrifying howl pierced the night, louder than the pounding rain and thunder.

"Goddamn it! Let me shoot it!" Billy screamed, and Taylor and Martin both shouted for Del to let go of the arrow.

Although he held the gun and could call the shots if he desired, Del wasn't ready for that responsibility. He'd been taught to leave the lurkers alone, but what if that was wrong? And they'd already shot one. This wasn't up to him anymore. They were all grown men. All he could do was tell them what he knew.

A loud sucking pop, like the top being pulled off a can of tuna, drew their attention down below. The lurker held the arrow in its hand, a slimy black mass trailing from the tip. The body from which the arrow had been pulled began to deflate, large pieces of its mottled skin sloughing off and dissolving in the rising water that had already reached its chest.

"Jesus fucking Christ," Taylor said, looking like he might lose the fruity contents in his stomach.

Del let go of the arrow and turned toward the kitchen. A loud twang sliced through the air, followed by a series of cheers and high fives.

The weight of the gun was reassuring, but for the first time in his ten years of owning it, he wasn't comfortable with only fifteen rounds in the magazine. He wished to God he had brought along his extra boxes of ammo that were collecting dust back home.

Del knew they probably wouldn't listen, but he shouted anyway, "Everyone get inside!"

Only Billy responded, and it wasn't polite, so Del continued toward his room. As he passed the fridge, Taylor yelled, "There's another one!"

"There, too!" Martin shouted.

Billy said, "I see four of them!"

Lurkers weren't supposed to travel in packs, according to everything Del had heard. Some even claimed there weren't but one or two that existed. Del ran for the near wall and flipped the switches, turning on the flood lights. When he made it to the balcony, he counted six of the disgustingly strange beasts. Three were sloshing through the river toward the dissolving heap of yellow by the back door. The other three were already on the driveway.

"The Escalade! Fuck no!" Billy shrieked, nocking an arrow and taking aim. He released the arrow and it zipped past the nearest lurker and punctured the driver's door.

"They're too far away," Taylor said. "Get the ones near the house."

Martin agreed and told Billy to get the ones closest to the back door.

Billy turned to Del. "I'll take care of these. Get the ones out there."

A series of thuds came from the driveway. Though not appearing very solid, the lurkers packed a punch. In a matter of seconds, the Escalade was crumpled. "That's a seventy-thousand-dollar vehicle, you motherfuckers!" Billy cried and shot one straight through the neck.

"It's already ruined. You've got insurance," Taylor reminded him.

Billy was out of arrows. "Give me your gun," he said to Del.

Del shook his head. The sound of smashing glass and crunching metal mixed with the roaring river.

"Come on, you pussy," Billy said. "If you're not gonna use the gun, give it to me."

"I'll shoot them if they come in the house. We don't need to piss them off any more than we already have."

Another deafening howl tore through the night. Billy said, "They're taunting us."

"Let them." Del turned his back on the group. "I suggest you guys get inside."

"Fuck you," Billy said and started charging. Del spun toward Billy and shoved the barrel of the .357 at Billy's head. "Come at me again and I'll put a bullet between your eyes, you son of a bitch."

Billy glared at Del, but the Glock's barrel must have been too intimidating because he finally stepped back.

Still aiming at Billy's forehead, tempted to pull the trigger, Del said, "Do what you want, but you're not touching this gun."

Del spotted a quiver in the corner. So did Billy, but he kept eye contact with Del. "I'm not scared of them. Not like you."

"Yeah, and I'm not drunk or stupid like you," Del said.

Billy brushed past Del, grabbed an arrow, and ran for the front door. The guy was as dumb as anyone Del had ever met. Once Del heard the door open and close, he returned his attention to the back where the lurkers were still reducing the Escalade to a hunk of scrap metal.

"Hurry up, Del," Taylor urged, peering over the railing. "They're right below us."

"Back up and be quiet. Both of you." From the look on Martin's face, it was obvious that Martin didn't like being told what to do, so Del added, "Trust me on this."

Martin nodded and stepped away from the railing just as a shrill twang came from the driveway. The lurker who'd been caving in the rear of the Cadillac fell to its knees, the blue tip of the arrow sticking out the back of its head. Billy rushed onto the scene, grabbed a stray arrow off the ground. With the bow stretched to its limit and an arrow ready to fly, he swiveled towards the lurker on the passenger side and let the arrow loose. It missed its target and glanced off the demolished vehicle.

Billy looked around for another arrow. With the unnatural speed of a tsunami, the lurkers hurtled toward Billy from either side. Before he could do so much as scream, lurkers were lying on top of him, one ripping through his stomach, throwing heaps of intestines over its shoulder, while the other one clamped its massive jaws on Billy's face and began tearing out chunks.

Taylor was yelling something at Del when an enormous crash below shook the balcony. Del glanced over the railing, but he didn't see any of the creatures, only the water lapping at the house.

"What in hell was that?" Martin asked, his voice shaking worse than the balcony had.

"The door, I think."

"You think?" Taylor yelled. Before Del could tell him to back away, Taylor was on his hands and knees, his head between the posts of the railing, peering over the edge. "Holy shit. They knocked down the goddamn door! They're inside!"

"Come on," Del said as he watched the two lurkers in the driveway get up from their victim, leaving an unrecognizable mess where Billy had been only moments before. Both of them staggered toward the Escalade, grabbed hold of the rear bumper and heaved the SUV off into the brush. Del felt a sense of helplessness at their inhuman strength.

Taylor followed Del's gaze in time to see the Escalade crash onto its roof, its momentum rolling it into the river. "They're damming it."

Martin's eyes grew wider. "What do you mean dam?"

"Taylor, get away from the railing," Del ordered. "Both of you follow me. Come on."

Suddenly, a purple tongue the width of Del's wrist, and God knew how long, shot through the air, wrapped around Taylor's neck and started to pull him through the railing. Del yelled for Martin to grab Taylor's feet as he ran to the railing and stuck the .357's barrel against the beast's tongue. Taylor gurgled as he tried to pull away from the tongue with the gun just inches from his face. Realizing he had to risk damaging Taylor's hearing in order to save his life, Del pulled the trigger. The tongue blew apart, splattering the side of Taylor's face.

Martin yanked Taylor back and helped him tear at the dissolving tissue still wrapped around his neck, clumps plopping on the ground.

Del held the kitchen door open for them. "Inside! Now!"

This time there was no hesitation. Martin brushed by Del. Taylor cried out. He had been right behind Martin, but now he was reeling backward, one grotesque tongue gripping his left ankle, and another latched onto his right bicep.

Del reached for Taylor's outstretched hand, but he wasn't fast enough. Del heard a sickening snap as Taylor's lower back smashed into the railing, the agony on his face indicating that it was his back that had broken, not the wood railing.

Martin stayed pressed against the wall at the back of the balcony as Del ran to the railing, aiming with his right hand, trying to pull Taylor back with his left. There were five lurkers below; two were yanking with their tongues while the others waited patiently.

The lurkers were using Taylor to help pull themselves up. Just as Del was about to fire at the one latched onto Taylor's ankle, the creature next to it let its own tongue fly. Del swiveled and fired two rounds, both bullets striking the lurker's spongy forehead at the same instant the meaty tongue slapped Del's forearm and then fell to the floor.

Del turned back to his original target and fired two more rounds. The creature fell backward, losing its hold on Taylor's leg. Neither Del nor Taylor was prepared for the sudden release of tension. Taylor fell forward, his face bouncing off the floor. Del lost his grip, and Taylor was whipped off the balcony, his scream silenced abruptly when he splashed into the rising water below.

Pulling the trigger as fast as he could, Del killed the lurker that had pulled Taylor down, as well as the one whose teeth were buried in Taylor's neck. Before he could shoot the third, an explosion rocked the house. The indoor lights went out all at once, leaving the floodlight as the only thing between them and complete darkness.

The black seemed to amplify the smacking, slurping, and snarling down below. Del backed away from the railing until he bumped into Martin, shaking against the door. He stepped back into the pitch-black kitchen, bringing Martin with him and closing the door behind them.

"I don't want to be here," Martin whispered.

"The circuit breaker is down there. They took it out."

"We need to go away from here."

Del was just as scared as Martin, but he didn't like hearing the panic in his boss's voice. "You want to try running out the front door? I don't."

"My Porsche. It's in the garage."

Del looked around the dark room, unable to see past the kitchen's center island. "Even if the lurkers haven't gotten into the garage, the water sure as hell has. The car probably won't start."

"We try."

Del waited for a crash of thunder to finish before he told Martin to go right ahead and try to reach his car.

"We stick together?"

"Yeah," Del said. He sniffed the air. Something was burning.

"So we go to garage?"

"I didn't say that."

"Okay, I'll take gun."

"Hell no," Del said, having a difficult time hearing anything over the pounding rain.

Martin held out his hand. "Del, give me gun."

"I'm going upstairs. You can follow me if you want."

Martin grabbed his arm. "Hand over gun and I'll give you raise."

Del shook his head at the man's absurdity. "Find the flashlight. It's in one of those drawers by the sink. And hurry up," Del said, aiming the .357 at the kitchen doorway even though he could barely see past the tip of his gun's fluorescent front sight.

Martin opened a drawer. "I double your pay."

"Shut up," Del said. He listened. He thought he'd heard footsteps. A wave of smoke washed over him, stinging his eyes. "Hurry up. I think it's in the one closest to me."

One drawer slid shut and another opened. "Here it is," Martin said as he clicked the light on.

Del's heart caught in his throat as the lurker's bloated face appeared less than two yards in front of him. He pulled the trigger three times, erasing its twisted smile.

Martin gasped and the flashlight clattered on the floor, its beam shooting past Del's feet. He spun toward Martin, taking aim at the lurker holding his boss; the monster's arm covered the man's entire face. Before Del could get off a shot, he heard the sound of a tongue being launched from the far corner. Del ducked, crawled around the island. A cabinet door shattered.

Del fired three rounds where he thought the lurker was. It sounded as if two bodies fell to the floor. One was definitely Martin. Del heard his gurgled plea for help.

Aware that there was at least one more lurker in the room, Del bent over and picked up the flashlight. He brought it up and spun in a circle. A gang of yellow creatures surrounded him, and a dozen empty black eyes glistened in the dim light.

Del had three rounds left in the Glock, not enough to kill them all.

Changed Man

"I still love you."

That's the last thing Thomas told me. Now his head's by my feet. His eyes are open. His mouth's still moving, but there's no sound coming out.

I never wanted it to end like this. I'm sure Thomas didn't either. He got home from the factory around six, finished his third drink by seven. He was over by the fridge in his wrinkled, brown button-down and slacks. After he topped off his glass halfway with Coke, he said, "Have a seat. I want to talk to you."

When we first met, Thomas loved to talk and I loved to listen. For Thomas, talking used to mean something, it wasn't all grunts and groans. He wanted to know everything about me, would ask questions until the morning. He wanted to know why someone like me would want to be with someone like him.

Thomas still loved to talk, but now he demanded that I listen. Only it wasn't about anything real. We didn't talk about why I wouldn't have kids. Not about the future, what we'd do if one of us died.

The old Thomas never would've told me what to do, but ever since the accident I haven't known what to expect. If I hadn't been so tired, my feet swollen from a ten-hour shift at the diner, I might've stopped everything right there. Instead, I did what Thomas told me, but took my sweet time. I said, "So let's talk."

He shot me a quick glance, like I wasn't worth two seconds. "See that," he said. "That's what I'm talking about." He pointed at me and got flustered. "That. You taking all day just to spite me."

I noticed his cast was off and hoped he was just celebrating. I didn't yell at him for having that tone with me. I kept my voice cold and even, gave him plenty of warning. "I've had a long day."

"And I didn't?" Thomas put the Coke away and walked to the cupboard. "You say that like you're the only one."

Thomas had been an accountant, but got laid off, worked sixty hours at the factory and our ends still didn't meet. That's why I was at the diner, picking up doubles since Thomas totaled our car two weeks ago. I said, "We're both having a hard time. I won't deny that."

Thomas's fist was wrapped around the neck of the bottle. He poured the Jack to the rim, watched me with his baby blues for some kind of reaction. He said, "I don't want to hear it."

I had no idea who this new Thomas was. A man who'd talk back to me, treat me like dirt. I didn't think it could just be the alcohol. The booze might've made him brave, but not that stupid.

Thomas left the bottle on the counter and brought his drink to the table, dribbled a trail across the floor. He said, "Why are you so quiet?"

If Thomas had been acting normal, I would've taken his hand and asked him what I could do to help. We'd invested too much to just throw it away. But he wasn't himself so I kept both hands gripping the edge of the table. "You said you wanted to talk. I'm listening."

Thomas took a swig, set the half-empty glass onto the gas bill. He wasn't even wearing a sling. "Always so cute. That never gets old."

I was tempted to say something mean, maybe point out his old-man ear hair, his graying sideburns. I kept quiet. Now that I was paying attention, there was nothing to point out. Thomas looked ten years younger, his hair jet black.

He tried to keep his eyes on me. He found his drink more interesting and swirled it around and around. "This isn't working."

I wasn't ready to know what he was talking about so I didn't ask.

He said, "You just going to sit there?"

"Not all night. Say what you've got to say."

Thomas pointed at me, then himself. He used his left arm, the one that he'd shattered, like it was good as new. "This. Us. We're not working."

I thought I heard him wrong, almost asked him to repeat it. We used to be working. We worked for over ten years, the longest relationship of my godforsaken life. I buried my anger and said, "We're both under a ton of stress right now. We'll get through it."

Thomas didn't say maybe I was right. He didn't say he hoped so. He said, "I don't want to. Not the way it's been."

Thomas could've meant a lot of things by that, but the way he was looking at me like I was some kind of floozy, told me everything. I said, "You've got to be joking."

"It's my turn. See how much you like staying at home."

"Don't you dare. You knew that from the start."

I was afraid Thomas was going to deny I'd laid out my rules. It took him five seconds before he finally said, "I never liked it."

There weren't many men who would, but I said, "It was your choice. I told you."

"Not everything."

"I told you enough." There was never a reason to tell Thomas more. One man couldn't handle my needs. Not the man I loved. Thomas would've been used up in a week, no good to anyone else ever again.

Thomas finished his drink and set it down. He met my eyes for a moment and said, "Well, like I said, it's my turn now."

I gripped the table so I didn't lash out. Most people would yell double-standard, what a hypocrite, but I had my reasons. If Thomas stepped out on me, I couldn't stay with him. That was my rule and my rules couldn't be broken.

I needed the truth but acted like I didn't care. "So it's your turn, huh? Has it already started?"

Thomas crossed his arms. "Starting now it is."

I looked Thomas in his eyes, tried to remember if they'd ever been so blue. "So you haven't done it yet? You haven't been with anyone?"

He said no and I believed him. He was a good man and didn't lie. He was drinking to get up his nerve. He wanted to tell me because it was the right thing to do.

I said, "But you're going to? You don't care how I feel or what I say?"

"How *you* feel?" Thomas shook his head slowly. The scar that'd been on his left cheek wasn't there, the burn on his neck was all better. "It's always about how you feel. You do what you want."

I sat still, listened to the silence. Thomas's heart was pounding, pushing blood through his veins. 188 over 122. "Calm down, Thomas. I don't want this to happen."

He didn't seem to know what I was saying. "I'm sorry, but I have to. You should understand."

I understood better than he did. I just didn't want to believe it. It was the accident, all my fault for not wearing my seat belt. I went through the windshield, not that big of a deal, but it cut me bad. The wound was still open when I pulled Thomas free from the fire, the fear of him dying overriding the risk I might infect him.

I needed to hear it from him. "What are you feeling? Tell me the truth."

Thomas looked right at me, held my gaze. "I need more than you."

"You know what would happen if I let you do that?"

"Let?"

"What will you do to them? The women you're with."

"I'm not telling you that."

I said, "Isn't that what you want? For me to tell you everything?"

"No. I just said that you didn't." Thomas looked like he wanted to spit on me. "Why would I want to know what my wife's feeling or thinking or imagining when she's with another man?"

I sat up straight and cracked my knuckles. "Because I think you're probably feeling the same exact thing I do."

Thomas kept his mouth shut, gave off a new smell. His old fear was back, even more than usual. I bet he was guessing I shared some of his dreams. That I knew they'd come true if something wasn't done.

"You won't be thinking about me," I told him. "You won't be thinking about whoever you're with."

Thomas eased back from the table, the chair scraping the tiles.

I said, "All you'll be thinking about is ripping flesh from their bones, devouring every little bit."

He didn't ask if I was serious, if it was some kind of sick joke.

"You've done it," I said. "You've already done it?"

Thomas shook his head no, looked like he was going to throw up. "What are you saying?"

I got up from the table in case he attacked first. The old Thomas never would, but that man was gone. He'd changed into the thing I feared most. He was turning into me.

He said, "You're scaring me."

Since he was being honest, I said, "I never wanted this to happen. I loved you as a man. A husband. A friend."

Thomas rose from the table, stood taller than I'd remembered him being. "Loved?"

I said, "You're right, this can't work."

"You and me?"

I nodded and took a step toward him.

Thomas's heart was beating faster than before, but he didn't step back. He said, "I still love you."

I don't doubt that he meant it. I know that Thomas loved me. But he was giving off another smell. One that meant he wouldn't back down.

I told Thomas I was sorry, but I don't know if he heard. I was upon him, tearing at his throat, making it quick so he wouldn't feel much.

If Thomas knew what he was becoming he would have thanked me. I'm going to pretend that's what his lips are trying to say.

He was a good man and I'll miss him. But there can only be me.

Bad Habits

Burt Brighton was a mountain of a man, but it was his way with words, his power to persuade, that made him the best life coach in Arizona. He'd been in the business for ten years and had bettered almost a thousand lives. Bad habits die hard, but with Burt's perfect success rate, no one questioned his dedication and methods, at least not to his face. That included Walter Higgins who was sitting in a chair in this nondescript building at the Arizona/Nevada border. Burt knew this particular intervention wasn't going to be easy. Walter had sixty years of deep-rooted ways he'd need to break through, but, for Burt, failure was not an option.

There were plenty of places Burt would have rather been. He was supposed to be in Vegas, lounging at the pool, trying his luck at the tables, but Walter's wife had called in a panic and Burt couldn't turn down the opportunity to help correct someone's life. The $750,000 fee didn't hurt either.

Hot and hungry, Burt ignored his discomfort and thought about the job. Sure, the conditions weren't optimal, but he'd dealt with worse. The sooner he broke Walter's habit, the sooner he could get in his Porsche and drive to his hotel.

Burt positioned his face just inches from the trembling man's puckered mouth. He raised his voice and said, "Do not spit it out. You have to be strong, Walter, okay? Do not spit that out."

The look of pain in Walter's tearing eyes warned Burt to move, but he couldn't get out of the way quick enough. A mixture of tobacco juice and snot shot out of the man's nose and mouth, sprayed Burt's face.

Burt took a step back, calmly bent down and pulled a rag from the bag of supplies he'd picked up at the gas station. He counted to five and wiped off his face.

"Okay, so we're not off to such a great start." Burt smiled, kept his voice calm. "I know you must think that my techniques are a bit unorthodox, but let me assure you, they work. You may not realize it, Walter, but you've been given a once-in-a-lifetime opportunity to change everything." Burt took a swig from his bottle of sweetened green tea while Walter spat the remainder of the brownish-green concoction onto the dusty floor. "Did you swallow any of it?"

Walter nodded his head, looked as if he might throw up.

Burt said, "It's not nice to swallow something gross and disgusting, is it?"

Walter spit again. "I promise I won't…"

Burt shushed him by holding up his finger. "Don't make promises yet, Walter. I don't want to repeat myself again, so listen up. I talk and you listen. Got it?"

After Walter nodded, Burt pulled a 32-oz. cup from the bag and faced the back of the small room. He turned around thirty seconds later, careful not to spill the yellow liquid sloshing around in the cup.

Walter's eyes grew wide. "You're not serious?"

Burt swished the cup of urine in front of Walter's faded baby blues. "I'm not drinking that."

Burt gave Walter a friendly slap. "You need to see things from all perspectives. From Nancy's perspective."

When Walter began to protest, Burt pinched the old man's cheeks together and emptied the cup's contents into his mouth.

"Now before you spit that out, I want you to think about something." Burt kept pinching Walter's cheeks and tilted his head back so nothing poured out. "Do you see how someone else might not like this, Walter? Can you see Nancy's perspective?" He let Walter's cheeks go. "Can you see?"

Walter was on the verge of swallowing as he nodded. Burt walked back to his tea, finished it in one gulp. He pulled another one from the paper bag, along with a metal bucket that he set on the floor. When he looked back at Walter's bulging cheeks, he was disappointed.

"It looks like you're thinking of doing something very stupid, Walter." Burt grabbed his empty green tea bottle and dropped it into the bucket. The sound of shattering glass made Walter jerk. He probably would have jumped out of his chair if he hadn't been tied to it.

Burt held up his new tea and said, "If you spit that out, it would probably take me four or five more of these before I could fill up another cup." Burt chugged the entire contents and dropped the empty bottle into the bucket. "Neither one of us has that kind of time and I've got another hundred or so miles to Vegas." Burt pulled a 9 millimeter from his waistband. "Now swallow to get the full perspective."

Walter didn't swallow so Burt aimed the gun at Walter's face. "What are you more afraid of - swallowing some piss or dying?"

Burt pulled the trigger, but rotated the pistol to the left so the bullet grazed Walter's ear. The smell of gunpowder and piss filled the small room. The piss wasn't Burt's. It was the growing stain in Walter's expensive Fioravanti slacks.

"It's not easy to break habits, Walter, and I know a man like you isn't used to being treated this way, but that's exactly why your problem has continued to go on. People are scared of you, Walter. Your money scares people."

Walter spit the rest of the piss from his mouth. "You can have whatever you want. Whatever that cunt is paying you, I'll double it."

Burt popped open his third green tea and took a long swig. The desert heat was starting to get to him and this unexpected intervention was making him really thirsty. "Just when I thought we were making progress, you revert back to your bad habit. Thinking you can buy your way out. Look at yourself. You're sitting in your own piss. This is the bottom, Walter. There's no more bargaining."

"You won't get away with this!"

Burt didn't want to overreact to the old man's desperate outburst, but he wasn't sure how he should respond. While he considered his options, Burt finished off the tea, dropped the empty bottle into the bucket where it shattered against the others. Instead of reaching down and grabbing another bottle, he lifted a hunk of broken concrete from the floor. He held the jagged hunk in front of him and said, "Your money makes you think you have some kind of control over this situation, doesn't it?"

Walter's eyes followed the concrete up and down as it bounced in Burt's right hand, his left still holding the gun. Burt raised the rock and pretended he was going to throw it at Walter, but instead dropped it into the bucket where it crushed the shattered glass.

"I've got another idea, Walter," Burt said. "Now open wide."

Walter shook his head, pursed his lips.

Burt dug the pistol into Walter's temple.

Although he'd already cried and pissed himself, Walter pretended to be a hard-ass, kept his mouth closed.

Accustomed to dealing with difficult clients, Burt simply changed tactics, removed the gun from Walter's head and rammed it into his mouth, the sound of metal grinding against enamel. "I've learned a lot over the years, Walter, and there are two ways to go about things: the easy way and the hard way. It's totally your choice. The sooner you understand this, the better off you'll be." Burt drove the barrel farther into Walter's mouth. "You're going to swallow something, just like you made Nancy. Now, what's it going to be, a bullet or the glass? What do you want?"

Unable to speak, Walter frantically eyed the bucket before Burt could pull the trigger.

"Good choice, Walter. You're not ready for this to be over. You've got *chutzpa*. That's how you say that, right?" Burt withdrew the gun from Walter's mouth and told him to keep it open. He picked up the bucket, placed it to Walter's lips, tilted the bottom end up. "There you go. I don't care how you get it down, but just make sure you get it all. If even so much as one shard slips out, I'll make you finish the rest of what's in the bucket."

Walter's bleeding, distended cheeks didn't move.

"You're disappointing me, Walter. I was told you were a man willing to go the extra mile. Isn't that how you built your company? It's made a lot of people very rich, including your wife. And she needs your bad habits to stop. They're going to tear down everything you've built." Burt raised the gun. "Just picture Nancy. You remember your niece, don't you? She's your bad habit, Walter, and you need to put an end to it. Now chew."

Burt stood back and opened a pack of gum while Walter worked on the glass, wincing as slivers embedded into his cheeks and gums. Shards shredded his tongue and throat. Burt left through the back door and called over his shoulder, "Don't stop chewing!" He came back a few minutes later with a five-gallon gas can. "All right, let's see."

Walter opened wide to show all the glass was gone.

"Wow, that was messy."

Blood dribbled down Walter's chin. "Go to hell."

"I know you're mad, but pointing your finger at me, trying to blame others, that's not going to help end your addiction. That's why we're here, to correct inappropriate behavior." Burt cocked his head. "Well, that and to make sure your wife doesn't lose her fortune because you can't stop diddling little kids. You're wife's not a saint, actually she's kind of a bitch, but I see her point. I mean, who's going to hold onto stock in a company run by someone like you?"

"I'll never do it again. I swear. I fucking swear!"

"I know, Walter." Burt forced Walter's head back and stuck the gasoline can's hose down his throat. "You might as well relax. This thing's full."

When he reached the half-gallon mark, Burt decided that was enough and backed away. The color drained from Walter's face. Burt warned him again about throwing up. "Remember, mind over matter. You can do this."

Burt was impressed that the old man kept the fluid down for so long, but he knew it was just a matter of time before he retched. He walked behind Walter's chair and said, "I think you've learned your lesson, haven't you?"

Walter violently nodded yes.

"That's what I like to see. I'm proud of you, Walter. Now, I've just got one last thing I need you to swallow." Burt reached into his pocket and pulled out a book of matches. He tore one free and lit it, the flame jumping to life and burning bright.

"WAIT! What are – I swear I won't do it. I promise to God and my grave. I'll never do it again. Please!"

Burt set fire to the entire matchbook, held it by the corner. "It's okay. You're almost done. Well done, in fact." Burt's face crinkled at the bad pun, wished he could take it back, but the matchbook was already falling into Walter's mouth.

Every Precious Second

The numbers on this stupid cell phone are so small that my finger punches the nine every time I shoot for the eight. My granddaughter tells me I should upgrade to one of those new smart gadgets, but it already takes me ten minutes to dial when there are actual buttons. This old hound dog's not learning any new tricks, especially on one of those virtual screens.

"Leave it alone, William. If it comes, it comes," Rose whispers. She pauses for a second to gather her breath. "If it doesn't, it doesn't." It hurts her to talk. I turn up the volume on my hearing aid and ask if she wants some water.

"I want you to put down that phone."

"I made plans. Plus, Billie already paid for the shipping. It's not right if the package doesn't come."

"We shouldn't have involved her. This whole thing's wrong and I feel torn up."

I hold up the cell, squint over my glasses. "I'll just be a minute."

"It's too early there. She's still in bed."

I glance at the clock. It seems to run faster with every passing day. "She's up," I say and concentrate on pressing the eight. "It's already noon."

On the fourth ring, Billie answers with a yawn. "Hi, Grandpa. Is everything okay?"

"Everything's fine, sweetheart."

"You sure?"

"Of course." The afghan is slipping down Rose's thighs. I pull it up to her waist. She's so frail you can hardly see her legs under the blanket. I ask our granddaughter, "You weren't sleeping were you?"

"No." Another yawn.

"I wanted to catch you before your classes begin."

"I need to be getting up anyway. My Biochem final is at eleven. I was up pretty late last night studying for it."

"I completely forgot about the time difference. You're so far away."

I don't even have to look to know Rose is rolling her eyes. I never remember the time difference.

"I wish I wasn't so far away, Grandpa. I'd leave today to see you guys, but Mom and Dad won't let me miss my exams."

"I told your father I'd tan his hide if he did."

"I'm still flying out next Thursday, right after my last test."

With my hearing aid up, I hear Rose breathing from five feet away. It reminds me of dry leaves rustling. As much as I want to deny it, Rose isn't making it until next Thursday, she might not make it two days. But you don't say those sorts of things to your medical school standout, the little girl who used to steal butterscotch candies from the tin and wrap them up as Christmas gifts for everyone. I say, "You don't need to worry, Billie. You just focus on your tests. We both know how much you love your grandma."

"But I want to see her. I want to say goodbye," Billie says, her voice quivering. "Can I talk to her?"

"Of course you can." I turn to Rose, her blue eyes shiny with tears. "But I just had a quick question about the package."

"Didn't it arrive?"

"Not yet. Do you think maybe they have the wrong address? I just wanted to make sure it's coming."

"Hold on." She reads off the correct address. "I have the tracking number. I'll call them right now."

"Thank you, dear." I'd do it myself, but with all that button-pushing, I'll end up getting instructions in Spanish or talking to some guy in India.

"Remember what I said, Grandpa. Only take one every four hours. That's plenty."

"Of course." I crane my neck to see out the kitchen window, no UPS truck, just the snow-covered street. "Thank you again for this, Billie."

"It's the least I can do."

"Let me put on your grandma."

"I love you."

"I love you too, dear." I shuffle around the table and hold the phone to Rose's ear. She jerks back like she's being attacked, before realizing it's just my cell.

Rose holds the phone to her ear, traps it with her neck and trembling hand to keep it there. They talk while I stare out the window. I check the grandfather clock in the living room. It's been in the family since I was a baby. Several minutes have slipped by.

Rose says her goodbyes, and I fiddle to press End. She's biting her lower lip so I tell her not to cry. I say, "Come on, what's the matter, beautiful?"

"It's not right, we shouldn't be doing this to her. What if she gets caught? She'll get thrown out of school."

"No one's getting thrown out of anywhere." I'd already played out this scenario a dozen times after Billie first told me about the pills. She went on and on about studies and chemical-whatchu-do's, but all I heard was, "Time stops, Grandpa." She corrected herself and said it actually just slows down perception, but I just kept thinking, time stops.

I stroke Rose's good hand. "Try not to be sad. Why don't I make you some tea?"

Rose flashes that smile I'll never forget. "I'm not sad. Just worried."

"Well, stop." I look down at the phone. "Let me just make one more call to…"

"No, put it down, William."

"I just want to make certain that UPS has our correct address."

"You're like a dog with a bone. This is almost as bad as that decoder ring of yours, Captain Midnight."

I hadn't thought of that cheap, plastic ring in over twenty years. "I waited six weeks for that."

"Standing out by the mailbox every single one of those days."

"I did, didn't I?" I'd sent away for it from one of those ads in the back of *Boy's Life.* "You and your mother brought me in when it started snowing."

"We didn't want to see a dead kid out on the lawn."

"And your mother made that pecan pie."

"You were the only one who would eat it."

Rose and I spent that entire summer fishing by the creek, walking through Dover's Canyon. We had our first kiss behind St. Gabriel's Church. I nearly passed out because my nose was all stuffed-up from a cold, and I didn't want that kiss to ever end.

After a sip of water, Rose looks at the wall, all those memories playing in her head. She says, "Isn't this nice?"

I don't know if she's talking to me right now in this room or me as a young man.

The grandfather clock chimes. I look out the frosted window. Nothing. "I'm calling them. This is ridiculous. Billie paid good money for it to arrive and it hasn't."

"Calm down, William."

"I'm not going to let them rip her off like that."

"Please." She touches me. Her hand's shaking so much it tickles.

"I'm sorry," I tell her, "but it gets me so mad."

"Darling, they're just pills."

I can't have this conversation. I know where's she's leading, so I stand. She asks where I'm going.

I force a smile. "I've got a surprise for you." Package or not, I can't let this ruin all my hard work.

"What surprise?"

"Just some things. There's one for each of the next three nights."

"What are you up to, William?"

I no longer have to force the smile. I've been waiting months to show her. Suddenly, I hear a ringing. I look at the phone in my hand. It's not that, so I peek around the corner at the landline on the wall. The little red light isn't flashing either.

"Did you hear something, William?"

"No, I guess not." I wonder if my hearing aid is on the fritz again just before a series of bangs come from the living room. I hurry to the window. A brown-clad man, holding a small box, is walking back toward the UPS truck idling at the curb.

"What's wrong?" Rose asks as I try to hurry out of the kitchen.

I concentrate on the floor in front of me, wishing my slippered feet would move faster. My labored breaths make my chest feel like it's burning. I reach the door and go to pull it open, but the deadbolt and security chain are fastened.

My fingers tear at the chain, slip it free. I twist the lock and open the door as a blast of cold air knocks the delivery slip from the screen door. The yellow scrap of paper blows off the porch and towards the truck where the deliveryman is already behind the wheel.

"I'm here! Stop!" I wave my hand, nearly slide right off of the icy porch. The snow seeps through my slippers.

The truck pulls away from the curb as I hobble down the slick stairs, gripping the handrail.

Another gust of wind picks up the small slip and carries it into Peterson's bushes across the street. I prepare to step off the curb when the UPS truck circles back. I'd been in such a panic I hadn't realized he'd have to make a U-turn at the end of the cul-de-sac.

The deliveryman pulls right up next to me. I wave once more because I can hardly breathe. He asks, "Mr. Hanneman?" I gulp and nod.

The deliveryman hops down from the truck with a small package in his hand. "It's freezing out here. Let's get you inside."

The man offers his outstretched arm, and as much as it makes me feel like a damn fool, I take it. It's like we're going to prom. I mumble a thank you and try to keep pace as he helps me up the walkway, then the stairs. By the time we make it onto the porch and into the house, my slippers are completely soaked. I kick them off, turn, and reach for the package, but the young man is holding out the electronic pad.

"Sign here first, please."

My arthritic, frozen fingers can't even pick up the pen. I want to scream, cry, and punch the guy in his face. I guess my frustration shows because he tells me it's okay, hands me the box, and scribbles a name on the pad. This might actually come in handy should the authorities ever track this down. *No, Officer, I never signed for drugs.*

"Sorry about you having to chase me down," the delivery man says. "You get warm and have a great day."

With the box in my hands, I'm suddenly no longer cold or anxious. "You've made an old man's day. Thank you."

I close the door, head over to the hutch, grab my wooden box of secrets, and carry everything to the kitchen. Rose is still sitting in her chair, shaking. At first, I think it's another stroke, but then realize she's freezing. I left the door wide open chasing down the deliveryman. The entire house has turned into an icebox.

I set both boxes on the table and hurry over to the hallway closet. My feet are still wet. I find her favorite red quilt on the top shelf, pull it down, walk back, and wrap it around her shoulders. "I'm sorry, honey." I place a gentle kiss on her forehead. "Is that better?"

She nods, and I take a seat. I pat my little wooden box. "This one's from me. And that one's from Billie."

She eyes the one I'm tapping. "Open it for me?" Her smile is back, warmer than a radiator.

"In a minute. Let's just make sure this is okay." I scrape my thumbnail on the UPS package. The tape is stronger than it looks. After a few attempts, I set the box down, angry I can't do the simplest of things. Rose, always prepared, passes a butter knife across the table. It takes half a dozen tries, but I carve through and find a bottle of Extra-Strength Advil.

"Advil?" Rose says. "All this for Advil?"

I struggle with the cap and dig out the cotton ball, dump the blue pills into my hand. "Billie couldn't very well put a label with the real name on it, could she?"

"I don't know. We never took drugs before. Not once."

"You smoked a joint at Barbara Wilcox's Christmas party."

"That was forty years ago."

"These are fine, Rose." I slide the pills back into the bottle. "They're no different than your heart medicine."

"Then why are they illegal?"

"Darling, trust me on this. We don't have much time left together. These pills will help us enjoy every precious second. Billie said they'll intensify our perceptions and feelings."

"That sounds terrifying."

"It does not. One minute is gonna feel like an hour, one hour will feel like a day." Something splashes against the back of my hand. I realize it's a tear. "And that's exactly what I need right now."

Rose bites the inside of her cheek, like she always does when she's about to give me an earful. Only this time, she says, "You really sure about this?"

"Positive."

"Oh, Lord, I hope you're right."

I thank her and open the wooden box, take out the plastic case with a DVD inside it. "This is a slideshow. Pictures of our family and friends. All of our memories. Vacations, weddings, anniversaries, Billie's birth. Everything you can imagine."

"All on this disk? Oh, honey, that's so thoughtful."

"We'll watch this one tomorrow." I then pull another DVD from the box. Rose asks what's on it. I say, "This one is all videos. It's for the third night. Sandra, Jimmy, Elaine, and Frankie helped me edit it. I used to hate it whenever they would get out those recorders, but now I'm glad they did."

Her faded blue eyes sparkle. "Third night? Why not tonight?"

"No. Tonight we have this." I pull out the final plastic case. "This is a recording of all of your favorite songs." I motion towards the door to our enclosed back porch. "We'll have a nice evening out there, listening to it as the sun sets."

"I don't want to wait."

"Well, I'm afraid that's just too bad. I've got some setting up to do and it's about time for your nap."

"Oh, you sure do know how to spoil a treat." She pretends to be upset, her grin giving her away like always. I swear, the woman would be the world's worst spy.

I close the box, get up from the table, and offer my hand. "Let's get you rested. You're all mine tonight." I help her to her feet.

"You devil. You've never changed."

"And you never needed to."

Rose pats my hand and we make it a few steps before she grimaces, quickly covering it with a smile. I start to ask if she's all right, if she wants to stop, but she hushes me as we head into the bedroom.

The grandfather clock strikes five just as I finish setting up the back porch. The CD player is on the coffee table next to the pitcher of sweet tea, along with two glasses. There are two napkins, each with two blue pills. I turned the thermostat up to a toasty seventy-eight, a nice contrast to the winter wonderland on the other side of the plate-glass window. The entire back acre is covered with virgin snow, the sun almost ready to drop behind it.

I take one last look making sure I haven't missed anything, then head to the bedroom. When I open the door, I see Rose is still in bed. Any other night, and I'd let her sleep.

"Rose, dear," I whisper softly, then again, a little louder. Her good hand is resting over her heart. She's not sleeping. I ask if she's okay.

"Just so tired."

"I know, sweetheart, but do you think you can get up?"

She gives a weak nod and I help her to her feet. "Take your time," I tell her, but I'm practically pulling her out the door.

She says, "Someone's got ants in his pants."

"I'm wearing a robe."

"Oh, you think you're so cute."

I don't respond, just help her cross through the kitchen. "Now let's have ourselves a nice time."

Two minutes later, Rose is in her chair and I'm pouring her a glass of tea.

"No wonder we don't come out here much," she says. The trip from the bedroom clearly exhausted her. "I feel like we walked to Vermont."

I hand her the glass. "It's nice, though, isn't it?"

Her blue eyes seem to gain color as she looks out the window. "It is, dear. It really is. Thank you."

I pluck two blue pills off her napkin and hold them in my open palm. "Are you ready?"

"Didn't she say only one each?"

"If one is good, two is better."

Rose looks at the pills. I worry she's going to back out, but she opens her mouth and sticks out her tongue. Gently, I place them. Two swallows of tea and they're gone.

"Here's to us," I say. I pop mine in and wash them down with a swig. Then I push the play button and "From You I'll Never Part" starts.

Rose sighs. "Our wedding song."

I start to sit when I realize I've forgotten the final touch. I head up the three stairs into the kitchen. A sharp twinge of pain shoots down my leg. My sciatic is acting up. Doc would tell me to rest, that I've overdone it, but I can't think about the pain.

"Where are you going?" Rose asks. "The sun's setting, and our song's on."

"Won't be a minute." I hurry around the table and reach my hand into the little sliver of space between the cabinets and the top of the icebox. A single white rose. I picked it up from the grocery store yesterday, had to sneak it in when Rose was napping. It's a little dusty. I blow on it and gently wipe it with my finger. The soft music floats in from the porch and I can't wait to get back to my wife. I shuffle towards the back porch with the rose in one hand and the other running along the wall to steady myself. It's so smooth and cool to the touch. I look over and see the rose, a streaming trail of petals carving through the air.

The wedding song stops, snaps me out of this trance. I realize I've been sliding back and forth across the floor in rhythm to the music. The next song begins, "Gone but Not Forgotten." I stare out the window, mesmerized by the sunset. The purple strip of sky between the snow and the clouds reminds me of the nights that Rose and I snuggled on the couch, holding each other as darkness descended.

I reach the porch and hold onto the handrail for support, and there's my wife. This woman, so full of love, so full of kindness, that's cared for me since we were children. Her soft cheeks, the deep smile lines showing anyone and everyone how she had spent her life, always laughing, always thankful for what's in front of her.

Rose turns her head, those blue eyes piercing through me as I make my way down the stairs. That look melts my heart. Tears are sliding down my cheeks, in and out of my wrinkles. I have to explain to her before she goes that she's made life worth living.

Each silver hair on her head sways back and forth. They're soft and fine like a baby's. I want to caress them and assure her that everything is going to be okay. I'm not going to let her go. I'm going to keep her here with me forever.

The world starts to tilt. I'm falling, my foot catching on the step, my weight tumbling forward. I try to bring my other leg underneath me to catch myself, but it's too late.

Rose screams this melodious roar as my right wrist snaps against the floor, the crackling echoing in my ears. I can't look away from her as the rest of my body seems to hover in mid-air. Rose pushes off the chair, her long-sleeves barely rippling. My hip crunches into a thousand shards of terrific pain. Waves of agony wash through me when my head cracks off the carpeted concrete. My fragile skin splits, a warmth slowly spreading along my face as Rose falls back onto the chair.

My fingers crawl along the fibers, trying to push myself off the ground, but my hip feels like slivers of glass digging into my flesh. I can only raise my head an inch, warm blood dripping down my lips. Rose clutches her chest. Her screams soften with the song as the sun slowly dips beneath the horizon. The last streams of light slide down her body, leaving her once-bright blue eyes forever sparkling in the darkness.

To Feed an Army

Until he joined the Army, Private Edwards had only seen the jungle on TV. He wasn't prepared for the heat, and the air was so damn thick you could practically sip it. It hadn't rained in days, but everything just stayed wet.

Edwards had been moving all morning, alone on the run. Even though he'd lost most of his baby fat in basic training and these six months in the shit, Edwards felt just as heavy as he did in high school, when the kids used to point at his white, lumpy stomach and call him "Curdle King."

The sweat probably added another five pounds to his uniform and gear. When Edwards could go no further, he leaned against a tree and threw off his pack. He didn't sign up for this. He didn't want to be a soldier. He just wanted to survive, maybe learn a skill. That's why he'd requested to become a medic.

Something moved to his right. Edwards grabbed his M-16 and aimed. The sunbeams coming through the canopy played tricks on his eyes. He heard squawks and the distant cry of a monkey. He figured it was nothing, but Rex was still out there. Edwards forced himself to stand. His feet began to tingle like he'd tied his laces too tight.

Something fluttered. A rustling. Edwards wanted to take off running, but he stayed still, scoured the ground for tripwires. There was always something waiting to turn you into wet confetti.

It was hard to believe that it'd been less than twelve hours since Edwards foolishly thought the real danger was gone. It'd been gruesome, but the worst of it was over. Their squad had taken the village and secured a massive food supply, Staff Sergeant Rex doing things Edwards spent the entire night trying to forget. But they were safe and just had to wait for the convoy. They'd be supplied for three months.

Everyone knew Staff Sergeant Rex was a dope-fiend and had issues long before any of them had landed in country. But he was their superior and this was war. No one thought Rex would ever intentionally do anything to jeopardize their lives. There was talk that this was to be his last mission. Maybe that's what sent him over the edge. Or maybe it was the heat. Or maybe he was just an evil piece of shit.

Whatever it was didn't matter. Edwards just wished he could get Rex's knife tricks out of his head.

An hour after breakfast, Rex had called everyone over to the open-walled hut where Ornalez, Shipley, and Curtis lay sleeping. Edwards was squatting in the bushes, halfway through a shit that was more of a spray. He almost yelled he'd be right there, then noticed no one else was hurrying. Jennings was last to join the group, his hand holding his stomach. Neither Rex nor Jennings said a word to any of the men still sprawled on the floor.

Nothing special happened, there was no provocation. Rex just started blasting. Jennings and McKinney, headshot, headshot. Everyone else got one in the chest. The entire squad dead in seconds, tendrils of smoke curling from the barrel of Rex's gun.

That shit saved Edwards' life, but he knew he had to keep moving. If he didn't, he'd end up like the others, so Edwards started running again. He didn't check for traps or hiding gooks; all those drills and training evaporated in the clammy mist. Sweat cascaded down his back and legs, dripped into his socks. He wiped his forehead and a chill ripped through him. A wave of nausea stopped Edwards short, and he doubled over in pain. Invisible hands were twisting his guts like they were wringing a wet towel. It was just like the time he'd had a bad oyster on vacation with his folks, his stomach cramping so hard he saw stars. But he'd barely touched the powdered eggs for breakfast. And last night he only had coffee and cigarettes, unable to eat after watching Rex's wet work.

Another sharp abdominal pain dropped Edwards to his knees. The M-16 fell from his hands, and he grabbed his throat. It was closing up. He gasped but just barely. Something was moving near him, crunching over branches. He reached for his gun, but he fell onto the muddy leaves.

He didn't even try to get up, just curled into himself. His rifle lay a few feet away. Sweat rolled into his eyes, and he realized he couldn't blink. Something awful was coursing through his veins. A spider or bug must have crawled into his clothes. He hadn't felt anything bite him, but that had to be what happened. In training they'd been given a little book of dangerous insects, but he'd lost his the first week.

Edwards tried to sit up but he couldn't move. It was like he'd been filled with cement. If the enemy found him like this, he wouldn't even be able to turn over. He'd just have to stare into his executioner's eyes. He prayed it wasn't anyone that'd escaped from the village. He knew what they'd do to him.

Now everything was black. His eyelids had finally shut. He listened to the crunching steps coming closer. Closer…

He struggled to look, but only a sliver of light came through before another round of darkness. He could hardly breathe. He prayed the birds were drowning out his sickly wheezing. He listened for the steps, wondered if he'd hear a growl or voice before the inevitable, but the crunching steps were growing faint. Whatever or whomever was angling off. Edwards figured he must still be hidden. His paralysis might actually be a blessing. If he could have moved, he'd have been spotted.

Tiny pinpricks jittered up and down his fingertips, then hands and wrist. It wasn't much, but his thumb was starting to bend. Maybe lying down was slowing the poison. The pinpricks were becoming more painful, but at least a sense of feeling was coming back. If the poison passed, Edwards could get to his pack. There was a vial of epinephrine. Why the hell had he taken off his gear?

Again, he tried opening his eyes. It was like lifting a rusted roll-up door on a cargo truck, but he could make out glossy leaves. His vision was still blurred and he couldn't turn his head, but he was sure he was lying next to a slow-moving black stream. He didn't remember a stream before he'd fallen, but here it was, washing over him. He could feel it moving up his hands. It made no sense, but it had to be freezing, because the pinpricks spread over his arms and neck.

Edwards tried to tilt his head to get a little of the water into his mouth. It was so close. A few pinpricks hit his chin. He wanted to scream. Then another loud crunch came from nearby. Another rustling. Edwards hoped it was a small, cute animal, that he'd open his eyes and see a cartoon fawn lapping at the stream. But he remained realistic. His luck, it'd be an anaconda.

Then he heard a voice, a voice he knew. He'd heard it every day for the last six months.

"Goddamn, Eddie. You come all the way out here to take a nap?" Rex's words were mumbled. It sounded like he was wearing a gasmask. "If you wanted to sleep in, all you had to do was ask. You could've invited your friends here. Had a sleepover."

Edwards didn't know what the lunatic was talking about, but he was actually relieved to hear the staff sergeant's voice, especially so friendly. Maybe Rex didn't want to be alone in the jungle. Rex could open his pack, inject the epinephrine. Even if it didn't work, he might be able to carry Edwards to the village.

"You feeling okay there, Eddie? You're not looking so hot."

Edwards tried to speak, but all he could squeeze out were wheezing puffs of air.

"I can't hear you, bud. You gotta speak up."

Edwards tried to swallow, and Rex just laughed.

"Ah, hell, I'm just fucking with you. You just lie still, buddy. I mean it, don't move a muscle."

Edwards couldn't see, but it sounded like Rex actually slapped his thigh. Any relief Edwards had quickly dissipated. Edwards curled his fingers, imagined them wrapping around Rex's throat, but he gave up and tried to look in the direction of his pack. He couldn't actually see it, but hoped that resetting his gaze and quickly looking left might get Rex to stop fucking around and help.

"I gotta say, Eddie, for a blubbery piece of shit, you sure can move. I don't know how you made it this far." Rex started stomping the ground.

"Goddamn, man, I don't know how you aren't flipping the fuck out, right now. That shit would be driving me crazy."

Edwards lifted his finger a few inches. He hoped he was pointing at his pack. Black beads of water slid towards his knuckle, then strangely crawled up the nail and twisted around his hand defying the laws of gravity.

"I just figured if anyone was going to finish their eggs, it'd be a big fuck like you," Rex said. "But I guess I'm lucky. If it'd been McKinney or Barklett I'd still be running my ass off."

The powdered eggs had tested almost metallic. Edwards had just assumed it was the water from Rex's canteen. Now, he knew the truth. They'd been poisoned. It's why Rex had been able to take everyone out. Barklett was the fastest draw in the squad.

Rex started cursing, smacked at his skin, and hopped around like he was on fire.

A water bead trickled down into Edwards' ear and burned. And that's when Edwards saw the undulating black stream thinning on the ground in front of his face. Little droplets spread out and crawled towards his eyes. It wasn't water. It was ants. And they weren't the kind you'd find at a picnic. They were devouring Edwards, and there was nothing he could do but blink.

"Now this is an army," Rex said. "There might be twenty million in this one colony. All working together." Rex spat on the stream of ants. A few got stuck in his loogie. Others scattered. But they all found their way back towards their goal. "Now, that's loyalty. They know what's important. It's not the individual. It's the team." Rex bent down and lowered his head so Edwards could look him in the eye. "I knew you all were going to talk. You forced my hand." Rex shook his head. "No, our boys have lost enough…perception-wise. I had to put us on track again. For the greater good."

The M-16 lay a few feet away. Edwards tried to fling his arm, but it barely moved. He felt an ant crawling up his cheek and closed his eyes. It gnawed at the thin layer of skin until bits of red light filtered through.

Edwards tried to cry out, which sent a battalion of ants into his mouth. He gagged, almost puked. Rex stood, walked over to Edwards' M-16, and picked it up. "I am sorry though. I want you to know that." He forced a little laugh. "What you wouldn't give for a can of Raid right now, huh?"

Edwards swallowed a mouthful of blood and managed to eek out, "Please..."

"Ah, man, I wish I could. Truly. But if anyone finds you, I can't let it get back to me."

Edwards blew out strings of bile and ants. Then he tapped his finger onto his chest. Rex gave a little nod.

"Okay, alright. But you got to do this on your own." Rex bent down and placed the rifle in Edwards' hands. The barrel was just under Edwards' chin. "All you gotta do is squeeze."

Edwards' finger fumbled for the trigger. Rex told him he was almost there. Edwards dragged the gun a little higher, strained to lift his head a few inches. There was a fleeting thought he might be able to take one shot at Rex, but it didn't last long. He just stared at what was left of his hand, the tendons and bones. A cluster of ants, clinging to some remaining flesh, plopped down onto his chest and carried away the meat. Edwards' finger started to slide off the trigger, but Rex held him firm, even placed his own finger over Edwards' bone.

"They're army ants, Eddie. Just like you and me."

Instant Terror

Susie Cohen had no one to blame. If she hadn't procrastinated, she could be asleep, instead of walking the three blocks to the computer lab in the middle of the night. Her twelve-page archaeology paper was due the next day at one o'clock, one-fifty if she turned it in at the end of class. But Susie had barely finished the introduction, and even that was pretty sketchy.

The freezing wind sliced across Susie's face. She adjusted her scarf to cover more of her nose, but the thin material did little to protect her lips and skin. Instead of braving the streets, she cut through the campus, the slush seeping into her boots with each step. Two of the lampposts were out, and a third flickering, but there was a blue-light safety phone just up ahead.

The crunch of hard snow came from behind. Susie acted like she hadn't jumped, and casually glanced over her right shoulder. No one was there. It was just her imagination turning crackling ice into the steps of some crazed stalker. No more horror movies for her.

Susie concentrated on the task in front of her, a flight of ice-slicked stairs leading down to the lower quad. Not about to slip again, she pulled both hands out of her pockets, one gripping the metal railing, the other pressing against the brick wall. Susie had already made a fool of herself outside the cafeteria. She found out the hard way how much a bruised tailbone could ruin late-night extracurricular activities. Her boyfriend, Tom, hadn't been too happy about that.

Maybe boyfriend wasn't the right word. They had been together for nearly two months, but she wasn't sure what he thought of her. Susie liked Tom a lot, maybe even loved him, but it was hard to believe he could feel the same way. He was a senior, captain of the football team, and could have any girl he wanted. And if the unpleasant rumors were true, he nearly had. Still, he was with Susie now and that was what mattered. Tom swore to her that she was the type of girl he was looking for: someone loving, sweet, and selfless, the exact opposite of his last ex. That crazy chick had refused to give him back his varsity jacket and actually tried to stab him when he broke it off with her.

Two steps to the bottom, Susie heard the fall of footsteps again. The crunchy splash was unmistakable. No longer caring what she looked like, she whipped her head back to catch a glimpse of her attacker before he lunged down at her. She was too low to see anyone. The guy was probably waiting just out of sight.

Susie hurried down the stairs and made it halfway across the block when she heard someone. She spun around and spotted the bundled body exiting the stairway. The guy was large dressed completely in black, and he was heading right for her.

He'd catch her in less than a minute unless she ran. Susie knew she was overreacting. The guy was probably a student. Why else would he be on the quad? Unless he had just committed a crime. Or wanted to.

Susie hated herself for listening to her roommate who'd told her to leave her cell phone behind so it wouldn't be a distraction. She couldn't even pretend to call the police and there wasn't a blue-light around. Susie wasn't going to run, but she also wasn't about to wait for the guy to catch up. Without checking for traffic, Susie jumped off the curb and darted across the street.

Judging by the sound of it, the guy had stayed on his side. A quick glance confirmed this. The only problem was that he was mimicking her pace, keeping a few steps behind. He had been in such a hurry and now he wouldn't pass. If he crossed the street, she would run. The computer lab was now only a block away. Surely she could make it there before he caught her.

The two of them continued down the street, matching step for step. Susie passed the chapel and finally saw the lab's angular glass roof slicing into the night sky. Usually it was closed by ten o'clock, but during finals and midterms the lab was always open. Susie hoped she wouldn't be up to see the sunrise, but she knew that would probably be the case.

The lab had never looked so inviting. Bright light flooded out of the two-story building, a warm welcome for anyone stuck out in this crappy weather. She started up the stairs and took one last look to see where the man in black was. He was crossing the street, headed right for her.

Susie scampered up the stairs and threw open the building's front door. She felt trapped inside the small, heated entryway. She yanked off her glove and pulled out her cold, plastic student ID card, slid it down the electronic reader. The light flickered red. The guy was almost there. Susie looked at the card, realized her error, flipped it around and slid it through again. The light flashed green and she jerked open the door, slammed it shut behind her. Less than half of the twenty-or-so students bothered looking up at the noise.

Susie felt safer, but she still moved away from the door and checked out the building she'd only been in twice before. The computer lab was one large open room with a two-story high vaulted ceiling. There were twelve tables, six on each side of the room, and a bank of printers lining the eastern wall. The bathrooms and payphones were down the hallway directly underneath the stairs that led to an office overlooking the entire first floor. Susie saw the lights were on in there. That's where the tech-savvy students kept watch and were available for condescending support. Those nerds loved it when a computer-illiterate ignoramus, like herself, came to them with stupid problems.

Susie needed to pee, but decided against going to the bathroom, at least until she saw her stalker. She figured the safest place to watch from was the far corner by the printers. She would be kind of tucked away, but still able to see the entire room. She'd be safe. Besides, what could he do with all these people around?

By the time Susie made it to the corner, the guy in black had passed through the security door. That meant he had to be either a student or a teacher. Or he'd stolen a card.

Susie pretended to use the printer while she watched the man stomp snow off his boots. He pulled off his beanie and scarf as he started down the middle aisle. He didn't look familiar. Definitely a student, but older, probably a junior or senior. Maybe even a grad student.

The guy unbuttoned his bulky jacket. At the end of the last aisle he turned right. He was headed straight for her and reaching into his pocket.

Susie headed down the row of printers, barely stifling a scream. She reached the end of the aisle and looked behind her. The guy pulled a disk from his pocket and sat down at the last computer.

Susie's cheeks flushed. She felt stupid. How many people saw her do that? Hopefully, they were all too busy to notice. She quietly made her way to a computer station in the opposite corner of the room.

After slipping out of her backpack, Susie plopped down on the chair. She tried to slow her racing heart and took off her scarf and cap. Her forehead was slick with sweat and it wasn't due to the heat, although it was nice and toasty in the lab. Susie wiggled out of her jacket and tossed it onto the chair next to her. The guy was still sitting at his computer typing. It wasn't an act. How could she ever have been frightened of him? He looked harmless. Pudgy and a little dumb.

10:40 p.m. Time to get to work, but how could she concentrate after that near run-in, scare, whatever it was? Paranoia or not, her heartbeat was racing and she couldn't think straight. Unfortunately, she didn't think Professor Graham would accept that as an excuse.

Susie signed into the system and clicked on her email. She'd checked it before dinner, but most of her California friends wrote her later in the day because of the time difference. Josh, her boyfriend from high school, only sent her stuff at night. She hadn't told him about Tom yet. Maybe she would after Christmas. Probably not. Susie wasn't big on confrontations.

Everything was spam so she slipped in her flash drive and opened her paper. It was depressing to see those two small sentences surrounded by all that suffocating white space. What really pissed her off was that archaeology was supposed to be an easy class. That's why she took "Rocks for Jocks," figured it would be an easy A. If she had known it was going to be such a pain, she would have taken it pass/fail. But she hadn't so this paper had to be good. It was time to find some interesting stuff online and reshape it with her perfected practice of plagiarism.

Bling! An instant message window popped on the screen, a pleasant surprise. The screen name, URAHOTE, wasn't familiar. Susie sounded out the letters and smiled. Must be Tom. He was always being cute, but he was supposed to be at the bar. He must not have gone. If she hurried maybe she could make it back to his place by a decent time.

Susie clicked on the bubble to open the message. It simply read, "Up so late?"

"Paper's due tomorrow. Going to be a long night," she typed.

Susie sent the message and turned back to her paper, typed "Pompeii" in the search area. In a split-second, thousands of documents were at her fingertips, images of charred bodies curled in on themselves, panicked faces buried in the ash.

Bling! Another message popped on the screen.

She clicked it. "Want it long and hard?"

This time, Susie's fair skin burned bright. Tom could be dirty. That was one of the things she liked about him, but she had to get her work done.

She typed back, "Sorry but I'm afraid it's going to be long and hard enough without you."

Susie clicked on an article about erotic art. A quick glance promised some interesting points she might be able to rephrase in her paper, a dirty little statue of Pan giving it to a goat.

Bling! Another message but this time the screen name was different. IllBNU. Amused by the name, she clicked it open. "Why? Did you bring your baseball bat with you?"

Susie sat and stared at the screen. What did that mean? She scrolled back to her last statement and understood. Tom wouldn't be that dirty and surely it wasn't Josh. He was too sweet.

She typed a new message. "Who is this?"

Instead of checking out another article on Pompeii, she sat there, waited for a response. If it was Tom, he owed her an apology for pulling this when she was trying to work.

A few seconds passed. Susie started back on the paper when a message blinged onto the screen. It simply read, "Guess who."

She didn't know what to do. What if she wrote Tom's name and it was Josh, or vice versa? She didn't know what to write so she just sat there.

Bling! She opened the next message. "I said guess who, Bitch!"

Neither guy would write that to her. No way. Not Josh ever. Not even Tom when he was really drunk. Neither was that mean. She didn't know anyone that mean, male or female.

Susie typed, "AN ASSHOLE!" and pressed enter.

She had to concentrate on the paper and ignore the prick. Someone was just playing a stupid joke on her. They might not even know who she was for that matter. She'd created her screen name, 2HOT4U, when she was still in high school. It was a lit billboard for attracting unwanted messages.

The dreaded noise rang out again. Screen name, IH8U.

She didn't want to open the message but she felt compelled to. "Good guess. How'd you know? What a smart Ivy Leaguer. George and Helen must be proud."

He knew her parents' names. That meant it had to be someone from home. Maybe Karen told Josh about Tom and he went nuts.

The cursor was zipping all over her screen, her hand unable to steady the mouse. She finally guided it over the user's profile, determined to find out who it was and call him out. Hopefully it was Josh. It would make breaking up a lot easier.

The screen was blank. The user hadn't entered any information. There had to be a way to figure out who had sent it to her, but she didn't know how, and she wasn't about to go upstairs to ask the nerds.

If she wanted to finish the paper, she had to put the messages out of her mind. She still only had the two sentences and it was 11:03. She'd wasted twenty minutes. The messages were nothing but a distraction she had to block out, so she muted the volume on the computer.

Another message noiselessly appeared. Screen name, UAHO.

This was getting ridiculous. Whoever was doing this had a serious problem. But she wasn't going to play anymore. She refused to open the message and completely ignored the notification glowing in the top left corner of the screen. For almost forty seconds.

"Better start answering me, BITCH!"

"Fine," she mumbled to herself as she pounded on the keyboard, "You'll be sorry when I find out who you are. I'll go to the school police. You don't think they can trace these messages?" She prayed that they could.

Three seconds later a response came back. "Sending hate mail is the least of my worries if I get caught for the shit I'm gonna do to you, you prissy little slut."

Susie was stunned. The other stuff was mean, but that was scary. No one she knew could seriously want to harm her and none of them would take a joke this far. She hadn't done anything to anyone.

The sweat was rolling again and her throat was parched. She'd get a quick drink and try to cool down. Think good thoughts and try to work on the paper. No more opening messages. For real, this time.

Susie got up from the table, a little shaky, and walked over to the fountains. She took a long sip of the cool water, splashed some on her face and returned to her seat.

Four messages waited for her. She closed all four without opening them. A fifth one popped up. She was about to close it but then the screen name caught her eye. H2O4U.

The guy was here! It had to be that creep in black. Shivers ran down her spine. The message had to be opened.

"I like your jeans? What are they? Calvin Klein? They really compliment your fat, slutty ass."

He was in here alright. Susie rose halfway out of her chair. The guy in black wasn't at his computer anymore. She stood, took a quick survey of the room. There were only six people left in the room, and the stranger in question was nowhere to be seen.

Another message. She opened it. "See me yet? When you do, it'll be too late."

It was one of the six, but who? Only four were guys. Two were on the far side facing away from her. It would have been hard for them to see her get up.

The other guys didn't look like crazed stalkers, but then again, what did a crazy stalker look like? Was there a certain mold they came in? Did they have dark eyes, a shaved head and a goatee, or did they prefer those Poindexter glasses and a wild mop haircut? These thoughts spun around in her head, not making any sense, just making her dizzy. She forced herself to breathe as she slowly scanned the room. The payphones, over by the bathrooms. She needed to call the cops. Immediately.

Before she was out of her chair, another message blinked onto the screen. CUNHELL. She didn't want to open the message, but she was terrified not to.

"Don't bother with the phones. Didn't you see me go over there and cut both cords? Should have been paying attention. And don't even think of turning to these geeks for help unless you want their innocent blood on your hands."

Whatever bit of composure she'd been managing to hold on to, slipped away. Susie wanted to believe the guy was lying, but she knew he wasn't. She had to call the cops or scream or do something.

Another message, different name. ILCUDIE.

"Don't think about running. You probably wouldn't make it all the way to the Main Green. Too slippery, might fall on the ice. Definitely wouldn't make it to Wright House and I bet your life that you would never make it all the way to 308."

The guy knew where she lived. He knew everything about her. Like a rat hypnotized by the serpent's sway, Susie opened the next message.

"Remember, I don't have to be on a terminal. I can be on my cell. I could be crouching down in the bushes outside the front window. I could be standing right behind you."

Susie whipped her head around so fast she felt something snap. The searing heat barely bothered her now, but she knew it would hurt the next day, if she was still around to feel it.

No one was behind her and it was too dark to see past the hedge of bushes he wrote about. He could be hiding and she'd have no idea until he popped out and slit her throat. She continued to read the rest of the message.

"I could be waiting in the hallway. I could be in the bathroom. I could be the guy in the blue shirt sitting across the aisle. And if you make one noise, everyone is going to get it."

Susie carefully turned her head, the throbbing in her neck becoming much worse. She stared at the kid in blue. He was busy typing away, dividing his attention between the screen and his notebook.

Looking toward the heavens for an answer, she was greeted by a bright light. The upstairs office. The tech guys would have a phone. She could lock herself in and wait this out.

Susie slowly rose, watching to see if anyone was making eye contact. No one seemed to be paying attention. She edged away from the table. A message popped on the screen. She wouldn't open it. She took another step to the left and cleared the table. Someone at the back of the room stood up. It was just a girl.

Susie took two more steps toward the stairs. The guy three rows up on the right, fidgeted with his backpack, his hand deep inside it. She waited for him to pull out the gun and open fire. Instead he pulled out a candy bar.

She climbed the first step. There was movement by the hallway. The guy in black was walking by the security doors.

Susie sprinted up the stairs, stopping when she reached the second floor. She looked over the railing and saw the guy in black was headed back to his seat. It had to be him.

Susie approached the open door of the office. She looked behind her, having to turn her entire body because her neck was so stiff. No one had followed her.

A sick thought made her pause at the open doorway. She was walking into the guy's trap. He had killed the tech-workers and was now waiting for her inside there. Susie was about to run when she noticed a long mane of golden hair.

Susie knocked and said, "Hello?"

A pleasant sounding female said, "Come in."

Susie slipped into the room and closed the door behind her, locking the deadbolt.

"Is something wrong?" the girl asked, her voice full of concern. She was pretty, even in her thick glasses.

Susie walked past the blonde's desk and straight to the windows that overlooked the computer room. She closed the first set of blinds and looked for the guy in black. He was back in his chair, typing away. She counted seven others now; everyone accounted for.

"What are you doing? Are you okay?"

Susie crossed to the other window and told the girl, "I'm sorry, but there's some crazy guy down there that wants to… He's threatening me…sending these messages. I need to call the cops. He said he wants to kill me. Please I need your help."

"Guess. I was close."

Susie turned the knob to shut the blinds. She must be in shock. What the girl said made no sense. Susie turned. The blonde was now standing. Susie wondered why the girl wasn't calling the cops. She probably thought Susie was crazy. Susie knew she'd been babbling, on the verge of tears.

Susie tried her story again. "Some crazy guy's down there. He threa…." She stopped herself midsentence. Why was the girl smiling? And why in the world was she wearing Tom's varsity jacket?

Midnight Snack

Nick Decker sat on the toilet and flipped through the latest muscle magazine searching for the model with the tiniest bikini. He settled on brunette draped across the kind of chiseled monster Decker had given up on ever becoming. The brunette wasn't even as wide as the guy's leg.

Decker froze when he heard a rusty squeak. It didn't sound like the ward's front door, but the A and B wing doors were locked and no one else with keys was in the building. It had to be someone from the swing shift or one of the nurses from the front unit. Maybe it was that cutie with the short black hair. He didn't rush off the can for just anyone, but he would for her.

There were footsteps and a soft jingle coming from the ward. Decker was about to yell that he'd be out in a minute, then realized he might not have locked the control booth, grounds for termination. He didn't typically forget, but he'd been slacking off, especially since they'd stuck him back on graveyard.

Decker dropped the magazine and cleaned up. He ignored the sign telling employees to wash their hands and walked out the bathroom as he finished buckling his pants. An elderly doctor with a scraggly gray beard was struggling to find the right key to open the B-wing gate.

Keeping an eye on the doctor, Decker walked to the unlocked control room door and slipped inside. Speaking through the mesh wiring that served as a window, he casually asked, "Can I help you?"

Startled, the doctor looked up and stuttered, "Uh, no, forgot which… I didn't realize anyone was here."

Decker took a seat in his raised chair, positioned himself for a better look at the grizzled doctor. "I'm sorry, I don't believe I've seen you before. You work in one of the other wards?"

The doctor shook his head and shoved the keys into his lab coat. "No, I'm sorry, officer. I'm new. Just got hired today."

Decker didn't mention he was only a guard and not an actual law enforcement officer. "Yeah, I heard they hired someone. You're taking O'Malley's place, right?"

"Oh…yes, I believe that's the name on my office door."

"About time they hired a replacement. Been short a doctor all week. I'm Nick, but most just call me Decker."

"Oh, I'm Dr. Hoffman." The doctor stepped up to the window and a peculiar smell wafted through the mesh.

Unable to place the scent, Decker asked, "How much they tell you?"

"Tell?"

"About O'Malley. The gig."

"Oh, not much. The woman who hired me seemed preoccupied. Is there something I should know?"

"No, I was just asking," Decker said. "I was kind of hoping you'd tell me. O'Malley just stopped coming in. No one's heard from him."

"I take it that would be strange?"

"He just didn't seem the type to up and quit. But hell, it's not like people need a reason to leave this shithole."

"Oh?"

Decker laughed. "No, it's not all that bad. You'll get used to it. As long as you don't mind being around these crazy fuckers – not that…I mean…"

"It's okay. I have grown boys. I'm well-versed in insanity."

"Yeah, that's funny. Still, sorry for my language. One of the many reasons I'm here at midnight. They keep telling me I gotta be careful what I say in front of folks. Especially working for the state."

"Oh yes, I know this too well. I used to be over at Weatherly."

"Weatherly? Shit, must've been some time ago. That place burned down... What? Twenty years ago?"

Hoffman thought about it a second. "Yes, I suppose it's been a while."

The doctor's dingy lab coat looked as if it went back to his days at Weatherly. Decker asked, "Where else did you work?"

"Oh, all over. I've never been one to stay too long in one place."

"Well, glad they brought you in. Damn budget's so tight, I was half-expecting they'd let these bastards run the place themselves. Practically already do."

Dr. Hoffman laughed a little too hard at the lame joke. Decker didn't think he was being made fun of, but he didn't like it either way.

Seeming to sense his unease, the doctor said, "I am sorry to disturb you this evening."

"Yeah, there's normally not a doctor here this late."

The doctor shifted his weight. "I don't actually start until Monday but the lady that hired me, I forgot her name, said I could come in to check out the place. I know it sounds like something a teenager would say, but I guess I'm kind of nervous about my first day. I've actually been on sort of a sabbatical."

Decker finally saw why they'd hired this old timer. He was probably dirt-cheap. And though Decker wasn't the most sympathetic of men, Dr. Hoffman sort of reminded him of his grandfather.

"Nothing to be nervous about," Decker said. "We've all been the new guy at some point."

"I thought maybe coming this late might allow me to get a feel for the place, you know, when it's not so busy. I like to know where things are. Helps me seem not so much like a bumbling fool."

"Don't worry. Expectations are pretty low down here."

"Yes, well, if it's all the same, I was hoping to possibly get a tour. Obviously, it would be up to you. If you're busy, I can always…"

Decker studied the old man. He did seem eager. That's something Decker wasn't used to seeing in here. The poor guy probably didn't have anyone to get home to. "Yeah, sure. Time for my rounds anyway. I just need your ID."

Dr. Hoffman patted his lab coat, checked his pockets, his face reddening. "Oh dear, I don't believe I brought it. I must have left it in the office or possibly my car. I don't think I brought it home, but I was in such a rush to get here, I can't remember... I can go look. I'll only be a bit."

"Nah, forget it. You're here now."

"I don't want you getting in trouble."

"No trouble. You showed me your ID and I verified it. Simple as that. We scratch each other's backs around here."

"Oh, I do appreciate it. That's very kind," the doctor said.

"Not a problem. Let's get started," Decker said. He grabbed his metal flashlight and stepped out of the control room. Decker started towards B wing but turned back when he noticed Dr. Hoffman wasn't following.

"Is there a difference between the two wings?" the doctor asked.

"Yeah, the A wing is where we keep the semi-treatable schizos. B wing is a whole other story. All the psychos. Real sick fuckers. That is, until you cure them, right?"

"Yes, of course." Dr. Hoffman followed Decker through the gate and down a dark hallway. "Is it just you down here?"

"Yeah, just me and the loons."

"What if something happens? I mean, if there's a problem."

"You getting scared, Doc?"

"Oh...I'm always a little on edge."

"Don't worry. These cells stay locked unless I open them." Decker fingered the radio on his belt. "And I got this. We've got guards stationed in every ward. Someone's always less than a minute away."

"Unless they're in the bathroom."

Decker chuckled. "Yeah, I guess." He shoved his key into the lock on the metal door and had to jiggle it. Dr. Hoffman was practically on top of him, his disgusting aftershave even more pungent in this confined space. Decker finally recognized the smell. It was Sandoval. His old boss at the coroner's office used to slather himself with the stuff.

Decker locked the door behind them. "Now, just stay close."

"Is it always this dark?"

"Wing lights go off at nine." Decker pointed at the two open stalls on the right side of the hall. "Here are the showers. It's mainly for incoming inmates. Most of the long-terms rarely use them. Hygiene isn't a priority when you never see a woman." Decker stopped and turned to the doctor. "Look, I know you worked at Weatherly, but these guys can get a little rowdy. I just want to warn you."

"I appreciate it, but as I mentioned, I raised three sons. I'm sure it'll be nothing I haven't heard before."

"I don't know, Doc. These are some twisted fellas."

"So were my boys."

They passed the first set of dimly lit cells when the taunting began. It started softly, a whisper from the first two cells, number one on the right and ten on the left, but the rest of the wing was quick to join in. The hallway filled with the incessant wails of the inmates, Decker's own little rainforest of crazy.

Out of the rambling nonsense, came the inmates' favorite: "Here comes Decker, Decker the pecker-checker."

"Decker, Dicker, penis licker!"

The inmates continued the barrage, and Dr. Hoffman said, "Quite colorful, aren't they?"

"Yeah, not very original." Decker continued past the next set of cells. "Keep it down, gentlemen! Don't make this a long night."

An inmate's body banged against the metal door. With his face pressed against the square glass window, the guy screamed, "Shut the fuck up, Dicker!"

Decker pressed the flashlight to the window and flicked the button. Light blasted the man's contorted face, and he fell backwards with a scream, his hands covering his eyes.

Decker laughed and holstered his flashlight. "That asshole never learns."

"That happens often?"

"Don't worry. Doesn't hurt. Just keeps him quiet."

"Oh, no it doesn't, Ducker - you stupid motherfucker!"

Decker spun around and shouted, "You want the restraints! I swear to Christ, Homer. I'll strap you in for the next month."

"Oooooh. I love a good strap-on. But I'm more interested in the real deal, like the one Daddy's gonna shove in your ass."

Decker clinched his fists and started for the door, but he remembered the doctor. This wasn't a battle he could win and not the best way to make an impression. He kept walking and called over his shoulder, "Knock it off and go to bed."

They passed rooms four and seven, and a soft chanting began: "I know something you don't know. I know something you don't know…" It grew louder and louder until it seemed the walls were shaking. Decker's face turned redder, but strangely, he noticed, Dr. Hoffman didn't seem unnerved by the mind-numbing screams.

Decker yelled, "I'm not kidding. This ends now!"

The chanting grew.

"Do you mind if I try?" Dr. Hoffman asked.

Decker shrugged his shoulders, tried to hide his embarrassment and frustration.

"Excuse me, young men," the doctor said in a surprisingly firm and even tone. "Please listen to my words, for I will only say this once."

The chanting quieted, only a few murmurs filtered out.

"Thank you. My name is Dr. Hoffman and I want you to know I'm looking forward to meeting each and every one of you when the time is right, but right now I need your assistance. I would like to continue my tour without interruption. If you can do that, I promise it will not go unappreciated. Do I make myself clear?"

Decker couldn't believe it. Except for a couple hoots and hollers, the ward was silent. The ward was never silent. These psychos didn't listen to anyone but themselves. He didn't want to tell that to Dr. Hoffman though, so he just mentioned something about the cafeteria opening in a few hours. The doctor didn't seem to be paying attention. He was focused on the last door on the right.

"I wouldn't get too close to there, Doc. His food flap is broken. You get too close and that prick could reach out and grab you."

Dr. Hoffman kept his distance but bent forward to look through the window. Something was definitely stirring behind the glass. "He doesn't use his night light?"

"Doesn't have one. Broke it. We replaced it a couple times and every time he'd break it."

"Guess he didn't like the light."

"Yeah, and I called maintenance to fix the flap, but I can't even get one of those guys to sneeze down here. Especially with this one."

"Oh?"

"Name's Carter. A real freak. Takes three guards to restrain him."

Hoffman went up on his tiptoes to get a better look. "Have you tried talking to him?"

"Yeah, I read him bedtime stories every night. Come on, Doc. We should get back."

Still balancing on his tiptoes, Dr. Hoffman said, "Just one minute." He held out his hand and asked to borrow the flashlight. Decker handed it over and Hoffman shined it through the window. "Oh, I believe he's scared."

"Yeah, trust me, Doc, he ain't. Antisocial personality disorder. Fucker eats people's faces."

"Interesting."

"Doc, I really wouldn't get too close."

"It's okay. I can see him on the bunk. If he moves, I'll be sure to get back." Hoffman bent down so he could look through the opened flap. "Hello, son. How are you doing tonight?"

A loud thrashing erupted in the room, the metal frame of the bunk clanging as the inmate threw his body up and down.

Decker said, "He's been doing that all week. Stays on his bed and then acts crazy every time we do a check. It's like he gets so excited he can't control it."

"Kid's just got a lot of energy," Dr. Hoffman said a little too merrily.

"Well, he won't eat shit. Tosses out every meal we give him."

"Well, he's just particular." Dr. Hoffman pulled something out of his pocket. Decker thought it looked a little like hamburger, but it was hard to tell. What was obvious was Dr. Hoffman was trying to feed Carter. Decker grabbed the doctor's arm.

"What the hell are you doing? I told you, he's crazy."

"Oh, we're all a little crazy." Dr. Hoffman's eyes gleamed. Decker didn't understand it, but he looked taller. "It runs in the family."

Carter's lips pressed against the open slot. He whispered, "Daaaaaaad."

Decker realized this man wasn't a doctor. Hoffman pulled out the keys from his pocket. Each one was caked in dried flesh. They hung from a little black rabbit's foot keychain, exactly like O'Malley used to carry. Decker tried to block the key heading toward his face, but the small metal tip plunged through his pupil.

The inmates roared as Decker crumpled to the floor. They continued to shout every time the keys carved into his neck, face, and hands. Maniacal laughter filled the wing as the inmates banged their fists against the glass. Hoffman stood and faced them.

"Now, now. You'll all taste him soon enough. But my son goes first."

Hoffman yanked the keys off Decker's belt. He licked each one before trying them in Carter's door. Finally, the lock turned and the door creaked open. Carter fell into his father's arms.

"Yes, yes," Hoffman said. "Now, don't let this food go to waste."

Carter fell onto Decker's wheezing body and ripped off a chunk of Decker's cheek. Hoffman continued down the wing and called back, "Just make sure to save some for your brothers."

Shooting Flies

The fly wouldn't sit still. Raymond held his breath, pressed his eye to the viewfinder and tried not to move. Sweat beads rolled down his forehead, but he couldn't risk wiping them and scaring the skittish thing off again. Gina had been waiting for hours. The hunk of meat was almost dried out. This was it. He had to get the shot. He'd promised her perfection, but all he had to show were the dozen flawed photographs drying on the line. Blurred wings and bad light.

"Okay, there you go," he whispered. The fly's six little legs finally landed on the slab of flesh. Sadly, not a single photoreceptor was in view, just a giant shot of the fly's ass. Raymond waited for it to move. Without the eyes what the hell was the point? He stood perfectly still and tried to will it with his mind, but the fly refused to turn around. Slowly, Raymond slid his feet along the floor, tried to ignore his aching old man's knees. He kept his finger on the shutter release as he moved the viewfinder up along the arch of its swollen abdomen to the thorax, and almost to the head—when suddenly, another fly began to circle.

"No. Get away," Raymond whispered. "You had your chance."

An enormous eye crept into the frame. Finally, Raymond thought. He just had to maneuver around the table's edge and he'd have the full face in view. The light stand was precariously close, but Raymond stepped over it and held the shot. The fly began to feast. Just an inch to the left and Raymond would have his angle. His foot clipped the light. His finger mashed the release, but the fly was already in the air.

"God damn it!" Raymond threw the camera at the wall, but the strap caught the back of his neck. The Nikon banged against his chest. He closed his eyes. A dozen buzzing taunts echoed in his ears.

What made him think he could pull this off? It took him eighteen months just to talk to Gina. Whenever Raymond heard her voice in the office, even if she was simply complaining about the copier, his stomach would twist in knots. He went to great lengths to avoid her cubicle, at least when she was in it. He hadn't even stepped foot in the sales department in over a year. In fact, he'd go out the back, walk around the building and come in the side entrance just to go to the bathroom. Only in his dreams did he think he'd ever get a date with her, and now she was sitting in his kitchen, waiting for him to finish. And he was blowing it.

Raymond tried to breathe. All he needed was one good shot. That perfect moment – the delicate shadows, his careful composition and a motionless subject in tandem – and he'd capture a beauty and depth never before attributed to the common housefly. Gina would be so impressed by his brilliance, so stunned by his sensitivity, she wouldn't be able to speak. But that'd be okay. He'd just kiss her and never mention he'd only bought his first camera six months ago. It was the day after he saw her carrying a black-and-white photography book. Gina had told one of the office girls her dad had sent it as a present for her promotion. The cover was a picture of a little boy blowing a dandelion. Gina thought it was so cute.

"I guess so," Raymond had imagined himself saying as he casually sat on the edge of her desk and picked up her mug of pens.

"What do you mean, you guess so? It's cute."

"Sure, if you like generic."

"Oh, I didn't realize you were an expert."

"I dabble…"

She'd try to pretend she wasn't intrigued. He'd dismissively tap the book's cover. "It just doesn't say anything. I mean, if you're going to take a picture it should provoke…something."

Gina would cock her head, not think once about Raymond being twice her age. "Aren't you in accounting?"

"Just until I save up enough to spend a year in Naples." He'd stand and start to walk away when she'd call out:

"I'd love to see your work. Maybe I could even model for you?"

That was the fantasy, so far from the truth. Gina was way too beautiful and glamorous for a bumbling dipshit like Raymond. Still, he kept snapping pictures, actually getting a few decent angles of the city skyline and an action shot of two homeless guys racing shopping carts in an alley.

Raymond kept the photos in a manila folder, which he carried everywhere, waiting for the perfect opportunity to accidentally let them fall out in front of Gina. She'd help him pick them up and he'd ask her opinion.

Finally, one afternoon, he mustered the courage to follow her into the break room. As he prepared the coffee he didn't really want, Gina started frantically swatting at a fly. It landed on the wall, and Raymond, panicked and amped with adrenaline, squished it with his manila folder. When he pulled away, the splattered bits of fly on the wall looked like a burst of fireworks.

Gina screamed. "No! Oh my God, why did you do that?"

"What? I thought…"

"I was trying to shoo it."

"What?"

"Shoooooo it."

Raymond noticed the open window, and he was suddenly the little kid who disgusted his poor, old mother.

"I'm sorry," he said.

"It's a living creature." She walked up to the stain. "Awwww." She said it like she'd just watched a fluffy puppy's eyeball fall out.

Raymond mumbled an apology and slunk back to his desk, where he berated himself until the shame started to turn him on, which made him feel even more like a freak.

He looked for a new job, even went on an interview, but no one was looking to hire an old dog with no tricks. So he tried to avoid thoughts of Gina at all costs. He'd turn up his headphones when he heard her in the office. He no longer stood by the water cooler at that awkward angle so he could watch her wait for the bus. He didn't drive anywhere near her apartment.

The photography was all that remained of his infatuation. Raymond spent every second of free time taking pictures. Maybe his talent would one day outshine his dumb face. It wasn't impossible. This was a woman whose heart was so big she even loved a filthy little fly.

But time was running out. Raymond hadn't snapped anything good enough to even hang on a refrigerator, and Gina wasn't going to be here forever.

Raymond jabbed his thumb into the meat. He dug until a little pocket of pink flesh was exposed. Then he sat back on the stool and watched as one of the flies took notice. "There you go," he said.

But the fly swooped back and headed towards the corner. Raymond wondered if he should just get a can of Raid. He could arrange their lifeless bodies on the meat precisely the way he wanted. But that wouldn't be fair to Gina. She deserved more than some cheap lie.

Chuckles let out a low growl behind the bedroom door. Raymond realized he hadn't fed him dinner. The smell of meat had to be driving him crazy. Raymond had locked him in the bedroom because Gina had a thing about dogs licking her. He'd considered letting Gina in the studio with him, but he couldn't work with someone watching, judging every move. Gina probably wouldn't be critical, but it was better this way. He was already panicking and sweating. He just hoped she would stick around a little longer. If she left before he finished, he didn't know what he would do.

Maybe he should check on her? He needed a fresh piece of meat anyway. This was the third piece he'd had to toss out, and of course, the flies swarmed the moment it thunked in the bin. Raymond wiped his hands on his shirt and opened the door. Chuckles jumped against it, his claws scratching.

"Cut that out or you're not getting dinner." Raymond tried to sound tough, but he couldn't help smiling as Chuckles wagged his tail across the carpet.

Raymond knelt down and let Chuckles lick his fingers. A tiny sliver of bone fell off Raymond's shirt and Chuckles snarfed it down in one bite. "Be careful. You don't want to choke, silly."

Chuckles' mouth was stained red with meat juice. Raymond shook his head and told Chuckles to stay. He didn't need Gina freaking out from the dog bounding in and slobbering all over her.

Raymond slipped into the kitchen where Gina sat at the table. Chuckles' whimpers seeped under the door as Raymond headed for the fridge. "Hey there, beautiful." He brought out two energy drinks and said, "I think this will be my best work yet. Trust me, you are going to love it."

He popped the tab on one of the cans and took a long pull. "I know you're upset I'm not finished yet, but there's no reason to cry. I'll be done soon. I promise." Raymond downed the rest of his drink and opened the second one. "But...I do need a new piece."

Gina tried to scream, but the dirty dishtowel muffled her cries. Raymond reached down and grabbed the power saw under the table. Her open stumps were beginning to fester. A few flies dipped in the soft, gooey tendrils. They must have snuck in through the vent.

Raymond grabbed her remaining arm. Gina tried to pull away, but the restraints kept her in place. "Hey, it's okay," he said. "I promise, fourth time's a charm."

Surviving the Holidays

At twelve years old, Paul began to suspect he was jaded. He wasn't entirely certain he knew what it meant, but that's the word that popped into his head and it felt right. What other explanation could there be for a kid hating Christmas? Paul just couldn't wait for this day to be over, the squeals of his brothers and sisters rummaging through presents only making it worse. He didn't want to be this way. In fact, he envied his younger siblings. He wished he could feel their joy. But in the Harrison household, when you reached a certain age, Christmas lost its innocence, presents no longer mattered. That time had come for Paul and his older brother, Ron, who was slumped next to him on the couch. They had both seen too much and remembered too well.

Jonathan and Francis, the blue-eyed twins, rattled boxes to their ears, trying to guess what was inside. Emily fluffed a bow that had gotten smashed in the stacking. And Tina, who'd just turned five, was begging for help. She'd somehow gotten herself tangled in a string of garland.

Mother let out a little snort from the kitchen. "Ron, help your sister."

Ron grabbed an end of the garland and twirled little Tina around and around until she was finally free. From the laughter and cheer, you'd never know the family had lost five children on this very day. There were reminders though: their stockings still hung above the chimney; their homemade ornaments dangled on branches; the slips of paper with everyone's names, and Tommy's misshapen star on top of the humungous fake pine. But these reminders were nothing compared to Emily's missing index finger or Jonathan's wheelchair. Ron wore a long-sleeve t-shirt to hide his scars, but Paul had seen them all before. The fifteen-year-old looked like he'd run naked through a field of barbed wire. And finally, there was Tina and the puckered pink skin around her little glass eye. She was the only one who didn't remember how she'd gotten hurt. Paul envied her the most.

Only five minutes to midnight and Christmas would officially begin. Then they'd vote and open presents. Paul wondered if other families had stupid rituals like theirs.

Francis stood up. Paul had seen his mangled face a thousand times, but it always looked worse at night in the shadows. Francis said, "I'm going to clean up this year. Who wants to bet?"

Jonathan said, "It's a little hard to tell. Yours are pretty heavy, but I bet you anything Emily's are worth more." He whispered, "She asked for jewelry."

Emily pushed Jonathan's wheelchair. "You can't tell people what I asked for! You know the rules!"

Jonathan stuck out his foot to keep from crashing into the wall.

Francis dragged a box out from behind the tree. "Check this one out. It's the biggest one. It must weigh over fifty pounds."

"No way." Jonathan spun back and said, "Maybe Mom got me the weights I wanted."

Francis said, "It's Paul's."

Paul ran over and read the tag. "It's a mistake," he said. "That's not mine."

"It has your name on it," Emily said.

"It's not mine. I only asked for clothes."

Francis tried to shake the present but it barely budged. "These are some heavy clothes."

"Only clothes. That's all I asked for. I swear."

Ron said, "Why would we believe you?"

"'Cause I'm telling you. It's not mine."

Jonathan did a quick count. "It is yours." He pointed at a pile of boxes by the ottoman. "And these are your others."

Paul told himself weight didn't mean anything. Two years ago, the wrapping on one of Brian's gifts had been torn, revealing a new computer box. But inside were only rock-filled socks.

Less than a minute to midnight and Paul still hadn't made up his mind. Sometimes it was better not to, just go with instinct, but this year he felt he should give his decision a little more thought. Now that Tina was old enough, things could get interesting.

A loud 'ho-ho-ho' bellowed from the hallway and out came Paul's mother and father, both dressed as Mr. and Mrs. Claus. His dad adjusted his fake beard and grabbed his gut.

"Merry Christmas, children!" He slung a red velvet sack over his shoulder. It sounded like metal clanging inside.

Mrs. Claus handed everyone a pencil and piece of paper. The kids scattered and started scribbling. Paul looked over at Emily, who covered her slip.

Tina asked, "Why do I have to vote? I don't want to."

In a deep Santa voice, Dad asked, "Do you want presents?"

She shuffled her feet and nodded. Mom guided her to the table and helped her hold the pencil.

"Do you want two extra presents?" Mom whispered.

Tina's eyes brightened. She nodded even faster.

"Then vote for whose presents you want."

She eagerly looked around the room. "Anyone's?"

"That's the rule," Mom said.

"But that's not fair," Jonathan whined. "She doesn't even know what her vote means."

"I do too," Tina said.

"She's five now. Those are the rules and it's already after midnight," Mom said.

Dad took off his Santa hat and bopped Tina's head with the fluffy white ball. "Hurry up," he said. Tina plopped to her knees and scribbled a name. The other kids dropped their slips into the hat. Emily dropped hers as if it were on fire. Ron tossed his in. Paul still hadn't decided.

"Tick tock, Paul," his mother said.

Francis threw down his pencil. "You do this every fucking year. Just write down a name."

Mom smacked the back of Francis' head. "Language."

"Ow!"

Paul felt everyone's eyes. Could they have actually picked him this time? He'd figured he'd had another year, at least. He'd always sworn if his name was called, he wouldn't be like the others. He'd go out with a fight. But now his legs began to shake. Paul remembered he was the one who cried because he'd only gotten one Christmas present. It's how this all started.

Dad shoved the hat into Paul's chest. Paul finally dropped the name. It seemed to fall in slow motion.

Mom took the hat and stepped into the middle of the room. "Okay, listen up," she said. "We're only counting this once, unless there's a tie." She pulled out a handful of the slips and read the first. "We have one for Paul." She held it up for everyone to see. She turned the next paper over and sounded fairly surprised when she read Paul's name again. "That's two."

Paul's name was called a third time. He sunk back into the couch. One more vote and that was it, but he still had the chance for a tie.

His mom looked at the next slip and turned to Paul. "Aw, I'm sorry, honey," she said.

"Can you read the rest?" Paul asked.

"It doesn't matter," Jonathan said.

"I just want to know," Paul said.

"He's stalling," Emily said.

Mom looked at the last two slips. "Wow. Six votes."

"That's unanimous," Francis said.

Dad grabbed Paul's arm. "You voted for yourself?!"

Paul stared at the slips covering the table. He always voted for himself because he didn't want to feel responsible. He just never thought it'd actually come back to hurt him. He'd assumed he was the likable one.

Paul's mother picked up the red velvet sack and dropped it on the table. His father continued to berate him for not being man enough to write down someone else's name. Paul just stood there watching his mother dump out the gleaming contents of the sack.

"Okay," she said, "who wants Paul's presents?"

Tina and Emily dove for the table. Jonathan rolled over Francis' foot.

Francis punched his brother's neck. "Are you stupid?"

Paul leapt toward the table, knocking both of them out of the way. He reached for the wooden handle of the jagged bread knife.

"Hey, he's supposed to wait!" Tina said.

Paul's father grabbed his shoulder and dug his big, meaty fingers deep into Paul's clavicle. Instinctively Paul spun, bringing the knife up, and slicing through the Santa suit. The sound of the blade carving through his father's stomach was muffled under the padded costume, but he was no longer the invincible titan of Paul's childhood. His father took hold of the knife, tried to stop Paul from twisting it, but Paul dropped a little lower and drove the blade against the bottom rib bone. His father began to falter.

Paul pulled the knife out, slicing through his father's palm. He went to stab his old man again, but a blinding white pain ripped through his lower back. Paul whipped around, his knife tearing through the air until it met Francis' cheek.

Francis cried out and dropped his butcher knife. Paul turned back to his father, who was now on his knees. Another blade tore through Paul's arm, but he concentrated on his father. He stood over him, stabbing in and out of the soft, bulging skin at the back of his father's skull. The blood poured and dripped through the fake beard.

Paul's Achilles snapped and he fell. He saw the bubbled flesh of his forearm as he raised his knife to all five of his brothers and sisters. He didn't want to hurt them. He knew they felt the same, or at least that's what he wanted to believe as Ron plunged the wooden skewer into Paul's chest. Francis drove his knife into Paul's left arm. Emily stabbed his right. No longer able to keep his grip, Paul's knife clanged to the ground.

Tina stepped forward and dragged her tiny steak knife across his throat. Paul smiled and took the weapon from her trembling hands. Gently, he made Tina turn and face his pile of presents.

Book of Revelation

Professor John Warrington stood in the middle of the driveway, an eight-foot-high gate towering before him. To his right was an intercom console. Its red button had faded considerably since he'd last been to this house more than five years ago. That was a day he would never forget, no matter how hard he tried.

Not yet ready to announce himself, not sure if he'd ever be, and thinking that maybe it would be best to just turn around and go home, John tried to peer through the wrought iron gate to glimpse what awaited him. But the once-immaculate gate was now an impenetrable wall of ivy and brambles. The only metal showing was the sharp, rusted points that begged for blood, taunting the foolish to climb over them, hoping they'd slip and impale themselves on the menacing spikes.

John wondered again what he was doing here, why he had agreed to the old man's invitation. They hadn't spoken since that day five years before, when Hazelwood, John's former professor, mentor, and friend, had let John know exactly what he thought of him. Not only had Hazelwood kicked John out of his house and out of his life, but he'd threatened John with far worse. The old man had been seventy years old then, and appeared physically incapable of carrying out the vengeance he'd threatened, but his words still echoed in John's mind.

People change, John told himself. They get older. They calm down and realize they had jumped to conclusions and overreacted. Hazelwood had probably decided to forgive John and didn't want to take his grudge to the grave.

At least that's what John tried to believe. The old man's threats replayed in his mind as John glanced over his shoulder to the car he'd left at the bottom of the winding driveway.

He should be at home, sitting next to the phone. Even though he had his cell phone with him, and the police had promised they would alert him immediately if there were any new developments, it didn't feel right to be away from home while Susan was missing. She'd been gone since January. John had come home one afternoon to find their front door wide open. There was one suitcase missing and some of her clothes, but John had never believed she'd packed it herself. There hadn't been a note, and Susan would never have walked out without saying goodbye. She was many things, but not someone who just ran.

John rarely left his house since she'd vanished. He'd done nothing but pace the halls of their home, barely eating, sleeping less than a few hours at a time. The police, along with his friends and family, had encouraged John to go on living his life as best as he could. They said sitting at home wouldn't bring Susan home any faster, and the last two months had proved their case. He knew that everyone believed Susan had left him. She was half John's age, gorgeous and intelligent. But Susan loved him; of that much John was certain. They were going to be married in the fall.

Hazelwood's invitation was the first John had considered since Susan disappeard. His old mentor had sounded so excited on the phone that John had agreed immediately, despite his better judgement.

Truthfully, John needed the distraction. There was still the nagging feeling this wasn't a good idea; but John was out of the house now, and if he didn't go through with the visit, he would never find out what Hazelwood had to tell him. Maybe the old man wanted to apologize after all these years, or maybe he expected one from John?

Perhaps Hazelwood needed John's advice on a book. The old man would be reluctant to turn to John for assistance, especially after the so-called betrayal, but Hazelwood was getting on in years and might be desperate enough to ask for John's help. Word on campus was that Hazelwood had been living as a recluse for the past few years, rarely venturing from his property. Rumor was he'd finally given up his search for the mysterious books he once dedicated his entire life to finding.

John shivered against a sudden chill. Not only was he nervous about the impending reunion, but in his haste to leave the house, he hadn't thought to grab a jacket. Twilight had turned to dusk, and he found his lightweight polo shirt lacking. John pressed the button on the intercom. Almost instantly Professor Hazelwood's voice sounded from the metal box. "Is that you, Jonathan?"

John greeted his old mentor, surprised by the pleasantness in Hazelwood's voice. He was unable to detect any of the anger that he'd heard on their last visit.

"Then come on in, old chap," the professor said as the gate began to hum and slowly creak open.

John took a step forward and then stopped suddenly, stunned by the full view of the professor's lawn and gardens, which had once been meticulously manicured. Now everything was overgrown or dead. Images of southern graveyards came to mind, but even those places had some order to the flora. This looked as if nature had been given free reign to do whatever it liked.

Still teetering on the edge of turning around and leaving, John thought of the Berretta 9 mm hidden on the top shelf of his closet at home. He'd considered bringing it after he accepted the invitation to visit the man he'd nearly destroyed, but ultimately told himself he was being paranoid and left it locked in the security box. Now, whether or not the old man had been serious, John couldn't ignore the fact that Hazelwood had threatened his life the last time the two had met.

The intercom buzzed and Hazelwood's voice came across. "The tea is getting cold, Jonathan."

John scanned the grounds for the camera that was allowing the professor to monitor him. He found it hidden halfway up a pine tree to the left of the intercom. Hazelwood had been watching him the whole time. Not willing to look any more ridiculous than he already did, John started up the driveway, the gate closing slowly behind him.

There was still beauty in the garden; it just had to be found: a solitary rose blooming amid the thorny brush on the left side of the driveway, a young sapling emerging from the wall of weeds to the right. Good can survive with the bad and life does go on, John thought, but then he looked to the rotting tomato plants and realized everything comes to an end.

The door to the professor's house was just ahead. Now was the time to deal with Hazelwood and see what this was all about. Susan would be fine.

The black maple door opened just as John raised his hand to knock. Hazelwood appeared, dressed in a shabby dinner jacket. The yellow crest on the pocket was fraying. So was Hazelwood. Thin wisps of silver hair stuck out in every direction. He was a tiny shell of the man John had studied under nearly two decades ago. His back hunched, making him look like a turtle, especially the way his small head with its beady eyes poked forward from the collar of his shirt. Hazelwood pushed his glasses up his nose and smiled. "You can put your hand down, Jonathan, unless you mean to strike me."

The old man's sly smile and questionable sense of humor worried John. He had betrayed Hazelwood's loyalty when he published *The Book of Revelation; Exposing the Truth*. He'd gained the man's trust, learned all he could about the sacred and secret tomes, and then wrote a book systematically disproving their existence. In doing so, Hazelwood's life's work was ruined. He still had his tenure at the university, but he'd lost all credibility.

John hadn't set out to deliberately hurt the old man; he simply saw the fallacy in what Hazelwood espoused. At the time he was researching and writing it, John had told himself that Hazelwood would be dead before the book hit the market. But he'd obviously been mistaken and the book's publication had crushed Hazelwood. Now the old man was smiling up at John as if nothing bad had happened between them.

John lowered his hand and scratched at the scraggly, unkempt beard he'd been meaning to shave for several weeks. "Good to see you, Professor. You look well."

"Thank you, Jonathan. I would say the same, but then you'd know I was lying." Before John could respond, Hazelwood continued. "But that is to be expected. I read about Susan's disappearance. Are there any new developments?"

John could only shake his head.

"That's a shame. I did enjoy her company." Hazelwood moved out of the doorway and waved John inside. "I don't want to waste any more of your time than I need to. I heard you're writing another book, and I wouldn't want to impede your progress."

John winced at the dig, then entered the house and waited while Hazelwood closed the door behind them. John admitted, "I haven't written a single word since she disappeared."

"Sorry to hear that." Hazelwood shuffled down the hallway and motioned for John to follow. He led him into the bookcase-lined study where they used to meet every week to pore over manuscripts and letters from antiquity. Hazelwood pointed John to the seat at the head of the long oak table.

John walked behind the chair and studied Hazelwood's emotionless face. "What's this about, if you don't mind me asking?"

"Actually, I do. It's a surprise. Now have a seat while I fetch the tea."

John wanted to protest, the idea of a surprise made him feel ill, but there was no sense in pushing Hazelwood. The old man would talk when he was ready. He'd learned that lesson a thousand times over the years. Might as well take a seat and relax.

A few minutes later, Hazelwood reentered the study pushing a small bronze cart. After pouring the tea and maneuvering the cart into a corner of the room, Hazelwood said, "I let go of the help. In case you were wondering."

Instead of saying that he had gathered that much from the garden, John simply nodded and took a sip of the Da Hong Pao tea, a treat he hadn't had in five years. It tasted just as delicious and exotic as he remembered.

Hazelwood shuffled to the other end of the table and took the seat opposite John. Looking over the top of his steaming mug, he studied John's face.

John waited as long as he could. "What is it, Arthur?" he asked impatiently, forgoing his usual formalities. "I don't have time …"

Hazelwood held up his hand to quiet John, finished sipping his tea, then set down the mug. "You'll want to see this."

"I don't see anything," John said, irritated as he looked about the room. John knew he was being rude, but all he wanted to do was leave. Just seeing his mentor's face brought back the feelings of guilt.

"Maybe you can't see what you don't believe."

John pushed away from the table. "I'm sorry. Maybe I shouldn't have come."

"John, sit," Hazelwood said with the same force he used on his more unruly students. "You don't want to help me?"

"I'm sorry. Tell me what you want."

"I want the expert of rare books to verify my greatest find, the one you and I have been discussing since the first day we met."

John perked up, recalling his first visit to Hazelwood's office. John had been a sophomore and was desperately trying to get into Hazelwood's class, Lost Books of the Ancient World. He tried to remember the list Hazelwood had compiled and hung on his office wall. "Which one? You haven't found the unedited *Taming of the Shrew*?" Shakespeare had always been Hazelwood's favorite, even though he'd spent the better part of a decade trying to disprove the Bard's authorship on classics such as *Macbeth.*

Hazelwood shook his head and got up from the table to take down the painting that hung between the two largest bookcases. A safe. He dialed in the combination. "Even better."

John couldn't begin to think what could be better. Shakespeare's *Comedies, Histories & Tragedies* had sold for over six million dollars, a dozen times more than John's most lucrative find. If it was better than that, it explained Hazelwood's friendly disposition and forgiving attitude. "Don't tell me it's da Vinci?" John guessed as Hazelwood opened the safe's door.

"You won't guess." Hazelwood slipped on a pair of latex gloves he kept in the safe.

John leaned forward in his chair but couldn't identify the cover of the thick book Hazelwood extricated from the safe. Its glossy black binding with bright red letters looked to be something from the latter half of the twentieth century. Whatever it was, it couldn't be more than sixty years old, and as far as he knew, nothing of much value had been produced that recently. When he looked at Hazelwood's crooked smile, he wondered if perhaps the old man had lost it.

Holding the book so John couldn't see the title, Hazelwood handed him a pair of gloves. Once he had them on, Hazelwood set the book on the placemat before John.

Stephen King's *The Stand*. Complete and uncut, not even a first edition, and probably only worth the twenty-seven dollars any store would charge for it. "If this is a joke, I don't appreciate it," John said. "You said this was something I had to see."

"How many times have you been told not to judge a book by its cover? Surely, you of all people should know that."

John breathed through his nose, reached into his shirt pocket, and pulled out his reading glasses. As he slipped them on, he examined the cover, searched for anomalies and imperfections that could raise the value, but he couldn't detect a single one. "What exactly am I looking for, Arthur?"

Hazelwood returned to his seat and took another sip of tea. "Open it. Tell me what you see."

Exaggerating in order to humor Hazelwood, John lifted the cover with the utmost care. The smell of rotten meat wafted up from the title page and immediately brought tears to his eyes. John turned his head to the side and slammed the book shut.

"What the hell was that?" John wiped the spit from his mouth, realized he could no longer smell the foul stench. All he smelled was the tea.

Hazelwood offered his infuriating smile. "You tell me," he said, ever the teacher.

"It smelled like death inside a toilet."

"That's aptly put," Hazelwood said, almost to himself.

"So what is it?"

Instead of answering John, Hazelwood instructed him to open the book again. John steadied his stomach and prepared for the gut-wrenching smell as he opened the cover, but this time there was nothing except the aroma of aged paper.

"But it ... ," John trailed off helplessly, looking up at Hazelwood for an explanation.

"Read the details inside the cover. See anything interesting?"

John wasn't familiar with many of King's works, but he had read this book after the miniseries had come out. Everything, as far as he could tell, seemed in order as he scanned the page. Then he came to the copyright date. "19666." His first thought was that someone had accidentally hit the 6 key one too many times, but then he considered the newer looking cover. "How old is King?"

"Sixty or so."

"He wrote this as a teenager?"

"Not quite. The official copyright was 1978."

"Interesting," John said, not all that impressed by one mistype. "How many of these were printed with this date?"

"You're looking at it."

"Just the one?"

Hazelwood motioned to the book. "Keep going."

Annoyed but more than intrigued, John turned the page and read the dedication aloud: "'To all my true believers: May your fate be revealed.'"

John looked to Hazelwood and asked, "Do you have another copy of this book?"

As if reading John's mind, Hazelwood recited, "'For Tabby, this dark chest of wonders.' That's the original dedication. The one I'm sure you'd read as a younger man."

John didn't want to jump to an irrational and impossible conclusion. He needed more proof before he would even acknowledge the question the dedication sparked. He'd heard this dedication countless times, but it'd been years since Hazelwood discussed it. *To all my true believers: May your fate be revealed.*

"Anything else?" John asked, knowing he needed more than a dedication to even begin to entertain what Hazelwood was suggesting.

Hazelwood nodded. "If you need more convincing, that is no problem. Be assured, you have *The Book* in front of you."

With one hand ready to turn the page, John said, "Professor, you and I both know it doesn't exist. This might meet some of the so-called criteria, but this is not …

"All I ask is that you hold your judgement until you've finished the examination."

"That is what you want me to believe, isn't it? That this is *The Book of Revelation?*" John wasn't referring to the one from the Bible, but the original written a century before the New Testament. Legend said it'd been burned over a million times, but it couldn't be destroyed; instead, it found its way into other books, hiding in the pages of lesser works.

"That's not what I want you to believe," Hazelwood said. "It's what I want you to acknowledge. It's what I want you to verify."

"I can't verify a myth."

"Yes, you can and you will. You'll verify that it is real, that it is here, and that both you and your book were mistaken."

John started to close the cover, but Hazelwood told him to stop.

"What are you afraid of, John? If it is just a hoax, as you claim, then *The Book of Revelation* doesn't exist. But there is no harm in checking, is there? It seems to me that you would want to do that. Look at it as me giving you another chance to disprove me, to embarrass me once again."

"I didn't write my book to embarrass you."

"But you did. Now verify my finding or disprove it," Hazelwood insisted, staring at John. This wasn't a simple request, and both men knew it. Still, Hazelwood wasn't about to let John walk out the door. "You owe me that."

An unexplainable panic surged through John's body, urging him to run. It had been a mistake to come here, but he was here. The professor deserved his time. Even though John's book had been accurate, he still should've told his mentor what he was publishing. Hazelwood had discovered his pupil's writing the same way as everyone else—in the newspaper.

John acquiesced, figuring he could do a quick examination of the book and be done with the whole mess.

John looked at the book, then back at Hazelwood. "After I prove this is not the book you've been spending your whole life in search of, you'll let me go and I'll owe you nothing?"

"Let you go?" Hazelwood laughed. "You're not being held. I'm simply requesting a small favor from an old friend, the preeminent authority on fakes, forgeries, and fables."

John's guilt reached nauseating proportions. "Fine. Let's do this." He turned past the author's note and browsed over the preface. "What else is there? Another typo? An inscription?"

"Turn to a page in chapter one."

John did as he was told. "So what am I looking for?"

"What page are you on?"

There was a number one in the middle of the footer at the bottom of the left-hand page, but a five on the page beside it. John began speed-reading the page, searching for any kind of abnormality. Everything appeared just as he'd read in his dog-eared copy when suddenly, across the page, five nonconsecutive words transformed from black to bright red. The words then made their way toward the header. John mumbled his disbelief.

"Yes?" Hazelwood said giddily.

"What is this?" John asked. But before Hazelwood answered, John looked at the old man and said, "Nice trick. Okay. Well done. How'd you manage that?"

"I didn't do anything."

"The ink turns color when the air hits it, or is it just the temperature change?"

Hazelwood smiled. "It's no trick. What does it say?"

Reluctantly, John read the highlighted words to himself:

respect, don't, him, you

Always quick with puzzles, he reversed the order of the words: YOU DON'T RESPECT HIM. Instead of telling Hazelwood though, he shook his head and said, "I'm surprised you'd sink so low."

"There's no deception. I have no idea what it reads."

"Then I'm even sadder, because either you've been duped this easily or you think I'm an idiot."

Hazelwood didn't seem bothered by John's disbelief. "Try another page."

"Which one?"

"Your choice."

Figuring Hazelwood would direct him to specific doctored pages, John was surprised to be given a choice, but only slightly. "Don't tell me you fixed every page? This had to cost some money."

"Not to mention the amount of time it would take to do what you are suggesting I did."

Hazelwood made a good point, but it only made the situation more pathetic. "Any page, right?"

"Any one you choose. Be my guest."

John flipped through a few dozen pages before stopping. Hazelwood asked him what number he'd landed on. John said, "It should read 47, but there's only a 2. A mistake, but not a very revealing one."

"It's no mistake. You don't see anything else?"

John adjusted his eyes. Seemingly random words slowly turned from black to red, then moved to the top of the page.

back, is, coming, she, not

It didn't take John long to rearrange them: SHE IS NOT COMING BACK. John fought to keep from grabbing the heartless bastard by the throat. Gritting his teeth and staring at the old man, he said, "This is no longer funny."

"I agree; it isn't. Recognize what you have in front of you. Or are you truly blind?"

John's hands couldn't stop shaking. Even after what had happened because of his book, John was unable to believe the old man would cross the line and bring Susan into the hoax.

"If you recall, you stopped at that page. I didn't direct you to it. Please, tell me what it reads." His voice seemed to be truly interested, not a trace of malice. Hazelwood had never been a good bluff, so John started to wonder if maybe he wasn't trying to pull off some sinister prank.

"It says she's not coming back."

"Do you think it means Susan? Or might there be someone else?"

"There's only Susan." John remembered they were talking about their honeymoon plans that morning before she'd vanished. He'd finally given in and told her they could go to Fiji like she wanted. "But it doesn't matter what appears, because either you or one of your friends put this here."

"You suppose it's luck that you turned to that exact page?"

John motioned toward the book. "It's probably on every page."

"Oh, I assure you it isn't."

"So you admit you know what's on the pages?"

"What I admit is that *The Book of Revelation* is able to draw the chosen to it. It must be calling to you. Do you feel its pull at the back of your mind?"

John wanted to tell the old kook he was out of his head, that he should be locked up in an asylum; but there was a tug, one that made him want to turn the page. He shook his head to clear his thoughts, upset that he had been so gullible as to consider Hazelwood's suggestion. There was no pull. It was just a book.

"Why don't you try another?" Hazelwood asked. "Afraid of what you might find?"

"This doesn't prove a thing. You are worse than one of those TV psychics. These revelations could apply to anyone."

"Turn to another page. I won't take much more of your time."

John flipped through the book, and stopped a few pages into chapter forty-two. Even though he was more than a third of the way through the thick book, the page number in the footer was only 3, the one next to it 389. If the next page he turned to was 4, then he had to at least consider the possibility of the book's legitimacy. He could not think of any way Hazelwood might have rigged the pagination.

"What page are you on?" Hazelwood asked.

"Your guess is as good as mine."

"What does the number say?"

"Come on, how'd you do it?"

"Do you remember what I taught you?"

John flashed through the years of information he'd gathered during their chats, many taking place right here in this room. He tried to remember anything concerning the book and pages. Something clicked. There were some who said the book would give only four revelations a day, each numbered accordingly.

He pushed this realization from his thoughts and examined the red words on the page. This one was too simple:

scared, is, use, to, he, pistol, the

John had completely forgotten about the nickel-plated derringer that Hazelwood had kept on his desk. It was a hundred years old and always under glass, but Hazelwood had claimed it still worked.

"Anything interesting, John?"

John shook his head and continued to stare at the book, trying to collect himself. As he stared at the blood-red words, an internal alarm sounded, his logic and rationality struggling to hold precedence, but it was a losing battle. The book kept calling him, warning him to beware, to stop the crazy old man before it was too late.

"John, I need to know. It looks as if you found something of interest."

John picked up his mug and drank as he observed the professor. He hadn't noticed it before, but there was a small bulge under Hazelwood's jacket on the left side of his chest. It was probably just a notepad or a handkerchief, but John supposed it was large enough to be the derringer.

In an attempt to distract the old man, John asked Hazelwood if he would mind getting him some more tea. The old man answered that he would be glad to.

Hazelwood got up from the table with his eerie smile and turned his back to retrieve the teapot. John looked around for a weapon. On the remote chance that Hazelwood was carrying a concealed gun, John would need something. Hazelwood was old and slow; still, he couldn't forget that that feeble man coming back with the tea had threatened to kill him the last time they met. Hazelwood had seemed very definite on that subject.

As Hazelwood poured John's tea, making a point not to look at the book, John leaned forward trying to peek inside his mentor's frayed jacket. He couldn't tell what was inside. Then Hazelwood returned the pot to its cart.

The old man's wife had died shortly after the release of John's book. It wouldn't be surprising if the professor blamed John for her death as well. A devastating loss could change a man and make him do things he wouldn't have considered before. Now that Susan was gone, John knew this to be very true. Before today, he rarely entertained violent thoughts, but inside this study he was dreaming of strangling the demented son of a bitch sitting across from him.

"You're not going to drink it?"

"I was just letting it cool." John picked up his mug and brought it to his lips, wondered if the tea could be poisoned. Could that be what was causing the violent thoughts, making him consider the book to be real? "Actually, I think it needs another moment." He set the mug in front of him.

Hazelwood shrugged and drank from his own cup, the same tea that was in John's mug. Or was it?

"What do you say to opening up one last page? I promise it'll be the last one."

"But it only gives four a day, right? Are you sure we should rush to the end?" John's eyes drifted to the cart and the small butter knife. He wondered if he could reach it before the old man drew.

"Four per person, yes," Hazelwood said.

"So maybe we should do yours next."

"Not necessary. I just need you to verify that it is *The Book*. I take it that you're still not convinced."

"That it's *The Book of Revelation*? You told me yourself that it only gives revelations to one who has killed another. I've never harmed a soul in my life."

"Physically, maybe," Hazelwood said, the overwhelming sadness in his voice hanging over the room.

Feeling he had the man on the ropes, John said, "At least tell me how you did it?"

"Turn to a new page and I promise to explain everything."

John agreed and flipped further into the book, stopped and stared at the 4 in the footer that should have read 932.

Hazelwood stood and said, "If the book is not real, then how do you explain this?"

"What?" John asked, distracted as he studied the letters changing color in front of him:

going, He's, *Kill*, to, you

"Will you agree that the book is real if its revelations prove to be true?"

John looked up from the book in time to see Hazelwood reach for the object inside his jacket. Before the old man could pull out a gun, John shoved the table into Hazelwood's chest. John, now on his feet, came charging and grabbed the old man.

Hazelwood caught his breath, motioned to the hand beneath his jacket. "What do you think I have in here?"

"Don't move."

"Well, this isn't going to be very fun. I have something to show you."

"Don't move," John repeated.

"You're acting like I'm going to kill someone."

"Are you?"

"I'm not going to kill anyone." Hazelwood grinned. "Not anyone else," he said.

Anyone else. Anyone else.

"What are you talking about?"

"Don't worry, John, I won't hurt you."

"Shut up and slowly bring your hand out from the jacket."

"I had to do it, Jonathan," Hazelwood said without making a move to withdraw his hand.

"Shut up!" John screamed, pulling Hazelwood's hand away before reaching in himself.

"I wasn't an evil man, I swear it. They say you have to be evil to get it to work. They say *The Book* calls you if you look long enough." Hazelwood tried to reach in his jacket.

"Stop!" John shouted. "Leave your hand where it is!"

"But it's the proof you need in order to believe. Go ahead, take it." John felt something in his hand. Not a gun, but an envelope. It was black.

Hazelwood let out a raspy sigh and licked his lips. "You'll want to see this."

John simply stared at the professor. Then his eyes moved to the envelope.

The old man's fingers pushed it toward John. "Open it. I offer your proof."

John tore it open.

"Thank you, Jonathan. Thank you for coming tonight. For heeding the call."

John hesitated, wondered what could be inside the black envelope. Slowly, he tipped it to the side and caught the necklace sliding out. He didn't need to see the engraving on the locket to know whose neck it had adorned. Another small object dropped to the floor and bounced off his shoe: Susan's two-carat engagement ring. John turned on the professor, ready to grab him by the neck and squeeze.

"In the envelope, Jonathan. Look," Hazelwood whispered.

He let the necklace fall from his hand and peered inside. There was a folded Polaroid. It had caused the lump under Hazelwood's jacket.

Hazelwood struggled to keep his eyes open. "Go on, Jonathan. Go ahead and look inside."

John pulled out the photo, the envelope fluttering to the ground.

"I do thank you, Jonathan. Taking her enabled me to find this book. And soon you'll take its burden from me." Hazelwood took a ragged breath. "Tell me, Jonathan, when did you know where she was? Was it before or after you walked into my house."

That smell. Susan's perfume. He'd been paying too much attention to Hazelwood to realize that it was his fiancée's. The blood-red words. Hazelwood had caused her death.

John turned the photo over in his fingers, unable to open it and look at the image inside.

"I did what I had to, Jonathan. Isn't that what you once taught me?"

John unfolded the photo. Susan lay on her back, her eyes open. There was a hole a few inches above her right eye. Blood pooled beneath her beautiful blonde hair splayed on the hardwood floor, the same floor he was standing on.

Shaking, his mind numb, John reached out and wrapped his fingers around his mentor's throat and squeezed, felt his thumbs denting his larynx, the fleshy tissue stretching under the pressure as Hazelwood's breaths turned wet. John's eyes stayed locked on the old man's face as Hazelwood's fingers clawed at his wrists. He lowered the old man to the floor and continued to squeeze until he felt his fingers tingle. The life finally left his old friend's eyes and John turned to the book, which had fallen to the floor. Page 166 was now numbered 1. The words changed color before his eyes.

her, Goodbye, tell, run

The words made chillingly perfect sense. This truly was *The Book of Revelation*. John walked out of the room and saw his love's body curled up under a table. He fell to his knees and kissed her cold hand. He said his goodbyes and stifled his sobs. He sat there for hours until his legs fell asleep. Then he lay down next to her and recalled the final word:

RUN

Shades of Death

I wake, the concrete cold against my cheek. Everything's black. I can't see my hand even though my palm is touching the tip of my nose.

I have no idea how I got here. I don't even know where 'here' is. I'm indoors, that much I'm sure. I remember being at home, falling asleep on the couch. Someone must've grabbed me. Maybe the Feds, but I don't think so. This isn't a cell. I smell something cooking. Maybe chicken. Someone says something in Spanish. Julio must've found out I can't ever pay him back.

Seems like my head would be sore from a knock on the head. Or I'd feel bruises. Or I'd be groggy from being drugged, but I can think fine. I just can't see.

I whisper, "Hello?" My voice bounces right back. There has to be a wall pretty close. I whisper again to the right and then straight up, each time the same echo. No wind, just my voice and the one in Spanish. It's a guy. He's laughing now, or maybe he's screaming.

My eyes start to adjust. It's not completely dark. On the wall in front of me are the outlines of two large rectangles. It looks like someone carved through the wall with the thinnest laser so just the hint of sunlight could tease me.

I get to my knees. I'm not tied up. I stand and take a step to the left. The tile's cool against my fingers and a bit damp. I stick out my arm, wave it back and forth as I inch toward the smaller rectangle. There's no sound other than my shuffling feet now; no laugher, no Spanish, just my hurried breath. I'm close enough to see the rectangle's a window with a drawn shade.

The fabric's disgusting and sticky, and I imagine the web of a giant spider whose feet are silently scurrying across the ceiling. I know there aren't giant spiders that prey on people, but my mind prefers to think of eight-legged death than whatever is on the other side of the wall.

Twisted Reunion

As far as the explanation for how I got here, I'm guessing it's pretty bad. If it really is Julio, I'm fucked.

I need to know where I am, so I tug and release the shade and the bright fluorescent light from another room blinds me. I assumed I'd see a streetlight or some trees, somewhere to escape.

It takes a moment for my eyes to adjust to the harsh light. The other room is larger. There's no furniture, and there's a naked Hispanic man cowering in a corner, his belly round and legs so spindly it looks like he might collapse. No sound carries through the window, so I can't hear his panicked yells as he waves his hand at the two snarling pit bulls in the corner of the room.

The dogs bare their teeth, snap at the man. There's a speaker above them. The second I see it, the savage barking comes blaring into my ears. It's coming from behind me, another speaker in my room.

I turn back to the window. The blue brindle drips bloody saliva onto the tiled floor next to a stringy piece of raw meat. The man moves in my direction and I see where that morsel came from; he's missing a large chunk of his right thigh, the white bone glistens under a layer of shredded tendons and muscle.

The man spots me, and he's screaming in Spanish. The black pit leaps, clamps its jaws shut on the man's left hand. It tears through the index and middle fingers, gulps them down like a tasty treat.

The man tries to run, pushes off with his injured leg, slips on the slick tiles, and hits the ground. The pit attacks, but the man kicks out with his good foot, nails the dog square on its nose.

The other pit snaps at the man's mangled hand, but he draws it back just in time, punches the pit's massive head. Both dogs are still stunned, and the man's back on his feet, hobbling toward me.

He waves me away. His mouth's open, but I can no longer hear his screams. Someone's controlling the speakers. He's reaching to the left of the window towards the outline of the larger rectangle. It has to be a door, but I don't feel a handle. Still, I brace myself against the rectangle. Sorry, but I can't let in the dogs.

235

His contorted, sweating face is back staring at me. I can't look at him. On the back wall behind him are two windows, black shades drawn. In the middle of both there's a door with a shiny silver knob. I point to it, but he doesn't seem to comprehend. The dogs are back after him.

The black pit flies through the air, turns its enormous head to the side, chomps down on the man's right hamstring. The other latches on his arm, thrashes back and forth. The man keeps his eyes on mine, his jaw set and brow furrowed as he drags the dogs toward the glass. The black pit loses its grip, then charges and bites down on the man's Achilles, snapping it in half.

Somehow the guy keeps coming, bent over like an old man dragging a ball and chain. A chunk of meat tears free from his leg and he stumbles forward. His forehead slams into the middle of the window. I feel the faint vibration, but still can't hear anything. His tortured face slides down the glass, leaving a trail of sweat and blood. He disappears below the window.

The door shakes. I move back, put everything I've got into blocking it. Feeling like a coward, I yank down the shade and throw myself back into darkness. I slide down the door and scream, "Stop shaking!" I've never been so scared. I tell myself the dogs aren't getting through that window. I tell myself the man's suffering is over.

I wait for a minute. Two. I'm sitting on a damp spot. Is it sweat? Piss? I slide my finger along the floor. I can't see. It doesn't smell like urine.

I fucking hate dogs. I got bit when I was three, and I still remember it like it was yesterday. I can't stay in here and wait for whatever this asshole is planning. Am I next? This isn't Julio doing this. He's fucked up, but not like this.

I've got to get out of here. Why didn't I think to look around this room while it was lit? I could've planned something. Instead I'm sitting here like a scared kid without a nightlight, not about to open the shade above my head. I'm not daring those dogs to attack.

236

I get up, drag my hand along the wall and hope I'll touch a knob, button, something. Finally, I find another shade.

I don't believe in God, but I'm praying as I yank on the shade.

The room's identical to the dog room; it has the same two windows at the back, each with a black shade drawn, and the same shiny doorknob. But this time there's an athletic twenty-something lying on his stomach in the right corner. He's naked besides a silver necklace, his face buried behind the crook of his muscular arm. There aren't any dogs.

I knock on the glass, hoping the guy can help. He doesn't stir. I back up and throw my weight against it. He still doesn't move, so I do it again, and something pops in my shoulder as I bounce off the window. He twitches.

"Come on. Come on, you big fucker. Get up!"

The man moves his arm, uncovers his face, the entire left side flush against the floor. He opens his eyes and stares at me.

I wave him over. "Come on!"

With the side of his face still against the floor, the guy places both palms on the ground and pushes. It looks like he's doing some sort of push-up where he keeps his head close to the ground. His neck strains and the skin on his cheek pulls.

Half an inch, an inch, the skin continues to stretch. He jerks his head and the skin tears, a large patch stuck to the floor, the rest dangling from the side of his face.

As he gets to his feet and staggers over, I see his entire body is blistered, rivers of sweat running between the bubbles. The crucifix hanging from its silver chain glows bright over the man's chest. A crazed, deranged look fills his wide eyes. Two more lurching steps and he falls to a knee. Patches of skin are missing from his forearms and thighs. Steam rises from his shaved head. He says something I can't hear.

I point to the wall. "The door! Try the door!"

He shakes his head, the crucifix burns brighter, and the steam rising off his head thickens.

My room's still cold and damp. Even the glass is cool.

He keeps coming for me, waving me away from the window. His feet leave patches of flesh with each step.

I spin away. The light from the furnace room illuminates the walls. There's the shiny knob. I can't see the door, only the knob. I grab it and twist it but it just spins in my hand. It's hard to see in the shadows, but I can't make out any cracks in the wall, no sign of a door.

I turn as the light dims. The blistered man's steaming silhouette fills most of the window, blocking the fluorescent lights. I feel like an ass, but wave him away and turn my back on him.

He stays there for another second, and then falls to his knees. The light in his room flickers out.

My heart's racing. What the fuck's happening? Someone turned off those lights. When would my light go on? What's going to happen if it does? Maybe I'm just here to watch, but I'm pretty certain I'm not just a witness.

I keep feeling the wall, but there's no other door. There has to be an entrance here; I got in somehow. Was it through the one with the dogs?

I reach the corner and suddenly hear water. I keep moving. My foot splashes. I keep moving. The water hits my ankles. I keep moving. I'm back at the first window when the water reaches my shins. I drop to my hands and knees and feel along the tile. There's a current. It's coming from close by. I find the grate where the water is coming from. It's being pumped from below. I place my ass over it, but it's not enough, not even with my palms helping to block. The water's at my chest now. I have to cover the vent. I strip off my shirt, wad it up, and smash it over the grate, but I still feel the water pulsing through. My pants are off next, even though I'm sure they're useless. I'm naked and think of the men in the other rooms. Were they forced to strip themselves just like me?

The water's rising fast. It's at my neck. I have a minute or two before the room will be flooded. I paddle with my arms, push the water out of my way. "What the fuck do you want?" I keep asking that, but there's no answer. "I'll give you anything. Whatever you think I've done, I'll make it up to you. I swear." The water touches my chin, but I continue moving.

The bright outline of a rectangle blinks to life in the middle of the back wall, its lower third shimmering under the water.

I start swimming, I'm a few yards from the wall when I surface and take a deep breath. The water doesn't seem to be rising, but there's a hissing sound and the pungent smell of chlorine sweeps over me. I write it off as chemically-treated water, take one more breath. The metallic taste of pepper and pineapple stings the back of my throat. My scalp and face start to burn.

I lower my head close to the water, shut my eyes. My face no longer burns, but the back of my neck does. I've seen enough of the History Channel to know what chlorine gas can do.

My feet can't touch the floor any longer, I just float. The water's stopped at the top of what looks like another window. I plunge my hand to pull the shade, but there's nothing there, only slick, unbreakable glass.

I surface to breathe and everything burns. Plunging deeper, I feel some relief. The shade shoots up on the other side of the glass, and a woman, someone I've never seen, stares at me. She's still clothed. It's just starting for her.

I scream for her to help and point at the glass. I tell her to get something to break it, but she backs away.

My ears are ringing. I try to float to the surface, but the water's at the ceiling. I keep my eyes locked on the woman's. She takes another step back from the window and I don't blame her. Maybe I'm her first window. Maybe she'll find a way out.

Your Free Book is Waiting

Three short horror stories and one piece of nonfiction by Mark Tullius, one of the hardest-hitting authors around. The tales are bound to leave you more than a touch unsettled.

Get to know:

- an overweight father ignored by his family and paying the ultimate and unexpected price for his sins
- a gang member breaking into a neighborhood church despite the nagging feeling that something about the situation is desperately wrong
- a cameraman who finds himself in a hopeless situation after his involvement in exposing a sex trafficking ring
- the aging author paying the price for a reckless past, now doing all he can to repair his brain

These shocking stories will leave you wanting more.

Get a free copy of this collection
Morsels of Mayhem: An Unsettling Appetizer here:
https://www.marktullius.com/free-book-is-waiting

REVIEW

If you enjoyed these stories, I hope you'll take a moment to write a quick review. As an independent author, word of mouth and reviews are incredibly helpful. Whether you leave one star or five, honest feedback is truly appreciated.

And if you're on Goodreads or BookBub please stalk me. I believe the technical term is Follow, but I strive on anxiety and what better way to amp it up than thinking there are hundreds of strangers stalking me. Plus, you'll be alerted to all my new books and deals. Sounds like a win-win to me

TRY NOT TO DIE

Try Not to Die: At Grandma's House

It's Grandma's house – quiet, cozy, nestled on a little mountain in Virginia. What could possibly go wrong? A lot, actually.

So watch your back. Choose wisely. One misstep will get you and your little sister killed.

Try Not to Die: In Brightside

Mark and 10th Planet Jiu Jitsu teammate Dawna Gonzales continue the Brightside saga, bridging the gap between the first book and sequel, this time from the eyes of a female teenage telepath.

Try Not to Die: In the Pandemic

Mark and John Palisano take readers on the most intense hour they will ever spend on a cruise ship in this non-stop interactive adventure.

Try Not to Die: In the Wizard's Tower

Your name is Lucky and you're stuck inside the mysterious Wizard's Tower, mercy to its puzzles, traps, creatures...and magic.

Try Not to Die: In the Wild West

Mark and John Palisano join forces again, this time to take readers on a wild ride through the Old West.

Try Not to Die: At Ghostland

Duncan Ralston honored Mark by allowing the TNTD series to enter his incredible Ghostland world.

Try Not to Die: At Dethfest

Mark and Glenn Hedden take you to Dethfest, one of the largest heavy metal festivals of the year.

Try Not to Die: Back at Grandma's House

You escaped Grandma's House but you better hurry back.

Coming Soon

Try Not to Die: In a Dark Fairy Tale

Mark and Evan Baughfman take a pair of princes on a death-filled adventure. Late 2023.

Try Not to Die: At Summer Camp

Mark and Caitlin Marceau explore the Canadian wilderness.

Plus 15 others in the works.

Download Your Free Copy

Includes the first 2 chapters and 1 death scene from each of the first 7 books in the Try Not to Die series.

Out Now from Vincere Press

FICTION

Brightside

Across the nation, telepaths are rounded up and sent to the beautiful mountain town of Brightside. They're told it's just like everywhere else, probably even nicer. As long as they follow the rules and don't ever think about leaving.

Beyond Brightside

The exciting conclusion to the Brightside saga. Joe and Becky thought life was hard in Brightside, but beyond Brightside is even more brutal.

A Dark and Disturbing Collection

A boxset that includes 82 short stories taken from *Twisted Reunion, Untold Mayhem,* and *25 Perfect Days: Plus 5 More.*

Ain't No Messiah

The coming-of-age psychological thriller about Joshua Campbell: a man of death-defying miracles, whose father proclaimed him the Second Coming of Christ.

Nonfiction

TBI or CTE: What the Hell is Wrong with Me?

As a former fighter and Ivy League football player, Mark Tullius wanted to support his friends with traumatic brain injuries (TBI) and possible chronic traumatic encephalopathy (CTE). But when presented with a scan of his own grey matter, his life changed forever. After years of insisting he felt fine, the athlete had to face the fact that his time on the field and in the cage had caused considerable damage inside his skull.

Tired of throwing in the towel when challenged, Tullius worked tirelessly to make his recovery an adventure in health, happiness, and self-discovery. And now he's sharing his journey, research, and joy with you hoping that you, too, can recover and walk out of the darkness.

Unlocking the Cage: Exploring the Motivations of MMA Fighters

For his first nonfiction project, Tullius spent 3 years traveling to 23 states and visiting 100 gyms where he interviewed 340 fighters in his search to understand who MMA fighters are and why they fight.

ABOUT THE AUTHOR

Mark Tullius is the author of *Unlocking the Cage, Ain't No Messiah, Twisted Reunion, 25 Perfect Days, Brightside,* and the creator of the *Try Not to Die* series. Mark resides in Southern California with his wife and two children.

For more information about Mark's work, he invites you to connect with him on Facebook, Twitter, and Instagram.

Website - http://marktullius.com/
Facebook – http://www.facebook.com/AuthorMarkTullius
Twitter - https://twitter.com/MarkTullius
Youtube – http://www.youtube.com/MarkTullius

To hear free audiobooks and listen to Mark's weekly rant, be sure to look for his new podcast, *Vicious Whispers with Mark Tullius* which you can find on YouTube, iTunes, iHeart Radio, Spotify, Stitcher and other places podcasts are played.

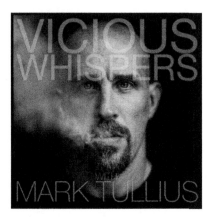

https://viciouswhispers.podbean.com

SINCERE THANKS

Special thanks to my editors, Anthony Szpak, my father, Michael Tullius, and my sister, Mary Nyeholt. I couldn't have reworked these stories without their help.

I'd also like to thank select members from Marked for Life who acted as the fourth and final editors on many stories. Their trusted input helped with critical decisions, caught some errors, and came up with new names for a couple of characters. If you had an issue with any of the stories please blame these guys:

Fourth Editors:
Chris Nicholson
Don Theye
Jasmine Thompson
Kim Hutto
Linda Moore
Meghan Thompson
Michelle Gilhouse
Rebecca Dotson

And finally, thank you to all the readers and reviewers for your support and encouragement. You guys are why I write these stories. And so I don't go crazy. I'm hoping to prevent that as long as possible.